Keep Going!

The Pleasure and Pain
of Perseverance

Keep Going!

The Pleasure and Pain of Perseverance

By

Piet W. Boonstra

Adventure Touring
Buchanan, New York

ISBN 978-0-9718589-5-4

Cover Photograph – Courtesy of:
Kenneth Gabrielsen, Gabrielsenphotography.com

Back cover portrait photo by Al Lemke

Acknowledgements

I am very grateful to Muriel Farrington, President of the BMW Motorcycle Owners of Vermont and Secretary of the BMW Motorcycle Owners of America, for her untiring efforts in proofreading the manuscript and for her words of encouragement.

I thank photographer Kenneth Gabrielsen for his kind permission to use the photo of me on the cover.

Dedication

I dedicate this work to the memory of my mother,
who was my greatest inspiration and role model
for personal integrity and perseverance.

Pietronella Dijkstra Boonstra Smith

(3/27/1896 – 6/8/1996)

Contents

"You may sometimes doubt his sanity,
but never his resolve"

Jim Moroney, 1995

Preface

As of this writing, I am in my 66th year of motorcycling, doing what I enjoy most while clocking more than 1¼ million miles on approximately forty different road and off-road motorcycles. That would average out to a little more than 19,000 miles per year for 66 years, but I spent two of those years in the Air Force during the Korean War, not riding at all, and I devoted 25 years to my enduro competition where I averaged less than 5,000 miles per year.

I didn't begin to concentrate on long distance touring and putting on the big miles until the spring of 1977 when I bought a new road motorcycle and gradually evolved from off-road competition into adventure touring and dual sport riding. Since then I've ridden on all kinds of byways in all kinds of remote areas of North America while clocking an average of 34,000 miles per year for the next 34 years on 16 different road and dual sport motorcycles.

I was in relatively good physical condition in 2005 when I turned 80, and I was enthusiastically anticipating at least another ten years of continuing to do what I loved most, in spite of a deteriorating case of glaucoma, some heart-related problems and a few of the usual geriatric-related issues, all of which I was quite capable of managing while I was on the road.

Soon after turning 80, I became totally incapacitated by a double whammy of Lyme Disease and ehrlichiosis; the latter being a relatively serious tick-borne disease similar to Lyme, originally known only to dogs. The combination of the two almost took me out of the game altogether as I was laid low for more than six months, in and out of the hospital. There were times that I was so weak I was unable to turn over in bed or lift an arm or a leg; and there were other times when I seriously doubted that my heart could stand the severe pain that overwhelmed the strongest of pain medications.

I survived the ordeal with prayer and with God's grace, but it left me with a whole new set of medical complications to manage, regardless of how far I might be from the comforts of home or from those who might be amenable to assisting in the additional care my aging body now needed. I hope to describe in this book, not only how I was able to do that, at least for a while, but also to attempt to inspire those with similar issues and concerns, and to suggest an alternative to becoming a slave to the dreaded tube or the easy chair – either of which could soon put a perfectly capable individual on the exit ramp of life, physically and mentally.

There is a beautiful world out there, created by God to be seen and enjoyed by all. I intend to keep doing what I love most for as long as I'm here on this earth, and for as long as I'm able to get a leg over the machine. I remember hearing while struggling to finish an enduro many years ago, "Keep Going! You're doing good!" I heard it even when I wasn't doing quite so good, but when I got to the finish line, I had the satisfaction of knowing that I had given it my best shot – and I had a lot of fun doing it.

Piet Boonstra, 2012

One

Alaska 8 – The Sheep Caper

July 14 – August 5, 2004

I got a call from Jake Herzog during the winter of 2003-2004 to say that he and Jim Hoellerich had been talking about riding to Alaska together. He called to ask if I might be interested in going along with them. He said it would be Jim's first trip to Alaska, and that Jim was quite enthused about going.

I had already ridden to Alaska seven times – two with Jake and others, and five trips alone, but I jumped at the chance to go again, even though I planned on going the following year for my granddaughter's graduation from the University of Alaska. Oh well, I suppose I could do it again next year, God willing.

I was 79 at the time, and other than my family's and my friends' concerns about my age and my failing eyesight, the only concern I had was with sleeping arrangements, since many motels along the way don't provide rollaway cots – and I, for one, don't care much about sleeping on a rollaway.

One way we sometimes dealt with it in the past was to rent two rooms, a double and a single, if both were available, and to split the cost three ways; but that can get expensive after a while, and I'm frugal by nature, as most of my friends know, having been brought up poor during the Great Depression. I still pinch my pennies.

Several years ago while traveling to Alaska with my two long-time buddies, Jake and Bud Peck, I bought a new inflatable mattress for sleeping on the floor in double rooms whenever there was no other option available, but that thing lost all of its air long before morning every time I used it. As soon as I got home, I returned it to the department store where I bought it and got a full refund, which put me ahead of the game, seeing that I had gotten a few partial nights use out of it in spite of its being defective.

I wasn't sure how we would deal with the sleeping arrangements this time, but the problem resolved itself when Jake called a few months later to say that he had to cancel – and for good reason – daughter Lynn was about to give birth to his and Arlene's first grandchild during the time we would be away. When I discussed this latest development with Jim, he was disappointed about Jake's not going, but he said he would still like to go, so without hesitation I agreed to go with him and began my preparations.

The first major problem arose two weeks before we were scheduled to leave when my primary bike at the time, a BMW R1150GS, blew the main bearing in its transmission during an impromptu trip I took to Rhode Island to pick up some old enduro photos for a book I was working on. As soon as I got back with the growling gearbox, I paid a visit to the two BMW dealers closest to my home, but I was unable to get either of them to agree to fix the problem prior to our date for leaving.

Westchester BMW of White Plains, a Motorrad USA dealership at the time, said that by giving it priority over routine service, they could probably get to it and get it back to me in a week to 10 days, but they couldn't guarantee the date because it was their busy season. Cliff's BMW of Danbury said they couldn't get to it for at least six weeks, and they wouldn't consider giving it priority over anything. Neither offer fitted well with our travel plans, so I looked for other alternatives.

The easiest solution would be to use the small 2003 BMW F650 Dakar that had been sitting in my garage for more than a year. I put a few thousand miles of dual sport and local riding on it during that time, so at least it was well broken in, and it was certainly capable enough, but I had a few concerns.

My first concern was that Jim would be riding his big R1150GS, and I would prefer that we were on an even playing field for the trip, with both bikes in the same class. The Dakar was not only much lighter and smaller than Jim's, but it was also smaller than any I had ever ridden on a long trip, let alone an Alaska trip of more than 10,000 miles. I never made the Alaska trip on anything smaller than a 750cc road machine, and as it stood, the Dakar was basically a dirt bike with knobby tires. The only facility it had for luggage was that I could strap on a tank bag and tank panniers, and I could pile stuff on the rear carrier. I'd have to pack light, for sure.

I had, in fact, thought about taking it to Alaska sometime in the future, whenever I could find the time for a more leisurely adventure, and when I had time to set it up properly, but the short notice forced the issue.

At one time I even thought of taking a trip to Alaska on something as small as a 200 or 225cc bike for the adventure and challenge of it, but that kind of trip would take much more than a month, and it's often difficult, even for a retiree, to find that kind of time.

I did in fact ride a Yamaha XT225 Serow to Goose Bay, Labrador on an earlier trip with Jake through northern Quebec, but that was a much shorter ride than going to Alaska and back. It would be a great adventure though, in addition to being an exciting experience and a real challenge, both for me and for the machine.

Since the main route to Alaska had been totally paved since its 50th anniversary year in 1992, I was sure that just about any size or type of motorcycle could make the trip without too much difficulty; and besides, I have often seen hearty souls out there riding bicycles along the Alaska Highway when more than a thousand miles was dirt and gravel. But of course bicyclists don't make six to seven hundred miles in a day like a motorcyclist can, nor do they make the roundtrip in less than a month.

On my most recent trip to Alaska for my grandson's graduation from high school, I rode the same BMW R1150GS that I still had. It was an ideal choice for the trip, in that it was strong, it handled well for the type of roads I'd be traveling, it was comfortable enough, and it had plenty of room to stow just about anything I chose to take with me. It was the bike I originally planned to take on this trip.

Having left home in mid-May on that trip, I faced the possibility of snow most of the way up and back; although as it turned out, the worst weather I hit was some blowing snow and a few inches of slush at the higher elevations in the Canadian Rockies during the return leg, which didn't become a problem. During one single 12-hour day on that trip, I was able to clock 760 miles on an almost-deserted Alaska Highway for an average of more than 63 mph for the day. I sometimes rode for up to an hour without ever seeing another vehicle of any kind in either direction, because it was so early in the season.

This photo was taken along the Alaska Highway during my seventh trip to Anchorage in May 2001. The highway was relatively deserted, and it was in excellent condition most of the way, except for some occasional frost damage.

All of my previous trips to Alaska were taken on road machines with much less handling capability than either the 1150GS or the Dakar; and that was back when the Alaska Highway was dirt and gravel, or being prepared for paving for more than a thousand miles in British Columbia and the Yukon Territory, and some of those work areas can make traveling a lot more difficult.

Construction areas like this were often more than 20 miles long, with deep mud most of the way.

I remember only too well my first two trips to Alaska in 1977 and 1981:

I took both trips with the same 1977 Suzuki – a reliable road machine, but it didn't handle well on any kind of gravel or other loose surface, especially the way I had it loaded. But on each of those trips I managed to ride on more than 2,000 miles of dirt and loose gravel, and sometimes through quagmires of mud for more than 20 miles at a time. There were other times during the trip that I rode through many miles of snow, and I still managed to do a fair amount of exploring. I certainly had my hands full on both of those trips, and I'm not anxious to take on that kind of challenge again very soon, especially at my age.

My 1977 Suzuki GS750, loaded for the 1977 trip, with far too much weight behind the rear axle. I was 52 then.

June 3, 1981 - Eagle Plains, YT - 231 miles up the Dempster Highway and only 12 miles from the Arctic Circle, about a week before the road was due to open for the season.

There was still plenty of ice in the mountain passes in the Northwest Territories when I attempted to make it to Inuvik in June 1981. This photo was taken at one of the passes along the Dempster Highway, several miles north of the Arctic Circle. The permafrost road surface was very slick in places.

It also brought back memories of my fifth trip to Alaska in 1992, which was the 50th anniversary year of the Alaska Highway. In spite of its being paved for its entire length, I rode my 1986 Honda Gold Wing on more than 2,000 miles of gravel roads to get to Anchorage and back while purposely avoiding as much of the main highway as I could, due to the heavy RV traffic that was expected to be using it that year – and also to satisfy a passion for exploring some of the most remote areas.

I carried extra gas in Prestone bottles on the back seat of the Gold Wing through the longest gaps in gas availability. I met my objective of avoiding the heavy RV traffic though, in that I saw practically no vehicles at all for days, and I was in my glory, riding all by myself in the far reaches of the Canadian wilderness, where I saw bear, bison, caribou, fox, lynx, and many other animals in their natural habitat.

1992: Mud on a deserted South Canol Rd in the Yukon Territory

Those many memories convinced me that the Dakar wouldn't be a bad choice after all – if I could get it ready in time. At least the stock Dakar seat was the most comfortable I had ever ridden for a small bike, and together with the much-improved long-travel suspension, the machine offered a very comfortable and confident ride – and although the engine was a mere 650cc single, it had been proven to be more than capable of maintaining speeds of 80 mph and higher all day, which was faster than I ever needed or intended to travel.

The Dakar handled exceptionally well on any type of surface, including the loosest terrain at just about any speed I chose to travel. My main concern was with its wind protection; although as it turned out, that was only one of many issues I would have to deal with and resolve before leaving on this trip.

Having bought the Dakar as an adventure touring machine, I had already carried the original small windshield to Gustafsson Plastics in St. Augustine, Florida in early March of that year during my annual pilgrimage to Daytona Bike Week, so that Leif, the owner, could use it as a template to make a taller custom windshield for the bike. I tried three different brands of aftermarket windshields and found them all to be far less than satisfactory. Now, all I had to do was to get Leif to finish it up and send it back to me in time.

Halfway through June, the bike was still without a windshield, and I was on the phone several times during those last few weeks trying to get him to finish it up and ship it. I explained my situation and pleaded with him to make a special effort and send it second-day air – or at least send back the original. In spite of having several other hot jobs going, he said he would try.

I ran into another problem while testing a set of leather throw-over saddlebags that I bought for the trip. I thought they would be a good addition to the tank bag and tank panniers for carrying just about everything I wanted to bring. While searching around for various types of heat shields to use that would protect one of the bags from the muffler, I noticed that the muffler had already burned a hole clear through the backside of one of the new leather saddlebags – and also through one of the Tingley slip-over rain boots that I was carrying inside.

I called Jake to see if he could pick up another pair of boots for me at his local farm store upstate where I bought the last pair, but unfortunately they were fresh out of my giant size, so I taped the burned-out hole with duct tape for the time being, and I hoped to find another pair before leaving.

I eventually decided to go without saddlebags. I could always pack the Tingley boots elsewhere – even under a bungee cord. But I eventually wore them for most of the trip to cut down on the luggage and to be prepared for unexpected showers.

I've found over the years that it's more convenient for me, and much less expensive, to wear a pair of athletic hiking shoes on my trips, and to slip the boots over them whenever necessary, rather than wear leather motorcycle boots, which usually aren't totally waterproof anyway, unless you spend a fortune. Leather boots are also heavier for walking, especially when wet. My experience with the Tingley boots has been that after riding in heavy downpours all day, my feet are still perfectly dry – and then in the evening, I can walk to dinner wearing the same comfortable pair of hiking shoes, rather than slogging along in a soggy pair of wet motorcycle boots.

I replaced the original knobby tires with a new set of Metzler Tourance dual sport tires that I hoped would go the distance, although I still planned on stopping at Phil Bourdon's farm in Wisconsin for a brief visit during our return trip. I had changed tires at Phil's on several previous occasions, but I'd rather not have to do it on this trip if I could help it.

Phil is a good friend and a charter member of our RAMS enduro club who moved to Wisconsin several years ago from Connecticut. I try to visit with him and his family whenever I'm passing through, which is usually during a return trip from Alaska when I need the tire that I already sent to him.

Changing the R1150GS rear tire at Phil Bourdon's farm in 2001.

I assumed that I'd be cutting it close with the tires this time by planning to make the trip on a single set. Even though I usually get more than 15,000 miles from a rear tire at home, I've noticed on earlier trips that tire wear seems to be accelerated on Canadian highways. It could also be from the weight of the luggage or the higher speeds that I travel, but I can never get nearly the same mileage on trips to Alaska that I get around home or on other trips.

I also thought that maybe the tire-wear on a single-cylinder motorcycle might be faster than what I was accustomed to on the multi-cylinder street bikes. But I still chose to deal with it later – and then only if I had to.

My custom windshield finally arrived late in the afternoon on the day before we were scheduled to leave. I quickly unpacked and installed it, only to learn from a test ride that it didn't do quite what I hoped it would – keep most of the wind and weather off my face, shoulders and torso. But it was better than any of the others I tried, and it would certainly be better than no windshield at all. At least it kept the wind out of my face better than the small stock windshield that came with the bike. I decided to go with it and hope for the best.

I was finally ready to leave on a four-week, 11,000-mile trip to Alaska with a dirt bike, a patched-up pair of rain boots, no saddlebags and a windshield that wouldn't keep the weather off of me. But I had a lot of confidence in the bike, and I was anxious to get underway on what I figured would be a great ride.

Needless to say, without the saddlebags I brought a lot less gear than usual and I packed exceptionally light; and I was well aware before leaving that it would be a rough trip for my 79-year-old body. But I called Jim and told him I was ready to go.

The 2003 BMW F650GS Dakar, as it looked on the Alaska trip. I was packed exceptionally light for a one-month motorcycle trip.

Here is most of what I wore and carried:

Blue jeans – (wore one, size 38; carried one, size 40)
    (larger size for extra winter clothes underneath)
T-shirts, socks, handkerchiefs (3 each)
Under shorts, undershirts (2 each – Wickers quick-dry)
Long-sleeve, white polypropylene T-shirt for hot
    summer riding.
Regular weight long-john top (Wickers quick-dry)
Double Force Damart long-john top (high-tech, heavy)
Double Force Damart sweats (bottom only)
Medium weight jacket (fits under the touring jacket)
FirstGear touring jacket, without liner
Gauntlet winter gloves and heavy gauntlet mittens
Damart glove and mitten liners
Lightweight riding gloves
Conventional rain gear, Hippo Hands, Tingley boots
Wear athletic hiking shoes (over-the-ankle type)
Baseball cap, warm stocking cap
Prescription sunglasses, spare regular glasses
License, registration, US and Canadian insurance cards
    (Now need passport or federal ID card)
Razors, toothbrush, toothpaste
Pen, pencil, pad, addresses
Sharpie pens for book signing.
Addresses, phone numbers, email addresses
BMW owner's manual and dealer directory
US and Canadian currency, credit and debit cards
Extra plastic (grocery) bags, two large kitchen bags
Duct tape, laundry soap, first aid kit, small flashlight
Spare bike key, extra oil, chain lube, bungee cords
Tube sealer, tube repair kit, CO_2 cartridges, rags
Medication, vitamins, prescription eye drops
Miscellaneous over-the-counter meds, sleeping pills
Granola bars, raisins, sardines
Small Brita water bottle, extra Brita filters

After returning from this trip, I decided that my advanced age warrants using an electrically-heated jacket liner and heated gloves, as well as waterproof touring bottoms, to go along with the touring jacket – all of which I got after returning from the trip, in addition to a few other improvements.

As we neared our departure date, Jake decided to ride along with us as far as Vintage Days in Ohio. My main interests in Ohio were the book-signing event and picking up a new pair of boots. Jake and Jim had other interests, mainly to do with the swap meet; but also visiting with friends, including guys from the Ossa and SMOG groups. Jake said he laid out a nice two-day course to get there that included several back roads across Pennsylvania, West Virginia and part of Ohio, which I was anxious to ride.

They left Jake's home in Slingerlands, New York around 8 AM on the 14th of July. I left around the same time and hooked up with them a few hours later at a rendezvous point in Royal, Pennsylvania where they were already having breakfast when I arrived.

We rode through several showers and thunderstorms on the first day. At the start of one of the heaviest, we passed under a bridge where we could have stopped to wait out the worst of the deluge, but since Jake probably thought I would call him a wimp if he ducked under a bridge, he proceeded to take us right through the eye of the storm.

He and Jim were much better prepared than I was for the heavy rain, with newer hi-tech waterproof riding suits. As a result, I got totally soaked, especially since my once-waterproof riding jacket was no longer very waterproof after having had more than 150,000

miles of exposure to all kinds of weather – which is
why I usually carry a traditional rain suit to slip over
it whenever it rains hard enough, like it was that day.
Unfortunately I never got the chance to put it on,
which I probably would have done if I had been
traveling alone.

Luckily I was wearing the rain suit bottoms from
when I left home, since occasional thunderstorms
were forecast for the day – although the bottoms were
pretty well worn too, and the seams at the crotch
were no longer waterproof – if they ever were. It was
not a surprise that my left foot got totally soaked
from the huge burn-hole in the boot. Needless to say,
the temporary duct tape patch didn't work for long in
the downpour, and I was reminded that finding a new
pair was an essential chore when we got to Ohio.

We reached Clearfield, Pennsylvania, near Dubois,
around 5 PM, for a total of 385 miles. Not bad
considering the weather and the twisty route Jake had
chosen, as well as our relatively late starting time. As
usual, Jake included what he refers to as an
"obligatory dirt section" in the Allegheny Mountains
that we rode in spite of the rain. We rode through two
strong storms that day with thunder and lightning
crackling and flashing all around us. I thought it was
a great ride though, and certainly exciting enough – I
enjoyed every minute of it.

I never did get around to putting on my rain gear top
and I felt like a drowned rat by the end of the day; but
in spite of it all, I still considered it to be a good day.
The only dry spot on me was the foot inside the
Tingley boot without the burn hole.

At least we arrived safely and we had some good laughs afterward while recapping the day's events over a few beers at the motel – part of the fun of traveling with guys like Jake and Jim, both excellent traveling companions.

Jake's second day included Ohio Rte 555, the famed "Triple-Nickel" – or infamous, as the case may be. I had ridden it several times in the past, as I think Jake also did. That particular part of the ride turned out to be somewhat anticlimactic for both of us because we had ridden several more interesting roads getting there, including Ohio Rte 255, which was just as twisty, scenic and exciting, and it might even have had a few less sand patches on the turns. Jake vowed never to ride the "Triple-Nickel" again, and I don't think I've been over it since then either.

A scene along Ohio Rte 255. How often does one see a freshly painted Mail Pouch barn anymore?

I remember the time when a patch of sand along Rte 555 surprised my friend Peter Davidson on an earlier trip to Vintage Days, back when the event was held in Westerville. Peter had been following me on his bike of

choice for the trip, a Yamaha SRX600, equipped with
clip-on handlebars. Joe Mitchell was riding with us on
a Kawasaki KLR 650. I leaned my big Honda Gold
Wing quite heavily into one of the tighter turns and felt
the rear wheel drift a little on some sand that was hard
to see – like black ice.

Seconds later, I heard the bizarre sound of metal
against blacktop behind me, as Peter hit the same
patch of hard-to-see sand while deep into his own
knee-touching turn; except that I think he hit a slightly
deeper part of the patch of sand than I did, causing his
bike to break traction altogether, skid out, and slide
clear off the road and into the adjacent field. He got a
few noticeable road burns on his right arm and right
leg from it, as did the vintage bike, but we were able to
resume our trip after stopping briefly in the next town
for a few first aid supplies and the prompt application
thereof.

It was mostly cloudy the second day with Jake and
Jim, with only a few light showers. We arrived at
Bellville around 6 PM where we would be staying for
the next few days. It was an hour later than we had
planned, but we rode a lot of good stuff getting there.
Our overall day's journey, including some of West
Virginia and the exciting ride through the hills of
southeastern Ohio, made our late arrival not only
worthwhile, but it was in fact a really nice ride, and it
gave us much to talk and laugh about that evening.

Jim had asked at least a month before we left for a
suggested list of items to carry, which I sent to him.
While the three of us were having a few beers
together in the room that night, Jim asked, "When are
we going to get into these sardines?" They were on
my list for when there is no place open for breakfast
– I would often stop for the night in remote areas

where there wouldn't be any restaurants around. The sardines work out well as not only a substitute for breakfast, but they're also a great source of protein for us old guys.

I answered, "Not yet, Jim. Why do you ask?"

He said, "I was just wondering because I packed 21 cans." OMG! – That would be one for every day of the trip after leaving Ohio. I didn't ask what he was thinking, but I hadn't specified how many, or when we might be getting into them. Actually we did get into the sardines several times during the trip, in addition to granola bars and raisins, which are also often on my list of things to carry.

It reminded me of my sixth trip to Alaska in 1996 with Jake and Bud Peck when we were a few hours out of Flin Flon, Manitoba, somewhere in north-central Saskatchewan – pretty much in the middle of nowhere. I had stopped in the middle of the scarcely-traveled gravel road for a nature break. We hadn't seen another vehicle or sign of civilization for at least an hour, and we left Flin Flon before any breakfast places were open. Bud naturally asked, "Where are we stopping for breakfast?"

I said, "I was thinking of right here," as I reached in the trunk of the Gold Wing for a tin of sardines that I was carrying.

Bud, who always looked forward to and treasured his sunny-side-up eggs with several strips of crisp lean bacon and a nice hot cup of coffee in the morning, said with an attitude, "You've got to be kidding!"

He refused to partake of the sardines and dug somewhat begrudgingly into his own bag for some beef jerky while Jake and I shared a can of the fish, and the three of us stood there having breakfast in the middle

of the road in a light drizzle with the temperature in the
mid 40s. It's certainly not the classiest of breakfast
places, but I think it worked out well enough under the
circumstances.

The two-day stay in Ohio with Jake and Jim was
interesting and enjoyable for the three of us, each in
our own way, albeit a little expensive for the frugal
Friesian. Our discounted room rent at the Ramada Inn
for the "special event weekend" came to more than
$160 per night for the three nights, not to mention the
nearby high-priced steakhouse that we chose for our
dinners two out of the three nights; but I do admit the
first-class accommodations and food were excellent,
leaving us with no real regrets.

I had called the AMA earlier to see what they could
do for us after I learned from calling several motels
in the area that everything was either fully-booked or
cost more than $200 a night. They graciously offered
the reservations to me from a block of rooms they
had reserved for VIPs attending Vintage Days. I'm
sure it was because I was doing the book signing.

I seldom reserve rooms ahead for any of my trips, but
I usually do the research to make sure there are some
kind of accommodations in the general area of where
I plan to stop – even sometimes for places where
there is only a slight possibility of my stopping,
especially when I'm not prepared for camping. This
was an exception, as I knew that thousands of bikers
would come for the weekend and they would have
made their reservations in advance, making any kind
of accommodations difficult to find at the last minute.

For huge events like this, it's not uncommon that I
would take a room as far away as 60 to 70 miles from
the activities, which is usually only a little over an

hour ride – and for me, the ride is what I come for in the first place, as opposed to the destination. I view it merely as putting a few hundred extra miles onto the trip total, doing what I enjoy most.

Jake graciously shared the room rent equally for the first two out of the three nights, in spite of sleeping on the rollaway for those nights. He left for home early Saturday morning to be back in time for our RAMS club's annual summer picnic the following day. We were sorry to see him go because we had been doing very well together as a group, and I had learned earlier that Jake is a great person to have along on an extended trip. My experience has been that some travel companions can get downright testy after the second or third week together, but it's never been the case with Jake. If anything, it brings out his sense of humor, in spite of some of the weird idiosyncrasies of others – including me sometimes.

On Friday, while Jake and Jim browsed the swap meet and chatted with friends, I managed to locate a Tractor Supply Company store in Bucyrus that stocked giant-size Tingley boots, and I bought a pair to replace the burned-out pair. I clocked at least 100 miles that day searching for them, but I met a lot of nice people along the way and had lunch at a small, friendly roadside stand in the country – which made it a nice overall experience.

The AMA Hall of Fame Museum had invited me to the book-signing event at their tent where two of my books were being sold. The event included some luminaries from the past, a few of whom I had met before. The overall turnout was disappointing due to a series of heavy rain showers that hit the area just prior to and during the time that the signing was scheduled. The museum people invited me to return on Sunday, but I declined because Jim and I planned to leave early that morning for Alaska.

During the time I was at the tent, I enjoyed making a few new friends and chatting with many old friends like Bill and Millie Baird, who have been dear friends for more than 40 years. Bill was a member of the AMA Hall of Fame Museum Board of Directors, as well as a member of the AMA Hall of Fame for his outstanding enduro career, including winning seven consecutive national championships. I also chatted with Don Rosene, the motorcycle dealer from Anchorage, who assured me he would be back home in time for our arrival there.

Among other Hall of Fame members who I met and spoke briefly with at the tent that day were Dick Klamforth, dirt track and road racing ace of the 40s, 50s and 60s, and John Penton and Dave Mungenast, both of whom I competed with in the enduros during the sixties and early seventies.

The event attracts many famous motorcycle people to Ohio, most of whom I've found to be friendly and easy to talk with, like Craig Vetter, who was inducted into the Hall of Fame for his innovative design, manufacture and marketing of the famous fairings and windshields that bear his name. I used one of his Windjammer III fairings on my 1977 Suzuki during my first two trips to Alaska, and I wished I had something nearly as efficient for this trip.

I located Mike Friedle at the BMW MOA booth. Mike, who is one of the officials of the group, had said earlier that he would bring along some anti-fog paste for my face shield – the type used by deep-sea divers. He graciously offered it the week before I left while we were having lunch together with a few other friends in Cold Spring, near home, after I mentioned that I was having trouble with my glasses and face shield fogging up in heavy rain. The paste worked out well on this trip and later, although we ran into a few cold, early-morning fog banks where I doubt if anything would have worked very well.

Jim and I left Ohio together early Sunday morning. It became somewhat of a time of reflection for me as I reminisced over the events of the last few days. I was focused on racking up some miles, rather than I was on the scenery and the thrill of the back roads, so we were heading north on I-75 at "warp speeds." I guess I was anxious to get started – I had the feeling that we were finally on our way.

A few hours later I lost my prescription sunglasses somewhere along the interstate when they flew out of the pocket of the light jacket I was wearing. We were running around 80 mph at the time. I felt them go, but there was nothing I could do about it, which is only one of the disadvantages of traveling on the super-slab. I blamed it at least partially on the poor wind protection from my new custom windshield, but I should also have put them in a more secure place.

Another problem I had with the windshield that day on the slab was the roar of the wind in my ears. My left ear actually hurt from it after a while. I had unkind thoughts about Leif Gustafsson and his windshield several times, as well as later on the trip, although I can't blame it on Leif because he gave me almost exactly what I had specified, and it was the best of several aftermarket windshields I had tried over the past year and a half. Jim offered a spare set of earplugs that he was carrying, which made riding at the higher speeds a lot more tolerable.

By using the interstate for about half of the day, we were able to cover more than 600 miles, reaching Escanaba near the western end of Michigan's Upper Peninsula well before nightfall. The weather was great most of the day with clear skies and warm temperatures, although it dropped several degrees a few times along the north shore of Lake Michigan – like it often does in that area.

It was in the mid-fifties when we left Escanaba soon after first light, and we quickly entered the Central Time Zone to gain an hour. Much of the two-lane roads I chose for the day had a third lane for passing about every five miles or so in Michigan as well as much of the way across Wisconsin and Minnesota. It turned out to be a nice ride.

I generally tried to hold the speed to a steady seventy most of the day whenever the conditions permitted, although I'm quite sure the posted limit was less in most areas. The area was sparsely populated for the most part, with very little traffic of any kind, so it wasn't like we were risking our lives or anyone else's for that matter.

My original plan was to find a motel in or near Warroad, Minnesota, hopefully on the Canadian side of the border. I figured the border would probably be closed at night and that the gate would be locked until 8 or 8:30 AM. I would rather avoid the delay of going through in the morning because I usually like to be on the road soon after first light.

I also figured we might be more likely to get a thorough screening in the morning, which I hoped to avoid. As it turned out, we reached Warroad in mid-afternoon, so we pressed on, taking less than a minute to pass through Canadian customs, like the old days; it's always been much quicker through the Canadian side anyway than coming back into the US where I've had a few of the thorough screenings.

After riding across about 70 miles of bleak scrubland in southern Manitoba, I spotted a motel in Steinbach, the first town of any size we came to. We covered more than 630 miles, most of it on two-lane roads, and I was beginning to get a bit weary.

The weather was nice for most of the day and it got quite warm during the afternoon, but the wind was strong from the side in some places and we rode through some light rain showers.

Jim probably wondered if I planned to push that long and hard every day, unless he was having much less of a problem with the wind on his bigger bike than I was with the little 650. Much of the problem with riding a lightweight across the prairie at the higher speeds comes from the frequent blasts of relentless side winds, usually out of the southwest. The tank bag needs to be lashed down securely or it'll get blown clear off the tank. I've found that if it's not lashed down well enough, it often ends up on my lap. I carry an extra bungee cord to hold it down tight whenever the wind is that strong.

Jim certainly had better wind and weather protection than I did, and possibly a smoother ride with the bigger bike, although I was happy with the comfort of the ride except when the wind made it a little tougher to control. I had concluded by this time that the Dakar would make an excellent long-distance adventure-touring bike as long as I avoided the high-speed interstate highways. I learned several things on this trip about riding a lightweight across the prairie at high speeds.

Jim never said anything about the 600-mile, non-interstate days being too grueling for him, nor did he complain about anything; but that day coming into Steinbach was admittedly a long day. Some of it was a little monotonous, and it would become a grueling pace under those circumstances. And that's without mentioning the extra hour we gained from the time-zone change, making it more than twelve hours of steady riding – not bad for two old geezers! I usually prefer to continue riding for that bonus time-change hour rather than spend it in the motel unless we especially needed the rest or the weather is bad.

Running at the maximum allowable speeds on the highway is certainly not my favorite way of traveling to Alaska and back, or anywhere else for that matter, but my main objective on this trip was to get there and back safely in a month without a great deal of adventure touring. I wanted to give Jim a sample of at least a day or two on some of the more remote gravel byways in the Yukon Territory and take in a few of the more scenic highlights that are accessible without venturing too far off the beaten path – like the Beartooth Highway in Montana and Chief Joseph Highway in Wyoming, to mention just a few.

I think we were both pretty well beat when we got to the motel around 6 PM. Jim went out in search of a six-pack, which he did just about every night. It helped us relax and defuse any tensions that might have built up during the day. I ended up drinking more beer on this trip than I have in the past 30 years.

The beer might have helped to relieve dehydration from some of the long, tough days against the wind too, but I suppose that's debatable, as alcohol is a natural diuretic. We learned from the desk clerk that cold beer wasn't readily available in Steinbach, so the guy gave Jim a map and some detailed directions on how to find it on the other side of town.

A few words at this point about my eyesight that had been getting progressively worse over the past few years: I was often unable to read road signs unless the sun was somewhere behind me and shining on the sign. The same applied to my instruments like the odometer that I needed for following my route sheet; and the bike's clock, both of which use pale LED displays. I couldn't read the route sheet on my tank bag either unless I came to a complete stop first, even though I used a 14-size font with bold lettering.

My eyes are on the borderline for keeping my driver's license that I can only get with a signature from my eye doctor – and she sometimes shudders when I tell her about some of my motorcycling experiences; but maybe she thinks I'm exaggerating to spice up the story!

I could rarely see the Canadian route markings during this trip, which are considerably smaller and less bold than most of those in the US. I can also rarely see motel and/or restaurant signs unless they're within less than 100 feet and I'm moving slowly. I usually had no problem with the "Golden Arches" though, which I suppose is one of the reasons they chose that particular symbol.

Whenever the light is subdued, as it often gets on overcast days, I have difficulty seeing cars coming

from the opposite direction for any great distance –
especially when it's raining and they're coming
toward me without headlights, which also makes it a
lot tougher to pass on two-lane roads. I almost never
execute the bold passes anymore for which I had
become known a few years back when my eyesight
and reflexes were a lot better.

Lately I would ride without my prescription glasses
whenever it got too dark for me to see well enough
through both layers of plastic – my glasses and the
face shield – like when it's heavily overcast or
raining. Using the face shield alone works much
better in the rain than glasses alone. Using the glasses
alone, the rainwater would get onto both sides of the
glasses, doubling the amount of raindrops I have to
see through with my one good eye.

Eliminating either layer of plastic allows for more
light to pass through to the retina of the good eye; but
without the necessary corrective lenses, I sometimes
see blurred and would still be unable to see oncoming
cars or trucks that happen to be running without their
headlights. Either way cuts down on my ability to see
and to pass safely, not to mention my overall safety
out there.

One advantage I'm fortunate to have is that I have a
fairly good memory of the routes I've used to and
from Alaska, and I have a pretty good sense of
direction. I can remember route numbers, landmarks
and where to turn from the many previous trips – or
at least from having studied the maps so often while
searching for new and different ways to get there.
One might say I should know the way by now. Of
course that's not so with adventure touring where I

would be traveling on seldom-used byways that I'd be exploring for the first time.

I could probably make the trip to Alaska and back quite easily without maps, prepared route sheets or a GPS. I'd be unable to read a GPS most of the time anyway because of my somewhat unique vision problem with LED displays. Then, too, I usually try to vary my route each time I go to and from Alaska to make it more interesting.

I stopped occasionally during this trip to ask Jim what route we were on, just to make sure that I hadn't missed a turn. In the beginning he wasn't paying much attention to route signs and he would shrug his shoulders like he didn't know; but after realizing how little I was seeing, he kept pretty good track of the route sheet I had prepared, and he would pull alongside whenever I missed a turn. That wasn't often, but it did happen.

Jim must have pulled up alongside dozens of times to tell me to turn off my turn indicator when I'd forget, which happened mostly because I had become used to riding the bigger machines with the automatic cancel function. After pulling alongside, he would use his left hand to make gestures like a quacking duck to tell me that the turn signal was still on. It worked, but I'm sure he got pretty sick of that chore after a while! I could almost never see the pale-green light flashing on my instrument panel to tell me that the it was flashing. I'm somewhat colorblind to green anyway, and I usually don't see green LEDs at all, unless they're extra bright.

That problem applies to the green LED traffic signals too unless they're also extra bright, or when I'm close enough. I can see red LED signals a little better but not much. I can usually see the yellow signals, which helps, because it gives me a clue that there's probably a light up ahead that's about to turn red.

Since I have several blind spots in both eyes just above the middle from glaucoma damage, I would sometimes see the "stop line" painted on the road before I would see the traffic light pod hanging from above, which is often too late if I'm traveling much faster than 20 mph. Many times I'd be too close when I finally see it, and I'd have to decide quickly whether to lock the brakes or go through the light. To cope with the problem in strange towns, I would usually move the blind spots around by moving my head around. That way I'd be scanning for hanging traffic light pods, giving me a clue that I might be approaching a red light. So far I've been able to manage all of these vision handicaps without having too many problems.

We had an early breakfast in Steinbach and a second breakfast around ten o'clock in Neepawa, both at McDonald's. I've heard that people who have read my *Motorcycling Stories* book sometimes say, "This guy must like McDonald's!" That may be so, but it's beside the point. The real point is that I'd much rather ride than eat, no matter how good the breakfast or lunch might be at some of the better restaurants or cafes along the way.

I'd much rather be riding my motorcycle any day and enjoying the scenery, than waiting impatiently for a waitress to bring a menu or to bring the food at a time when I could be out there enjoying myself. This is especially true when I'm traveling alone where all of the time I might spend sitting alone in a restaurant is quality time taken from the enjoyment of my trip. There's a time and a place for everything, and this is my time for riding – not eating. Whenever I'm on a trip, especially the solo trips, the greatest pleasure is the riding and enjoying the beautiful and interesting countryside as opposed to making my fat cells happy in some fancy restaurant.

We reached the outskirts of Saskatoon around 4 PM where I've stayed several times, and where I planned on stopping this time. But since we were running at least an hour ahead of my schedule and it was a nice day, I decided to pass through the city and get back onto the prairie. I thought it was beginning to look a bit foreboding anyway, and I remembered that North Brattleford, Alberta was about an hour from there. I realized it would put us a little out of sync with where we'd find the next overnight accommodations, but I figured I could deal with that when I came to it.

When we got about 20 miles out of Saskatoon, the crosswinds that we had run through most of the day suddenly picked up to around 40 mph with many stronger gusts, and I saw a rainsquall sweeping across the prairie out of the southwest that was heading directly toward us. My first thought was to stop and slip on my rain pants, although I thought it might already be too late. I decided to try putting them on anyway, and we pulled over onto the shoulder.

After stopping and putting the bike on the kickstand, the wind got much stronger, and I realized we were caught out on the open prairie with no haven from it – and it was bearing down on us like a freight train. I had difficulty getting the pants out of my tank bag while trying to hold the bike from blowing over at the same time, even though it was on its stand. I soon realized we were somewhat helpless out there at the mercy of the storm.

I managed to get the pants out, but I had all I could do to hold onto them as they flapped wildly in the wind. I eventually stopped trying to put them on, and I concentrated on holding the bike up by bracing myself against it. We were literally trapped until the wind abated, at least a little. Thinking back, this was not the first time I've been caught on the prairie in a rainsquall while crossing Saskatchewan.

It was quite a scene and a bit scary! I remember thinking at the time that I needed waterproof bottoms to go with the riding suit, and I vowed to get them as soon as I got back. But that would only mean that I would probably have tried to ride through it – a chore in itself that I'm glad we didn't do.

As soon as the wind abated and I was able to get the rain pants on, we found a small motel a few miles down the road just before another strong squall came through the area. It was certainly a scary experience but also a memorable one that becomes part of our overall adventure. I mentioned to Jim that night that we had passed our halfway point, which I usually consider to be Saskatoon whenever I go that way. I'm not sure if that little insignificant bit of trivia was of much interest to him at that point.

We ate our dinner meal and also breakfast the next morning at a nearby truck stop. I didn't care much for the dinner special, but the breakfast was passable – usually the case at truck stops. I thought at the time that a fast-food place would have been at least as good and certainly much quicker and it would have cost less. But I rarely choose a fast-food place for the dinner meal unless it's the only place around. Waiting for service at dinnertime doesn't take anything away from riding, so I don't mind if it takes longer – especially if there's someone to talk with.

It rained quite a bit while we slept and it was still raining in the morning – enough to get wet going to and from the restaurant both times even though it was only a quarter-mile ride.

We had been getting up regularly at 5:15, plus or minus about 15 minutes, and we would usually be on the road by 6:30 following breakfast and the bike-loading routine. A few hours after leaving the motel that morning, we rode through more rain showers for a little over an hour. The temperature hovered in the mid-fifties most of the way across Saskatchewan and into Alberta. I felt chilly most of the morning from the rain and the dampness, and I wondered if it would last all day.

It was still cloudy when we got to the Alberta line, but it began to warm up by the time we reached Trans Canada 16 – the superhighway that took us the last 30 miles into Edmonton. The skies finally cleared, and it became a really nice day. Even the wind died down as we got into the foothills of the Canadian Rockies. We stopped for a late lunch at a fast-food place that I spotted just before leaving Edmonton.

I noticed that my gas mileage was very bad. I figured that the strong prairie headwinds, combined with the speeds we had been traveling, brought our equivalent airspeed to more than 100 mph in spots, which I'm sure is what helped to drop it well below 45 mpg for the first time on the trip. I always try to watch the gas mileage closely because it can be an early warning of engine problems.

Saskatchewan gas was evidently part of the cause, which is something I learned from a guy I met while camping in this area many years ago. He said he worked in the Canadian oil industry and that the Saskatchewan gas is much less efficient than most, especially from the refinery in Moose Jaw that he said was a very poor grade, and that it would gum up carburetors on most vehicles. He named a few brands that were worse than others, but I don't recall the names.

I suppose that would also apply to fuel injectors, maybe even more so, although the refining process must have improved a lot since my first trip through that area almost 30 years ago. But I had been getting 70 mpg at home with the same bike and I was averaging 50-60 mpg on this trip, and now suddenly it's less than 45 mpg.

About a half-hour after leaving our lunch stop, we turned north from Trans Canada 16 onto Hwy 43. I noticed that Rte 43 had been upgraded considerably since the last time I went that way. I had heard it was now like a superhighway most of the way to Dawson Creek where the Alaska Highway begins, although the route I planned for this time didn't have us going that way.

At least it was finished to Grande Prairie where we stopped for the night around 4:45 after another 600-mile day. We gained an hour from another time-zone change too, making it one of our earliest stops of the trip. I favored Grande Prairie for the stop rather than Dawson Creek or Fort St. John, especially after I noticed the low motel prices. It seems strange that I could read the sign when I can rarely read any of the other signs, but this one was huge.

We rode through several brief showers that afternoon, although it had warmed up nicely during the day. Grande Prairie is one of several towns along the way that have grown considerably since my first trip to Alaska in 1977. Saskatoon and Whitehorse are the two that seem to have grown the most.

We chose a beautiful new motel that just opened for business. The room had housekeeping facilities, a mini kitchen, a working fireplace, and it was very reasonably priced. The motel also had its own first-class restaurant inside the building where we had two whopping 25-ounce schooners of Canadian draft beer for each of us with our meals. That's a lot of beer, but it was a special deal to go with their grand-opening celebration, so we availed ourselves of the bargain as well as the opportunity to join in on the celebration.

Later that same evening, Jim left the room to move the bikes around to the rear of the building for better security. He mentioned that he was leaving the door slightly ajar. He was out of the room for less than a minute when I heard a light tapping at the door, which seemed suspicious to me, so I got up to answer it rather than invite whoever it was into the room. The guy seemed surprised when I opened the door and his body language made me think that he didn't expect anyone to be in the room. I assumed that he saw Jim leave because it was that soon afterward. I didn't say a word at first but just looked at him.

He said nervously, "Oh, I thought Steve Walker had this room," which I assumed was a made-up name. It appeared obvious to me that our room was about to be rifled if no one had answered. Unfortunately many people get robbed that way when they leave the room unattended and the door slightly ajar, even for just a few moments. I could also have been in the shower at the time and not heard the light tapping. I said, "Check with the desk," and I closed the door in his face. I suppose I should have reported it, but I didn't.

It was sprinkling when we left Grande Prairie and a lot cooler than any morning so far – not uncommon for that far north. But the skies soon cleared, and it became a really nice day. We gassed up in Dawson Creek at the start of the Alaska Highway and Jim took a few photos at "Mile Zero" of the almost 1400-mile highway.

Jim's first experience with one of the infamous steel-grated bridges along the Alaska Highway with their deep grooves running in the direction of travel came that morning while crossing the Peace River. The grooves can be disconcerting to a motorcyclist and even turn the knuckles a little white if they're not expecting it, and Jim wasn't.

We ran through our first cold, zero-visibility fog bank in Fort St. John that morning. Truck traffic was stop-and-go and exceptionally heavy in town, causing us to lose about 20 minutes riding through a half-mile of thick fog and heavy traffic. I eventually had to flip the face shield up, remove my glasses and ride with bare eyeballs in order to see anything at all as we felt our way through town.

Once we got through the town, the fog cleared and we started the long, steady climb into the beautiful Canadian Rockies where the scenery begins to get spectacular. Some of the mountain peaks still had snow cover. The area between Pink Mountain and Fort Nelson is rich in wildlife, with beautiful scenery and practically no services. We stopped for lunch at an A&W later in Fort Nelson, and stopped again near the summit of Steamboat for photos of the beautiful panorama, but generally we pressed on.

Later we stopped at Summit Lake for more photos and again near Stone Mountain on our way down through the canyon west of the summit where many Stone's sheep of a thin-horn variety are often crossing the highway and standing around in the parking areas and the road. Many of the sheep can be seen climbing the sheer, rocky canyon walls from where they dislodge stones that often come tumbling down onto the road surface far below.

We spoke briefly with a small group of riders at the viewpoint along the canyon descent and learned that they were headed home to Alberta after having visited Alaska. One of the guys riding a big Honda ST-1300 sport-touring bike complained about the condition of Hwy 37, which they used for their trip north. He said they were now avoiding it, in spite of the extra time it was taking to go around. I asked him how much gravel was left on Hwy 37 because we intended to return that way. His answer was, "More than a hundred miles." I have been using Hwy 37, previously known as the Cassiar Highway, since soon after it first opened in late 1976, and it has always been one of my all-time-favorite roads. I've traveled that way on almost every one of my Alaska trips since then, either going up or coming back.

Jim at the viewpoint along the canyon descent, west of the summit. Some of the scenery in that area is mind-boggling.

Taken in early June 1977 at the start of the Cassiar Highway on opening day of its first full season in use. Ahead lie 480 miles of narrow gravel road through pristine forests of central British Columbia, a ride that offered some of the most beautiful scenery imaginable in an area once known as "Bigfoot country."

The photo was also taken along the Cassiar Highway in early June 1977 when it was unpaved for its entire length. I traveled for hundreds of miles that year without ever seeing another vehicle, house or any sign that anyone had ever been there. It was adventure touring at its finest.

I doubted his claim of 100 miles, although I didn't question him further, but I didn't think there could possibly be that much gravel left on the Cassiar because it was down to less than that three years ago when I last went that way, most of which was being prepared for paving – I suppose highway crews could have been upgrading when they went through.

Ever since my first ride on the Cassiar Highway, I've considered it to be one of my most memorable roads, especially back when it was devoid of civilization for its entire 480-mile length. The beautiful mountainous area that it passes through is sometimes known as Sasquatch or Bigfoot Country.

After Jim got a few photos of the scenery around Stone Mountain, and after we had ridden another 30 miles or so, we were approaching the small highway outpost of Toad River in northern British Columbia when I suddenly had my very ugly encounter with one of the wandering wild critters.

We were traveling between 70 and 75 mph on a fairly straight stretch of smooth highway alongside the Toad River when I first caught sight of two full-grown Stone's sheep headed for the other side of the road. They were walking close together and moving at a fairly brisk pace, almost running, and I could see to my horror that their intended path was on a direct collision course with my own; and they were completely oblivious to what was about to happen.

Jim was riding about a quarter mile behind for safety reasons because he was often sightseeing and wanted plenty of room between us in case I slowed for any reason, as I sometimes did. I instinctively locked both brakes with absolutely no hope of avoiding the inevitable because I was already less than 75 feet from impact when I first spotted the sheep – and there was zero time for me to change course or to do anything other than lock the brakes, hang on and leave the rest to God.

It's the moment that we all dread and hope will never happen to us. It comes with a feeling that's hard to describe, but once you've experienced it, you'll never forget it. The trouble with this particular feeling is that most people aren't around to describe it afterward. There was zero time to pray. The locked brakes threw the bike sideways a split-second before the headlight and windshield made initial contact with the head of the lead sheep. Meanwhile, the rear end of the bike whipped around and whacked the sheep full broadside a split-second later.

The powerful collision sent the sheep tumbling down the highway as I clung desperately to the handlebars as tight as I could, maybe even with super-human strength. I'm guessing that my speed at the time of impact was still around 50 mph, with the bike fully sideways and still perfectly upright. The force of the impact almost tore me clear off of the seat sideways, but I was somehow miraculously able to hang on.

My left leg got squeezed between the bike and the sheep's belly at the same instant that the left tank pannier, directly in front of my knee, took the brunt of the impact as it struck the bony area of the sheep's front shoulder. Luckily the pannier, which holds my overnight bag, was a few inches thicker than my knee, and it was fully packed, which is what saved my leg that otherwise would have taken the force of the crushing blow and probably broken it, and maybe broken my knee too. It was a miracle in itself that my leg and knee connected with the sheep's belly, which felt like a huge cushion.

The impact threw the tail end of the bike back to its original straightforward position, and I suddenly found myself facing forward again with the bike now rolling only about 10 mph or less. I was still hanging onto the bars as tight as I could. The whole incident took only a few seconds.

In spite of being in a slight daze and even before the wheels stopped turning, I thanked God, I thanked my angels and I thanked my family and my friends who pray for me. I was convinced that God had just bestowed one of His greatest miracles on me. It was certainly one of the greatest I had ever known, and I've had a few real beauties in my lifetime. I could hardly believe I had come through totally unscathed. It seemed that the end result for me was simply a slightly sprained ankle – the only physical injury I got from it, other than having the wind knocked out of me – and it certainly scared me half-to-death.

When the bike finally came to a complete stop, I felt like a NY Giants linebacker had just hit me, running at full tilt. I sat there and tried to comprehend what had just happened, as I took the inventory of myself. Aside from the wind being knocked out of me, and my left ankle slightly sprained, I was totally intact. I said another prayer of thanksgiving as I sat half-dazed, disbelieving what had just happened.

Feeling something warm and wet on my left ankle broke the trance that I was in. I thought as I looked down that it might have been oil because the oil tank is on that side, directly behind the left pannier that got hit and partially crushed. But I noticed that the fluid on my shoe was yellowish, which made me think about the poor sheep – that maybe I had knocked it out of him.

I reached down and put a finger in it and brought it to my nose and realized it was anti-freeze, which made me think that the impact might have ruptured the radiator. But after removing the side cover we found the rubber cap had been knocked off the expansion tank, causing it to belch out some fluid. A small piece of the lip that holds the cap had broken off, which we were able to seal with duct tape. At first it seemed that the bike was almost as fortunate as I was.

Starting to work on the bike after the collision.
Photo by Jim Hoellerich

Meanwhile, the sheep scampered up the rocky incline and stopped on a ledge far above the road, looking down at us. Jim picked up the sheep's horn that was knocked off, and we could see a bloody socket about two inches deep at its base, and we could see from the road that the missing horn left a two-inch red bloody spike on the sheep's head where the horn had been moments before. By this time the sheep was far up on the mountainside, probably still a little stunned.

The sheep that I hit was on the mountainside moments later with a single horn and a short bloody spike on the other side.

Photo by Jim Hoellerich

Jim handed it to me and said with a smile, "Here's a souvenir for you." He said that his first knowledge that something had happened was when he saw what he thought was a huge piece of cardboard tumbling down the road alongside of me. He continued, "…and then it got up and walked away." I have no idea what happened to the second sheep, but he was lucky – he got away with both horns.

We checked the bike over for other possible damage to see first of all if it was still ride-able. In addition to the broken windshield and minor damage to the neck of the expansion tank, we noticed that the headlight unit, which also holds the instrument panel, had been pushed back a few inches into its mounting and was now too close to the fork legs, causing a restriction in steering, but we lacked the proper tools to do anything about it out there on the highway. The left directional signal was also bent back, the lens was broken and the mounting screws were torn clear out of the decorative cowling that covers the oil tank.

We removed and jettisoned the broken windshield and side-cover, but not before I took the emblem and other parts that I could use later on a new side cover after I got home. One might say ironically that the final fate of the windshield, for which I waited four-and-a-half months, was an un-ceremonial burial in the Toad River. The words I spoke at the interment were other than words of praise but I was still sorry to see it go.

I started the bike and took it for a short test ride a few hundred feet down the road and back, during which time it seemed roadworthy enough while going straight, but the steering was being restricted by the headlight and instrument unit pushed way too far back into the triple-clamp.

But I thought as long as I don't have to make too many tight maneuvers between there and Anchorage, I could probably manage going relatively straight for the next two-and-a-half days. My main concern was riding without a windshield, possibly through many days of cold rain. I thought at the time that I'm getting too old for this, and I felt a little helpless for a moment; but I also felt very blessed, and the thought came to me: "The will of God will never take you to where the Grace of God will not protect you." I was ready to give it a try. I derive a great deal of comfort from my belief in a strong, spiritual, one-on-one, 24/7 relationship with God. He has protected me many times in my lifetime, motorcycling and otherwise, and I was ready and willing to take on the additional risk of the bike's new mechanical handicap.

After working on the bike at the roadside for about 45 minutes, including the test ride, we got underway with hopes of reaching Anchorage without too many more problems. As I began to increase the speed, I gradually gained confidence that there was nothing else seriously wrong mechanically that I needed to be concerned about, particularly with the handling and the engine. I thanked God again for the miracle, and for my life.

We got about a mile down the road when I noticed that a red warning light on the instrument panel was flashing. Being unable to see well enough to recognize the icon, I stopped and asked Jim. He glanced at it and said it was the temperature warning light, which wasn't the greatest of surprises at the time because it was obvious earlier that the expansion tank probably needed refilling after having lost some of its fluid.

We looked around for water and fortunately there was a pond nearby where Jim was able to use one of the thin plastic rain booties that he sometimes pulls over his motorcycle boots to carry a boot-full of water from the pond. We refilled the tank and rechecked the cooling system again for leaks before continuing our journey.

Another 15 miles down the road we were stopped by a female flag-person at the start of about 10 miles of road construction just east of Muncho Lake. A pilot car was in use at the site, and we became the first in line to wait for it to return from the other end of the construction area before taking us through. There was practically no traffic on the road. The pickup truck being used as the pilot car arrived a few minutes later, driven by another girl.

Jim snapped this photo at a later flag station along the Top of the World Road in the rain where I'm sure it gets lonely after a while, and I've often wondered about the young girl's safety.

We talked briefly with the female pilot car driver and the girl holding the traffic-control sign during the few minutes we waited. The girl holding the sign noticed the sheep's horn I was carrying, and after listening to some of the conversation, she asked if we had killed the sheep.

Jim said jokingly, "No, but it must have had one hell of a headache." She warned that I had better not try to "get that thing through customs" because if I were ever caught with it, I "would be in big trouble." The Stone's sheep are apparently a protected species.

The other girl smiled and said she thought it would be worth a try, suggesting that I could always claim I found it alongside the road and that I'm an innocent grandfather who planned on giving it to one of my grandchildren. Eventually I threw it into the woods because I felt I had enough problems already without tempting more – but not before posing for a photo with my trophy.

The sheep's horn that was knocked off in the collision.

I asked the girls about motels at Muncho Lake and specifically about the Muncho Lake Lodge where I remembered stopping with the RAMS in 1991. One of the girls said it was no longer there but said there was a small motel at this end of the lake that was by far the most reasonable in the area.

We got to the place around 4:30, to find that it was a real dump inside. It was a rustic old four-unit motel with no locks on the outside doors; the beds were old and swaybacked; the thin army-type mattresses were filled with lumpy cotton batting; the cot and bedding were badly worn and tattered; the small bathroom was old and smelly; the toilet tank was leaking; and the entire commode unit was loose from the floor. It ranked as the worst accommodations we had on the entire trip, even though the room was still quite expensive because of its location. I doubted that the girl who suggested it had ever been inside the place. The outside didn't look that bad. We were the only occupants that night.

Our tiny 4-unit motel at Muncho Lake
Photo by Jim Hoellerich

Our choice for dinner was either to eat Danish pastry, probably stale, in the lobby with our sardines, or to go a few miles down the road to a newly constructed lodge for a decent meal. Of course we chose the latter. The place was new and beautiful with a huge cathedral ceiling, and it was built entirely from logs. If my memory serves me right, I think it was located on the exact spot as the Muncho Lake Lodge that I had asked about earlier.

We both chose the Weiner Schnitzel, which was the lowest-priced entree on the pricey menu. The bill for our meal, which included a few beers, came to $85 between us. Actually the price wasn't that bad, in that the restaurant was certainly first class for the area and the food was quite good, as was the Canadian beer; and the prices were in Canadian dollars, which was an advantage at the time. It served as a celebration for me for having come through my recent unforgettable experience relatively unscathed.

I feel very fortunate for never having hit an animal of any kind in my first million miles of motorcycling. I've come extremely close to deer several times and to dogs and other animals, but this was the first time I connected – and I came through without a scratch. Considering the speed I was traveling and the size of the animal, and the fact that I was never thrown from the bike, is truly incredible!

The possible consequences of an accident like that at my age are scary to even think about, especially considering the blood-thinning medication that I'm on for one of my heart conditions – and my old bones have gotten much more fragile.

When I looked into my overnight case that night, I was shocked to find how much of the contents were crushed from the impact. The inside was a total mess, with ink, toothpaste, shampoo, broken pieces of plastic bottles and other miscellaneous paraphernalia intermingled with lots of loose pills. And to think – it could have been my knee.

I was able to salvage most of the pills, which were mainly vitamins from a broken plastic vitamin bottle, and I proceeded to thoroughly clean the inside of the case and repack it. Luckily my sardines were in the other pannier, or it would have made much more of a mess, not to mention the smell.

That night Jim named off several animals he had seen that day, including bear, elk, caribou, at least a few dozen sheep of different varieties and several other animals. I didn't see much of anything, and it's too bad I didn't see the sheep a few seconds sooner. I woke up at 3:30 AM and my mind went into high gear – and I couldn't get back to sleep. I concluded from all the midnight pondering that the best thing to do was to call Cliff's BMW in the morning and ask them to overnight the Cee Bailey windshield that I returned months earlier and send it to Don Rosene's shop in Anchorage so I might at least have some weather protection for my torso during the second half of our trip.

I certainly hoped for good weather for the rest of the trip because I knew from testing the Cee Bailey that the shape of it, as well as the mounting, directed a strong current of air at my shoulders, face and head. But I thought I could handle it with the full-face helmet I was wearing. I still expected it to make the ride much less enjoyable for the rest of the trip, but I decided to call Danbury rather than call home to have the small stock windshield sent, because I wasn't ready to break the news of the mishap to my family yet – they would only worry even more than they already do.

Every part of my body ached when we got up at our usual 5:15. My left ankle and my back hurt the most – my left ankle from the impact and my lower back from arthritis and stenosis, especially after sleeping on the lousy swayback bed and lumpy mattress. I didn't get much sleep. We had a sardine and juice breakfast because the nearest place for anything better was Watson Lake, three hours away.

I called Danbury at 6:30 AM local time from a pay phone on the wall outside the motel just before getting underway, which was 9:30 Danbury time on a Friday morning. I didn't think of the cost of overnight shipping with Saturday delivery, and I didn't realize until after getting my Visa receipt a month later that the UPS shipping charges alone came to more than $100.

Combined with the price of the little windshield, the total was well over $200. I certainly would have reconsidered calling home had I thought it through, since I had already tested that windshield and found it to be far less than desirable – to say the least. I knew I would never use it again after I got home.

The first thing I noticed that morning was that it was a perfectly beautiful day, although the temperature was in the mid 40s when we left Muncho Lake. There was barely a cloud in the sky until mid-afternoon. I felt very fortunate to be alive, and I gave thanks again to God for my life, for being totally uninjured, and for the beautiful day. I rode comfortably without a windshield – with the realization that, but for the grace of God, it could have been a lot worse.

A few hours later, not long before entering Watson Lake, we came upon a herd of about thirty bison spread out on the highway and both shoulders of the road. The dominant male was a huge, ugly-looking critter that stood stubbornly in the middle of the road as I carefully picked my way through the herd. He looked as though he was letting everyone know, especially me, that he meant to protect his girls. I sure wouldn't want to collide with the likes of him at any speed.

A herd of bison just east of Watson Lake in the Yukon Territory.

I believe some species of animals would have reacted unkindly to the way we rode through. The huge dominant male stared at me without moving a muscle while I rode slowly by, except that his huge eyeballs followed me. It seemed like he was saying, "Don't tempt me, old man!" I think if it had been a female moose with newborn, which I understand can get quite nasty when they feel their young are threatened, it might have been different. With some reluctance, I went back and rode through the herd again to give Jim a photo-op.

There was a lot of smoke coming from a forest fire in the same general area. I think the fire had been burning for a couple of weeks by the time we came through. I have no idea how much effort was being used to put it out – sometimes very little.

We had a stand-up second breakfast at a convenience store in Watson Lake where we got gas. Before leaving town we visited Signpost Park, which has been a tourist attraction there ever since the accumulation of road signs began during the construction of the Alcan Highway in the early 1940s. Families of WWII servicemen assigned to the construction project would send signs from their hometowns to remind them of home.

Signpost Park in Watson Lake, YT in 2004.
Photo by Jim Hoellerich

The area later became a famous park that has grown steadily since it all began. To this day, people still send signs of all shapes and sizes, including the names of their towns, route numbers, speed-limit signs, pedestrian crossing signs, etc. When I first passed through in 1977, it looked like there was only about an acre of signs. The park has grown since to almost 20 acres.

I survived my first full-day experience without any windshield better than I had thought. The wind bothered me a little at first as we rode at our usual 70 mph-plus most of the day, but I got used to it making a slightly louder noise inside the helmet. It actually reminded me a little of my early days back in the 1940s riding my first Harley, except that we didn't wear helmets then.

What bothered me most was the accumulation of thousands of bugs that kept splattering against the face shield, eventually covering it altogether between gas stops. Whenever we stopped for gas I would have to use the windshield-washing tool with soapy water to clean it. Since it was a beautiful day, I was able to tolerate the wind quite well, and I concluded that I could have easily ridden all the way there and back without a windshield as long as we didn't have to run through too much cold rain.

We got to Teslin around 1 PM. The long bridge across Teslin Lake with the deep steel grating has always been a memorable landmark and a thrill for motorcyclists. I wondered how the narrow, 21" front tire of my dirt bike would fare with the steel grating and if it might drop deep into the grooves. It actually did quite well. The excellent-handling little bike simply weaved gently from groove to groove as Jim and I rode across the long narrow bridge clocking our usual steady 70 mph.

Since the bridge is relatively narrow, the posted speed limit is much less, like maybe 30 mph, which would be more difficult for a motorcyclist to handle than faster. I think Jim was probably more shook-up earlier by the Peace River Bridge than he was about this one, which I had been psyching him up for. I hadn't mentioned the Peace River Bridge before we crossed it, so it was more of a surprise – and we went across slower. I figure he had also probably become accustomed to riding across the many steel-grated bridges by the time we finally got to the Teslin Lake Bridge, the longest by far of all the bridges.

We pulled into a combined gas station and grocery store in Teslin, just beyond the bridge. While getting gas, I suggested that we pick up a sandwich there for lunch. I had totally forgotten about the steering restriction from the headlight being pushed too far back, and while maneuvering the bike around to get it closer to the store, I committed my balance to a tighter turn than the newly acquired restriction would allow, which threw it off-balance – and I dropped it right there in front of the store.

The next thing I knew I was lying on the ground with my leg pinned underneath. Everything seemed to happen so fast! It made me think of Arte Johnson on the old TV show, "Laugh-in." Luckily I didn't break a hip. At least ten people came running from all directions to lift the bike off the poor old guy. A few even came running from inside the store and flew off the porch without using the steps.

Jim said his first thought when he looked over and saw me on the ground was that I had a heart attack. It was an embarrassing moment to say the least. It was the right-hand pannier that took the hit this time – and it was my right leg that was protected by it this time. A tin of sardines in that pannier got ruptured and created a real smelly mess inside that I cleaned out that night and washed everything, including the bag – but I could still smell sardines months later.

Less than two hours after our late lunch, we reached Whitehorse, the capital of the Yukon Territory, just as it began to rain. We got a room out on the highway rather than going into town. My recent experience has been that the center of Whitehorse has become a high-rent district with higher-class hotels and motels, whereas the travel motels are still reasonably priced out on the highway. Whitehorse seems to have grown tenfold since my first visit.

I planned all of our fuel and overnight stops before leaving home and I made changes as needed as we went along. Sometimes I would re-plan the stops a few days in advance based on my memory of motel and restaurant availability and prices, and how far we might have to travel to get to the next services. It all worked out well, even though there are still a few huge gaps in the availability of services on the Alaska Highway – but nothing like it was in the 1970s.

We checked into the motel early, at least partly because we were several hours ahead of my original schedule, and also because there was no need to press on in the rain. It would also give me a chance to see if there was something I could do to improve the steering before I fell again. After dinner, I lubed the chain and tried to come up with various ideas on how to get the headlight, speedometer and instruments back to their original position and clear of the forks so as to improve slow-speed maneuvering. It was certainly hazardous the way it was.

Jim found a 3-foot piece of two-by-four that we could use as a lever. He placed it behind the instrument unit above the triple-clamp, using the fork leg as the fulcrum. He held it steady while I gave the bars a healthy twist. The makeshift lever forced the entire unit forward and clear of the fork legs with one good pull. In short, we fixed the problem permanently.

We rolled out of Whitehorse at 6:45 the next morning with the temperature in the high forties. It was one of our coldest mornings so far, but we carried enough winter clothes to be prepared for those temperatures and much worse, in spite of my lack of a windshield. Our next sizable pocket of civilization where I also planned to stop for gas was Haines Junction, about 100 miles west of Whitehorse.

Twenty miles out, we went through another cold fogbank and for the next ten miles I rode with bare eyeballs and no face shield again, and this time it was with no windshield either. I could barely see well enough to hold the 60 mph that we were traveling. My eyeballs couldn't handle the cold dense fog at any higher speeds, nor was it safe to go much faster with the limited visibility. Fortunately the bugs weren't out that early to get into my eyes.

We passed through one of the normally colder areas of the Yukon just west of Haines Junction in a light rain shower. It rained again as we approached Beaver Creek, the last section of the Alaska Highway in the Yukon before crossing over into Alaska. It's a cold area that's always been a challenge for the road crews, as well as for travelers, due mostly to heavy frost damage to the pavement.

Much of the road was broken up when we went through, as it almost always gets when the ground thaws. Both our bikes were full of mud, and the mud was getting splattered onto the back and front of my jacket as well as on my face shield, making for very poor visibility. By the time we got to Tok, Alaska I was a muddy mess.

One section of highway not far from the US border was closed for resurfacing, and several plastic pylons had been placed side-by-side across the road to block and redirect traffic. There was a detour sign set up just before the pylons, directing traffic onto a temporary gravel road alongside the highway. The light was very poor from the rain and overcast and I had my face shield down with my glasses on, cutting the light down even more, to where I could barely see. I didn't see the detour sign, and I was only about 25 feet from the pylons when I finally saw them – and there I was, coming at the fresh soft dirt, loose gravel and who knows what at 70 mph. I thought: Oh boy. Here we go again, and so soon after the last time.

I instinctively hit the brakes hard, but when the bike began to swing sideways, my reflexes cut in quickly enough to prevent losing it. I released the brakes and regained control enough to guide it between the pylons and ride it out safely on the soft dirt until I could stop, which was at least a few hundred feet from where I first saw the pylons.

Jim was watching, probably with a big smile on his face, and he commented later that I sailed through the pylons in a partial slide like I was threading a needle. Thanks to the superb handling of the little bike I was able to survive the episode and get the bike safely over onto the temporary road where Jim was already riding. It was the third day in a row that I pulled something a bit too stimulating for a trip like this, and it led to some serious self-reflection.

It was still raining when we got to Kluane National Park, a beautiful area in the western Yukon. Kluane Lake, the largest lake in the territory, is nestled between spectacular snowcapped mountains – a great place for photos. I intended to stop so Jim could get some photos, but I didn't stop because of the rain.

So due to very light traffic and not stopping as often as I had planned, we built up another hour ahead of my original schedule, bringing us into Tok about three hours earlier than I expected. My original plan was to make Tok an overnight stopover because of the relatively low prices, but we stopped only for a quick lunch at Young's Café where I've stopped often in the past. We decided at lunch to press on for Glennallen, in spite of my remembering that it was somewhat of a high-rent district. I hoped there would be competition enough by this time to bring the motel prices down.

When we got there, the Caribou was still the only game in town and we learned that their lowest rate was $135. I inquired at the tourist center for an alternative, and they mentioned Tolsona Lake Lodge, about 25 miles farther west. I had seen signs for the place on earlier trips but I had never stopped there.

We found the lodge about a half-mile off the Glenn Highway, only to learn that they too, probably taking advantage of the monopoly of sorts in the area, were asking $125 – and the place wasn't nearly as nice as the Caribou. By bargaining for a senior discount I got the woman down to $100, but the room was a dump, second only to the small motel at Muncho Lake. There was a reasonably nice dining room in the lodge though, with a bar, so we had a few beers at the bar and dinner in the dining room. The dinner was good enough, but the bill came to $85 – and this time it was in real US dollars, unlike Muncho Lake where the bill was in Canadian currency.

One of the TV channels was running a "skin flick" that night, so Jim didn't consider it a total loss. Even though I've watched them in the past, it had been another rough day dealing with the rain, wind and cold, with no windshield and a lot of mud, so I opted for the bed instead. I also thought that in light of my most recent near miss at the construction area, it would be prudent to do something more in line with Proverbs 12:21, which says in part, "No harm befalls the righteous, ..."

We got up at our regular time and left around 6 AM in a light drizzle after sharing a tin of sardines in the room. I don't think the place served breakfast, and certainly not at that hour. It was still drizzling at Eureka Summit where I think in the dozen or more times I've been through that area, I only saw it clear once. On a clear day the panorama is spectacular. The elevation is only a little over 3300 feet, but with the northern latitude and being surrounded by so many scenic snow-covered mountain peaks, it can be quite beautiful, albeit usually cold and windy.

Road construction stopped us less than ten miles past the summit, and we had to wait about a half-hour for a pilot car to return from the other end. I think on weekdays they run two pilot cars; but at this early hour on a Sunday morning, it seemed like they were running only one. As soon as it arrived from the other end, it turned around and without further delay led us through many miles of construction, weaving in and out between huge piles of rocks and a lot of idle earth-moving equipment to the other end, near the Matanuska Glacier – a place I planned to visit when we came back through that way on Tuesday.

The area currently under construction originally had almost a hundred miles of twisty, two-lane blacktop from Eureka Summit to Palmer. It was along that section during one of my earlier trips on a Gold Wing that I experienced a strong earthquake. The tremor loosened rocks that came tumbling down from the steep canyon walls onto the roadway. It was the strongest earthquake I had ever ridden through, and I could actually feel the tremors while riding.

The construction crews have been cutting away huge sections of the mountain for years to straighten and improve the Glenn Highway, which will eventually be upgraded to modern standards from Glennallen to Anchorage – a distance of about 180 miles. We got to Palmer around 10 AM and stopped for a better breakfast at the McDonald's I've used on almost every one of my trips. Afterwards we rode the final 45 miles into Anchorage under crystal clear skies and milder temperatures.

We arrived at Rey and Becky's home around 11 AM on Sunday, July 25th, eleven days after leaving New York and roughly 7½ days after leaving Ohio – a relatively quick trip with a 550-mile-per-day average. My grandson Robyn was waiting with Rey and two of his and Becky's children. My granddaughter Asia was still at church while Becky and her two other children were helping out at a friend's home.

We were enjoying a snack on the patio when Asia arrived around noon. She and Robyn are the oldest of my ten grandchildren. Robyn was working at the time with a communications company out of Anchorage while Asia was in her final year at the University of Alaska majoring in Asian studies, including Japanese and Chinese culture and languages.

Becky had set up sleeping accommodations for Jim and me in their home, giving up their own bedroom. They also graciously fed us for two days as we rested and regained some of our strength. I'm speaking mainly for myself, although I suspect that Jim too, who I believe was 70 at the time, could also use some rest. That night we were treated to deep-fried halibut and chicken with beer batter that Rey prepared. He's an excellent cook, having once worked as the head party chef at the Elmendorf Air Force Base officer's club.

On Monday following breakfast, Jim and I rode over to The Motorcycle Shop to see if my windshield had arrived from Danbury and to visit with my friend Don Rosene. The windshield was there and I installed it, only to learn for a second time after a brief test ride that it was just as ineffective as I remembered. I can't imagine what size rider it was designed for. It certainly didn't fit me and I didn't have the time, tools or materials to modify the brackets and change the angle enough to make it right.

I realized it would have been much better to have called home and asked my son to send the original small windshield that came with the bike that Leif Gustafsson returned when he shipped the new one. At least with that one, the wind only hit from the center of my face upward, leaving only the top of my head unprotected, and my face shield would have taken care of that.

I soon learned that riding with the Cee Bailey shield was worse than riding with no windshield at all, especially after I had gotten used to riding without a shield. This windshield created a strong current of air that spilled off the top directly onto my face, head and shoulders. The only good thing I could say for it was that it kept the wind and rain off my tank bag quite well, for what that's worth.

Now that I had it on the bike, my only options were to keep it and use it, or to remove it, leave it there and continue to ride with no windshield at all for the rest of the trip. I decided I couldn't depend on having good weather all the way home, and it would at least keep the rain off my lower torso and tank bag, so I decided to keep it on and put up with the wind and rain for the rest of the trip.

I got a stiff neck the first day out of Anchorage from bracing my head against the current of wind at a steady 70 mph. The windshield finally found a home a few months later when Jim bought a smaller bike and I gave it to him. He redesigned different brackets for it and said it worked out well.

Asia, Robyn and I went to a Chinese buffet for lunch on Monday where I enjoyed quality time with my grandchildren. It certainly made the trip more than worthwhile for me; although I wouldn't want to downplay the great adventure I had in getting to and from Anchorage for the eighth time, the gracious hospitality of our hosts Rey and Becky, and the pleasure of traveling with Jim Hoellerich.

We got up around five on Tuesday and came out to the kitchen to find our hosts already up and fixing breakfast so that we could have what Becky called "a proper sendoff." They were certainly gracious hosts during our entire visit.

We were on the road by 6:20 following the first-class breakfast, giving us a great start; but I lost some of the advantage by missing a turn leaving Anchorage due to my poor eyesight and another turn later on the highway where recent road construction changed the approach to Palmer. We were off course in Wasilla before I realized it, and finding our way back to the

Glenn Highway took even more time because I was unfamiliar with most of those roads.

We still arrived at the entrance to Matanuska Glacier, about 60 miles east of Palmer, 15 minutes before the park was due to open for the day. The attendants at the entrance allowed us to pay and enter early and we became the first visitors of the day. Being alone in the park enabled us to get closer to the glacier with the bikes than we normally would have been allowed, which saved walking and saved time.

We picked our way along for at least two miles before parking the bikes, and then walked the rest of the way along a rough, rocky trail for another hundred yards to the glacier where we climbed onto the ice. It seemed to me that the glacier had receded a couple of miles since my last visit in the early 1980s.

Jim Hoellerich atop the Matanuska Glacier

After spending less than an hour there, we returned to the Glenn Highway and found that the construction crew had set up the flag station for the start of construction right there at the entrance. We got there just in time to slip in at the head of the line, between the pilot car and a huge string of waiting cars, trucks and campers. The pilot vehicle left immediately and led us back through the road construction to the same spot near Eureka Summit where we waited briefly two days earlier.

We stopped in Glennallen for an early lunch and stopped for the day around 2 PM in Tok, which was the last place I was sure of finding a room in the direction we would be headed in the morning.

Early the next morning we headed northeast on the Taylor Highway toward the Top of the World Road and Dawson City in the Yukon Territory, stopping only briefly for photos at the old Jack Wade Gold Dredge that sat idle in Bonanza Creek for almost a half-century. The dredge ceased operations in 1960, and I learned later that not long after our visit, it was dismantled and sold for scrap.

Jack Wade Gold Dredge in Bonanza Creek.
Photo by Jim Hoellerich

It was raining before we reached Chicken, Alaska, and unfortunately the weather continued to be lousy all the way across the scenic Top of the World Road.

This was especially disappointing because it was one of the scenic highlights I had planned for Jim. We rode through at least two heavy downpours and a lot of very thick fog for the last 45 miles to the Yukon River, making it almost impossible to see the road in a few places. But we pressed on, often feeling our way in zero-visibility fog at speeds between 20 and 30 mph.

I almost ran into the back end of a huge highway dump truck in the fog. Fortunately we were traveling less than 30 at the time. We got to the Yukon River with a few minutes to spare before the free ferryboat arrived. It quickly unloaded and reloaded and left the south bank to ply its way back across the swift river current to Dawson City. We were about the only ones getting on that morning.

The Yukon River Ferry arriving at the south bank.

We had a quick stand-up lunch at a convenience store in Dawson City at the same place we got gas. Jim and

I shared the last ham and cheese sandwich from the cooler and we immediately headed for Carmacks, 225 miles down the Klondike Highway. We ate on the run because we definitely had to make it to Carmacks that afternoon. I knew of no other place along that stretch of road to find a motel, and we had already lost so much time in the bad weather.

I was expecting a tough ride to Carmacks – gravel all the way and difficult to maintain any kind of speed. It rained steadily practically all the way, occasionally heavy, leaving many muddy spots and puddles in the road. At the gas stop in Pelly Crossing we met a couple from Ontario riding two-up on a BMW R1150GS, and we learned that they were headed for Inuvik in the Northwest Territories via the Dempster Highway. They mentioned having heard of someone hitting a sheep on the Alaska Highway a week earlier. It seems that news like that travels fast in the far north, originating from the two girls at the road construction near Muncho Lake.

The weather eased as we left Pelly Crossing, but not for long. It poured again for the last ten miles into Carmacks. The wet, slick gravel roads and the long distance made it one of our toughest days of the trip so far. The lousy protection from the windshield made it even tougher for me. We got in around 4:30, having lost an hour to the time-zone change leaving Alaska. The loss of the time-zone hours always tends to make the eastbound trip seem tougher because we try to travel the same number of miles in less time.

I was happy that we found a motel in Carmacks with a restaurant nearby, and I was especially happy that we got there minutes before they sold out their last room. This was a huge relief because I was totally exhausted from the 415 miles of rain, fog and soft, loose gravel, with the very poor weather protection. I felt every one of my 79 years and I'm sure I couldn't have gone much farther.

The crotch of my jeans under my rain suit was soaked for only the second time on the trip; the other being when I rode behind Jake in Pennsylvania – but it was much warmer then. The only part of me that stayed dry all day this time were my feet inside the Tingley boots. I hung the wet jeans in front of a fan that was in the room, and I set it on low and left it on all night. They were dry in the morning.

After a quick breakfast, we headed down the seldom-used south end of the Campbell Highway that was mostly slick gravel. It was the only piece of road on our trip that I had never ridden. We were about 15 miles into it, riding in a steady light rain, when I began to get a thin splattering of mud from the front wheel onto my face shield, and the current of air from the windshield was making it worse.

It got so bad that it was difficult to see through the mud on the shield. I wasn't wearing my glasses at the time because they cut down too much on the light. We didn't realize quite how slick the road surface was until we stopped to work on the problem and had difficulty maintaining footing on the road surface – much like wet clay.

We quickly fashioned a makeshift mud flap for the leading edge of the front fender from a small piece of plastic that Jim found alongside the road, and we used duct tape to attach it to the fender. I cleaned the face shield as best I could with water from a puddle in the road. I was literally covered with the mud.

The superb handling of the little Dakar helped me to get back up to 70 mph quickly on the slick surface. I noticed in my rear-view mirror that Jim lay back a little at first, until he gained enough confidence in the handling of his big 1150GS on the extremely slick surface, but he was soon right behind me, keeping the pace. It rained on and off for the entire 375 miles that we were on the Campbell Highway, almost all of which was the same slick surface.

We had to go into Ross River to refuel, about six miles off the main road. It took several minutes to find a gas pump. I remembered passing through Ross River on my fifth trip to Alaska when I traveled up the North Canol Road heading for the Northwest Territories, but I didn't get gas then – I had no idea where to find it. We finally found a pump outside an old repair garage on a gravel side street.

The final 230 miles into Watson Lake took almost five hours of continuous hard riding on the same wet, slippery gravel surface that also included a long muddy construction area. When I stopped once in the middle of the road around lunchtime to catch my breath, Jim broke out a tin of sardines and I think I munched on a granola bar as we stood quietly. I was too exhausted to talk.

We got to Watson Lake at 2:30 and had another light snack at the gas station – the second half of our lunch-break. My original plan for the day was to reach Dease Lake, which was still at least three hours away, bringing our daily total to 530 miles – most of those miles were wet gravel and mud. I was tempted to call it a day in Watson Lake, but it would have complicated finding accommodations for the next few days, so I chose to keep going.

Hwy 37, also known as the Cassiar Highway, was not nearly up to the same level of maintenance as the Alaska Highway, and the speed limit was set mostly at 45 and 50 mph – less in some places. Most of the surface was uneven and there were sections with no centerlines, making it very to maintain the higher speeds with confidence. We did manage to hold 65 and 70 most of the way into Dease Lake, arriving around 5:45 – my original target was five o'clock. I had hoped to give Jim a day on the gravel that he would long remember and that was certainly it. It was dual sporting at its finest! But it was admittedly more than I had bargained for.

I recalled what the guys from Alberta who we chatted with earlier on the Alaska Highway had said. I can see why they weren't too complementary about the Cassiar Highway. We were really tired when we finally got into the room, and I was glad that Jim was able to find a six-pack – maybe more so than any other time on the trip. It was a long, tough day for both of us – probably the toughest day of the trip. It would have been a worthy challenge for someone half our ages.

That evening I realized that the ride had practically destroyed the chain. The bottom rung was hanging way down, far more than it would normally have been for a single day of riding – even considering the wet gravel. It was obvious that the chain was on its last gasp. I had been lubing it every night, but that day on the muddy roads in the rain was more than it could take. My last glimmer of hope for it lasting the distance was fading fast.

If the bike was equipped with a center stand, I would have lubed it at least a few extra times during the day, but without the stand, it took several minutes each time; and I probably let it go far too long due to time constraints and the thought of having to push it every time in the mud and heavy rain to lube it.

I soaked it down with chain lube at the motel and readjusted it, but it didn't hold the adjustment for long. From that point on, I knew that I would have to readjust and lube it at least twice a day to make it last as long as possible. I was beginning to feel the strain of the growing number of problems. Having been in similar situations a few times before with others, I made a special effort to remain as calm and cheerful as I could, so as not to affect Jim and put him on the same track. I didn't want to mess up the excellent relationship we had during the entire trip.

A word about Jim at this point: From the onset, I could tell that he had read my first book. He did just about everything my way. He was an excellent riding companion for the entire 25 days. Every time I looked in my rear view mirror, I knew he would be there, even when my speed would inadvertently creep up over 80 mph on roads that one wouldn't normally travel that fast – especially the Campbell Highway with its surface like wet clay.

He was as agreeable as he could be with everything, whether it was where we ate, where we slept, what time we got up in the morning, how fast we got underway in the morning, how many miles we made in a day, or how late in the day we began to look for a motel: He never complained.

In the past, whenever I went on a trip with anyone, I was usually the first to have the bike loaded and running in the morning and the first to finish eating at almost every meal. On this trip I was the last at just about everything. I have seldom seen anyone who can pack his bags and load a bike as quickly as Jim, and I've never known anyone to eat faster.

He would let me make all of the decisions, and he'd be agreeable with every one. He never showed a bit of displeasure with anything that I decided to do, or did. He would even ask what kind of beer I would like before going out for a six-pack! How could anyone ever find displeasure with Jim Hoellerich as a riding partner? I certainly never did, and I certainly wouldn't want to do anything to mess it up; and I'm sure some of my idiosyncrasies must have annoyed him – at least some of the time.

We left Dease Lake before six after a breakfast of sardines in the room. There was no place open for breakfast, and we had many miles to go that day to get back to civilization. The temperature was in the low forties at the motel, and it dipped into the 30s at the higher elevations in the mountains within the hour.

There were only a few very short gravel sections left on the original Cassiar Highway, and much of it was covered with round, marble-shaped gravel. One of those gravel sections started halfway around a curve that I went into at 70 mph. Both wheels began to break loose and drift as soon as they hit the loose stuff, which brought my heart up into my throat for a second or two. Jim had similar problems, but we both got through without incident.

My face shield was beginning to get much more difficult to see through from having been hit with so much muddy water and by wiping smashed bugs off of it. Sometimes I wiped it without thinking first that the wipe would probably scratch it. Consequently, I came extremely close to hitting yet another set of construction pylons as I flew out onto some loose dirt and gravel, again at highway speed.

I stopped to check the chain more often that day, and at one rest area along the Cassiar I saw that it was looped way too far down after only a few hours of riding. I lubed it again heavily and readjusted it and began to get preoccupied thinking about where I might find a replacement. I was quite sure by then that it would never take me to New York, and I also strongly doubted it would make Phil Bourdon's farm in Wisconsin.

Soon after reaching Trans Canada 16, a major highway, we went through more road construction that cut considerably into our time. We were still able to cover 540 miles that day, despite the problems and extra stops to lube the chain. We found a motel in Vanderhoof around 5:45. It was a long, stressful day. Normally I would have stopped for photos of the beautiful scenery along the Cassiar Highway, but I was stressed out, over-tired and too preoccupied with the chain to give much thought to photos.

Jim noticed at the motel that my radiator was clogged with mud. I was able to clean it with a high-pressure hose that was already hooked up in the motel parking lot. Fortunately we had come through the last of the rough, muddy roads, and we should have nothing but clear sailing from here to the east coast.

We spoke with a biker at the motel who had just ridden in from Richmond Heights, Washington, having passed through Wenatchee on the way. He traveled in the exact reverse of a route I had originally planned to take into the US on this trip, but I had since revised it in favor of a more scenic route that would take us through the North Cascades. I've used this revised route at least a few times in the past and thought that Jim would appreciate the scenery, even though it added several extra miles onto the chain. I figured I'd have to get a new one somewhere anyway, and I supposed one route was as good as another for finding a chain.

The temperature was in the low 40s when we left Vanderhoof at 6:30, riding into the bright early-morning sun. I rode for at least an hour without glasses and with the face shield flipped up, putting my bare eyeballs in the strong current of air spilling from the windshield. Wearing a face shield and/or glasses would have created far too much glare that would be made worse by the cataracts that my eye doctor is reluctant to remove. It's my only good eye, and there's always a risk of something going wrong.

I knew that I would have to ride like that practically every morning until we got home, but I didn't think there would be very many bugs out that early. That and the lost hours from the time-zone changes are handicaps that are all part of the game traveling east. The only way to avoid the early-morning sun glare problem is to leave a few hours later in the day, but during the summer that means spending a few extra hours in the afternoon heat to make the same number of miles.

That day turned out to be my personal worst in several ways: my scuffed up face shield, the strong current of air in my face, the sagging chain, and a rear tire that was going bald faster than I had hoped were only the beginning. The bike's handling was also getting worse every day due to a bind in the head bearings. It was far too soon for head bearings to fail, but I've experienced head bearing failures on other BMWs I've owned, and I've heard that BMW has a history of head bearing problems.

It got quite hot as we descended from the higher elevations into the desert-like terrain around Cache Creek. I spotted a Subway, and we stopped for lunch. It got hotter after entering the scenic Fraser River Canyon where traffic was exceptionally heavy.

I had been passing cars, trucks and RVs almost as soon as we got to them most of the day as I continued to hold our 70 mph speed. At one point in the canyon I hesitated for a moment behind the last car of a long string of cars, trucks and campers and waited a few moments for a safe spot to pass.

As soon as we got to a long, straight stretch of road with no one coming from the other direction, I peeled the throttle open and started to pass the entire string about 10 feet before the end of a double-yellow line, and just before about a half-mile stretch of single dotted line with no one coming in the other direction. It was certainly safe enough.

The only problem was that the first car I passed was an unmarked police cruiser; and since I pulled out about 10 feet too soon for his liking, he flipped on the red flashing lights behind the grill and took off after me as soon as I was by his front fender. There was no talking to this guy, and I ended up getting a $109 ticket for crossing the very end of the double-yellow line, in what I considered to be a perfectly safe move, but it cut no ice with him.

Jim is not a mathematician but he offered later that if I were to spread that $109 over all of the cars, trucks and campers that I passed on double yellow during the trip, it would probably average out to about a nickel apiece.

It wasn't the end of my bad streak, and the day hit its nadir for me in Abbotsford. We had been riding along Trans-Canada One as I looked for the cut-off for Rte 11 to the US border. I couldn't read most of the tiny Canadian route markings, so I guessed at an exit and dove for it. I had seen a sign for gas and I figured we'd get gas and directions at the same time. It turned out that the gas station was out of gas, so I asked the female attendant for directions. She said we weren't far off, and she directed us via a few back roads to find the Rte 11 entry ramp. She said it was less than a mile and it would be much easier than going back out onto the highway.

The only trouble was that I missed the turn for the ramp and I had to make a U-turn to go back for it. Jim was right behind me and saw me make the initial U-turn but I made the second turn onto the entry ramp while he was still finishing up his U-turn, and he didn't see me make the turn onto the ramp.

I stopped partway up the ramp to look back, only to see him fly by. So I made another U-turn on the one-way ramp to go after him, except that he was already out of sight and I thought I had lost him!

I spotted a gas station on the left side of the four-lane city street and figured that rather than chase him, I would turn into the gas station and wait for him there. Since we had to get gas anyway, and he'd most likely return to where he last saw me, he would have to go by that spot. I checked both ways before making the left turn into the gas station, which was across two oncoming lanes, but suddenly an SUV came very fast over the crest of a hill in front of me as I was looking toward where I was going and I was already partway across the on-coming lane he was in.

I heard the loud screech of tires as the guy hit his brakes hard and swerved to avoid hitting me. It was the closest call I had in traffic on the entire trip, and it shook me up almost as much as the sheep incident. I thanked God again for protecting me. It made me think that dreadful things can happen in the blink of an eye, and it's a real blessing that God never blinks. This is yet another benefit of having an ongoing 24/7 relationship and keeping your nose clean.

Jim appeared as soon as I pulled into the gas station. I was still rattled from the near miss while we were gassing up. Later, while riding south on Rte 11, I saw a sign that said the border was only two miles from there, whereas my route sheet had 126 miles; so we gained more than 2 hours from my route sheet error. It seemed like nothing was going right for me that day, but at least this error was in our favor.

We stopped at Canadian customs to ask for a form to recover our GST for the tax we paid on motel bills while in Canada. The customs guy told us we had to walk over to the duty-free shop, a few hundred feet away and fill out the form there. After arguing with him on how ridiculous that sounded, he finally gave us the forms to take with us, which is what I had asked for in the first place.

We cleared US customs quickly and rode for another hour into Burlington, Washington, but not before I made a few more wrong turns and we got mired in heavy Friday night rush-hour traffic. We checked into a really crummy motel at the intersection of Rte 20 and Interstate 5. It was the first motel I spotted. As might be expected, the air conditioner didn't work, and it was hot and muggy that night – seemed like a fitting end to a really terrible day.

To top it off, the chain needed a major adjustment, and from the way the thing looked, it was obvious it would never make it to Phil Bourdon's. It was a very trying 12-hour day, with brutal heat from about noon on. Things began to look a little better after Jim got back with the beer – but not much! I was just glad the day was over.

I had originally planned to meet my friends in Wenatchee the following day and ride with them to Montana, but I got word that evening, relayed from home, that they were already in Missoula, and they would rather that we meet them there. Had I known earlier, I could have taken a completely different scenic route through Canada into Montana, and much of that worst day might never have happened.

Early the next morning we rode 40 miles through alternate patches of cold thick ground fog and bright sunlight. I rode with bare eyeballs for at least an hour again until we began to climb into the beautiful North Cascades, one of the scenic highlights of our trip and a change from my original route sheet. We stopped for photos at Diablo Canyon and again at Diablo Lake before reaching Winthrop around 11 AM, stopping briefly for gas and a quick snack. Winthrop seems to have become a favorite weekend spot for bikers. The town was filled with motorcycles, and I noticed that a lot of them had Canadian plates.

We reached Wenatchee around noon and decided to throw in the towel for the day, since the temperature was in the high 90s and we could take advantage of the low motel prices. I had originally planned to spend part of the day there with my friends – my reason for scheduling our arrival so early in the day. I finally managed to contact them directly, and we arranged to meet at the Days Inn in Missoula between mid and late afternoon the following day. Meanwhile, they planned to visit Flathead Lake earlier in the day.

I revised our route again in the morning and decided to avoid some of the gravel roads I originally planned to use over St. Joe Pass between Idaho and Montana. The chain had already taken just about all of the gravel roads it could handle for one trip – so we headed for Missoula over paved roads. Fortunately I was able to make the changes without the help of a map since I wasn't carrying one. I was familiar with most of the roads in the area.

We rode through miles of what seemed like clouds of very fine dust that morning, like in a mini dust storm, but there was no wind. It wasn't until we stopped for gas at an unattended gas station, set up for credit card only, that we noticed a thin layer of dust covering the gas pumps; and we realized it was, in fact, from a dust storm. It was otherwise a beautiful day in the wheat fields of eastern Washington.

We took a side-trip to the Grand Coulee Dam, mainly to kill time, and we were still able to reach the Days Inn in Missoula by 3 PM Montana time after losing an hour to another time-zone change at the state line. My friends pulled into the parking lot around 5:45. Meanwhile, Jim and I had already consumed our daily six-pack and were sitting around talking.

Jim Bellach and John Dey came by our room after freshening up from their ride. Jim and I began communicating after he learned from my first book that we had mutual friends in off-road competition, as well as other motorcycling experiences in common. This was the first time we met in person. He brought a gracious gift of California raisins and almonds. The raisins represent what he did for much of his life – raisin farming, and his brother grows almonds.

After introductions and time spent getting acquainted, we walked to a nearby restaurant where we ate and continued to talk. John insisted on picking up the tab for all the food and drink, after which we returned to the room for more conversation and bonding. When they left for their rooms, they said they had decided not to ride with us in the morning to avoid any possibility of holding us up, but not before we vowed to meet for a ride in the not-too-distant future.

Jim and I were up at 4:45 for one of our earliest starts of the trip. The complementary breakfast was ready early, so we were able to eat and leave shortly after six with enough food consumed to preclude stopping along the road for breakfast. It began to rain as soon as we got to the bikes, so we suited up in the parking lot and left in full rain gear.

We used I-90 for about 75 miles before the weather cleared and got a little warmer. We turned south on Rte 212 and stopped for gas in Red Lodge before beginning the long and very beautiful climb along the Beartooth Highway through a series of switchbacks and zigzags to the Continental Divide at Beartooth Pass (11,947 ft). The 50-mile ride from Red Lodge to the intersection of Wyoming Rte 296 was certainly the scenic highlight of our trip. It's considered by many to be the most spectacular ride in the country.

The little Dakar handled very poorly on the way up the mountain due to the worn head bearings, which had been getting progressively worse and taking some of the enjoyment from the ride. Every time I turned the handlebars even slightly, coming into or out of a turn, the defect would first try to hold the forks straight and then it would suddenly break loose, causing a jerk in steering as the bearings popped in and out of the worn spots in the bearing race.

The poor handling also provided a little excitement a few times, adding to the overall adventure. It was windy, rainy and cool at the summit, with patches of snow in the shaded areas. Jim took several photos – probably more than any other place on the trip.

We turned southeast on Rte 296 and rode the 62-mile descent to Cody on another spectacular road called the Chief Joseph Scenic Highway. I skipped the shortcut that I had originally planned partway down the mountain due to the deteriorating condition of the chain, the head bearings and the rear tire. I thought they all had just about as much as they could take of gravel roads on this trip – and we didn't really need the extra excitement, which would have added little to the overall adventure and enjoyment of the trip.

We were delayed along the Chief Joseph Highway by a group of real live cowboys on horseback driving a herd of more than a hundred head of cattle down the middle of the road, holding up a long string of cars and campers. After about 15 minutes of painfully slow riding, a car began to squeeze by on the right shoulder, so Jim and I followed and got through long

before we would have otherwise. After reaching
Cody, we turned east on Rte 14A and rode for about
25 miles to Powell where we found a motel just as
the sky was beginning to darken from an approaching
rainsquall.

The temperature was in the sixties when we left in
the morning. It dropped at least ten degrees less than
an hour later as we climbed into the Bighorn National
Forest. The climb was steep and twisty and the
scenery was spectacular. We saw large herds of cattle
grazing in the picturesque green pastures at the
higher elevations.

After getting onto I-90 near Sheridan, I noticed that
many of the ore trucks were running at 80 mph – and
some even faster. As much as I was tempted to run
with them, I didn't think it would be prudent to travel
at that speed with the chain and rear tire the way they
were, so I held it down to 70, which I felt might still
be a bit too risky under the circumstances.

From the time we got onto the interstate we saw
many motorcycles headed for the bike rally at
Sturgis, South Dakota, even though the start of
festivities there was still five days away. The
campgrounds around Sturgis were already filled to
capacity according to the signs we saw on our way in.
We ran through a few light showers around midday
and pulled over to suit-up, but we soon ran out of
them and rode across hundreds of miles of South
Dakota flatlands in bright warm sunshine.

The chain began to make horrible crunching sounds
around Chamberlain, South Dakota. When it sounded
like it was about to come off and might not last for
another mile, I pulled into a rest area to see if there

was anything I could do for it. It had more slack than ever and it was looped way down. Even after taking up the last of the available adjustment, there was still far too much slack. It was obvious that it might not last for another ten miles and we were still 550 miles from Phil's where I had hoped to get a replacement.

I asked at the travel center about motels in the area, mentioning also that I was having problems with the bike and I needed to find a motorcycle dealer quickly. The woman gave directions for a few motels in town and also to a Honda quad dealer, whom she was quite sure also worked on motorcycles. I figured he would have some kind of chain to fit, although probably wouldn't have the sprockets, but I could deal with those after I got home.

We decided to make it our overnight stop since it was already 6 PM and well past when I should be dealing with the problem. We went first to the quad dealer. We caught him just before his normal closing time, and I asked about a chain and if he would consider staying open long enough to install it.

The only chains he had were non-O-ring type, which would have to do under the circumstances. I bought one and the mechanic proceeded to grind the links to get the old chain off and fit a chain from stock, which I assumed was new, but I didn't see the box it came in. The chain didn't have a master link with it, which should have raised a flag for me. He searched around and found a removable-clip-type link, and he had some difficulty installing the clip – the other half of the clue I should have recognized.

Seeing the mechanic struggle with the link, I should have known that it was probably the wrong link for the chain, or the wrong clip for the master link, but neither Jim nor I gave it a thought as we were chatting with the owner and a few of the employees when I should have been watching the mechanic. Parts and labor came to around $100 and I tipped the mechanic for staying overtime to work on it.

After leaving the shop, we checked into a motel across the street and had a late hamburger and fries at a nearby Dairy Queen. I felt much better with one of my major problems out of the way – at least I thought it was out of the way.

The next morning we stopped at a small highway pull-off area about a hundred miles down the road to take a quick check at how the chain was doing and to adjust any initial stretch out of it. The first thing I noticed was rust coming from all of the links! It couldn't possibly have been a new chain. I think it was probably a used chain that had been sitting on the shelf for who knows how long. But I figured it would be futile to go back at that point, so I hoped for the best, doused it with chain lube and we continued on our way.

We ran through some cold, early-morning ground fog for about a hundred miles and crossed the Mississippi River at a small bridge near Wabasha, Minnesota, south of St. Paul. We got to Phil's in Augusta, Wisconsin around mid-afternoon without further incident with the chain.

We visited with Phil and Connie for the rest of the day. Phil gave us a grand tour of his farm, including his prize collection of antique farm tractors, his new barn and his collection of goats; after which we went to dinner with Phil and Connie in his huge vintage Cadillac.

Jim and I stayed at the Woodland Motel that night, just down the road. We wanted to get an early start without imposing on our hosts, especially since I was anxious to get on the road before the height of the morning rush hour for many miles around Chicago.

Before turning in, I checked the bike over to assess the probability of getting home without any more problems. We still had more than 1,000 miles to go and the chain had already stretched far more than it should have for only 550 miles – and the rear tire was almost bald. My conclusion was that the greatest risk was still the chain. I figured I could squeeze another thousand miles out of the tire and the head bearings.

I was sure by then that the chain was used when I bought it, and my only concern was for it getting me home. I lubed it again and took about four pounds of air out of the tire to change the wear-pattern slightly in an effort to squeeze a few extra miles out of it.

I didn't sleep well. We got up around 4:50 and loaded the bikes in almost total darkness. It was quite chilly when we left for a McDonald's that I remembered 15 miles down the road. After breakfast we got onto I-94 and were only 30 miles down when I felt a crunching from the rear, followed by the bike freewheeling and the engine revving, which I knew was the chain.

After stopping, Jim walked back several hundred feet for the chain where it was lying like a dead snake in the road. When he returned with it, he offered his bike to me to go back to Phil's and see if he might have a link to match it. I was quite sure he wouldn't, but he would know where I could get one.

There was no one stirring when I got to Phil's around 7:45, and there was no answer to my knock at the door, so I opened it a few inches and called out quite loudly through the opening. There was still no answer so I called a second time, much louder with the door opened a little wider. Still nothing! I noticed a huge bell on the porch with a piece of rope hanging from the clapper so I gave it a few healthy peals, which probably woke up the neighboring farmer a half-mile away! It woke Phil's son who was sleeping in the camper and it brought Connie running out of the barn where she had been milking the goats – but it still didn't wake Phil.

After Connie came up from the barn and woke him, we talked for a few minutes to give him a chance to wake up, after which he got dressed and got his bike out and led me through a series of back roads to Eau Claire, about 20 miles away. The first place we came to was a Sport Center that was also a dealer for Triumph motorcycles. We arrived just as the shop was opening for the day.

The guy didn't have any loose master links but he offered to sell me a link from a new chain package that he could replace later. The chain on the bike was a D.I.D non-O-ring type, which is what he had, so it should definitely match. After paying for the link, I thanked Phil and we said our second good-byes, after which I headed back down the interstate to look for Jim and the bikes. I almost flew right by as he stood waving frantically from about 30 feet off the edge of the highway. It was 10 o'clock by the time I finally got the chain on and we were back on the road.

Working on the chain problem alongside I-94 in Wisconsin.
Photo by Jim Hoellerich

Not long afterward, we were stuck in traffic for at
least an hour approaching the Illinois tollhouse near
Rockford. I've been through that area several times in
the past, and I don't think I've ever been through
without a delay. The heat was brutal and the oil in the
bikes was probably near boiling by the time we were
finally able to pay the toll and get back onto the road
where traffic was moving normally.

I was sorry I didn't choose a totally different way to
get home to avoid that congestion altogether – using
the Upper Peninsula would have been much quicker.
One of the disadvantages of stopping in central
Wisconsin is that there is no quick way to get around
the Great Lakes and back to New York State or New
England.

I chose a route that avoided downtown Chicago
where I remember from the past the many fast-
moving, five and six-lane interstate highways in the

city that have always given me problems, especially when the sun is behind the signs and I can't read them due to the glare in my eyes. As a result, I'm always in the wrong lane for the splits.

When we reached the Indiana state line, traffic was at a standstill with stop-and-go for at least 30 miles through horrendous construction delays. It was a very bad day for traffic that I could have avoided by taking US 2 across the Upper Peninsula.

It would have been even worse, except that partway through the construction in Indiana, a group of ten or twelve black "Hell's Angels" and "Wheels of Soul," riding big Harleys, went by us with the greatest of ease, weaving in and out of all the stopped traffic. The Wheels of Soul is known as the only racially mixed outlaw motorcycle club in America. That day they were passing cars and trucks on the left and right shoulders and making it all look so very easy, and showing us how we ought to be doing it.

Jim and I took the cue and tagged along with them and we "rode with the angels" for at least 15 miles. I was getting a kick out of the little good-natured guy at the back of the pack wearing a baseball cap turned backwards, as he expertly maneuvered his big Harley with its low seat and custom handlebars gracefully through the heaviest traffic while at the same time scanning in all directions for potential threats from the law.

He was apparently the spotter for those who might object to motorcycles weaving through the traffic and using the shoulders like that, but I assume most law enforcement would probably prefer to avoid the stop-and-go traffic jams that would make their job more difficult. The little guy motioned for us to ride in front of him, between him and the rest of the pack. I guessed it was so that he could keep a better eye on us too. He and Jim rode side-by-side for a while, chatting. They seemed like a good-natured bunch of guys to me.

We rode for at least 13 hours that day and finally exited at South Bend, Indiana around 6:30 where we were fortunate again to get the last room at a Super 8. It was late by the time we finally checked in and got settled – I was really beat. We ate our dinner meal at a nearby 24-hour Subway – the only eating-place we saw in the area.

My main objective for that day had been to get within striking distance of home before nightfall and I figured this was close enough. It was probably our longest day on the road, time-wise, due to the chain problem and the two major traffic delays.

We were up at 4:30 for our final day of the trip, and we were able to get breakfast sandwiches at the same 24-hour Subway, rather than getting off the highway later. The complementary breakfast at the Super 8 didn't start until six, and we had a lot of miles to cover, so we skipped it.

We were still a long way from home, but we were able to maintain a 70-mph average most of the day. We split along Interstate 84 near Middletown, New York where Jim stayed on the highway and headed for his home in Cheshire, Massachusetts while I exited and I headed southeast for my home in Buchanan.

The chain was completely worn out and sagging far more than it should have for less than two thousand miles when I pulled into my driveway. The rear tire was totally bald, although the casing wasn't showing yet. Of course part of the reason for the chain wearing faster was because it was a non-O-ring-type chain running at high speeds, and a part of it was also due to the badly worn sprockets; but I believe the chain was also practically worn out when I got it. It certainly should have lasted more than two days. I changed the chain and both sprockets the following week and was thankful that it got me home safely.

Jim said later that he purposely passed the road he lives on when he got there and went a few extra miles up the road and back so his odometer would read 900 miles for the day, which was the longest single day of his trip. Mine read a little less than 800 for that day.

The mileage for the entire trip according to my odometer was slightly more than 11,000. Jim had a few hundred more than that. We averaged about 525 miles per day for the 12-day return trip, in spite of several short days, the lost time-zone hours, and at least a few days of dual sport riding on muddy roads in the Yukon Territory.

It was certainly a memorable ride for both of us, and I learned a lot about traveling with a lighter weight motorcycle. Two noticeably different factors were the greater effect that high speeds and strong headwinds have on gas mileage, and the effect that strong side winds have on the handling; but neither affected the pleasure of my ride this time. The greatest negative factor was the use of a chain-driven motorcycle for long-distance adventure touring where the chain needs much more care and attention than shaft-driven machines, especially on gravel roads where mud is involved.

Two

Don't Fence Me In
June 8 – July 1, 2006

"Just turn me loose, let me straddle my old saddle underneath the western skies. On my Cayuse, let me wander over yonder till I see the mountains rise..."

I first began to sing that old Bing Crosby favorite on the fourth day of my trip as I rolled out of the Great Smoky Mountains of western North Carolina into Davy Crockett country of eastern Tennessee. My entire sensory system was alive and glistening as I headed my little Cayuse west on another of the long, solo, back road adventures I had come to love, and I was already anticipating seeing peaks of the Rocky Mountains on the distant horizon.

I planned to revisit California and the Pacific coastline on this trip as a guest of the friends I originally met through my first book, and later in Montana while Jim Hoellerich and I were returning from Alaska. Since I was in no hurry on this trip, my plan was to see and enjoy much of this great country along the way and to spend some quality time alone for self-reflection. It was the first long trip since my life and death struggle with Lyme disease the year before, and I had a lot to thank God for.

When I stopped earlier to visit with my daughter and five of my ten grandchildren in Virginia, she had birthday cake and ice cream ready to celebrate my 81st birthday while I was on the road doing what I enjoy most in life.

These long, solo back-road adventures are a complete change of pace from most of the trips I've taken to Alaska and from many of my other long tours – most of which were ridden solo. This type of ride is much more relaxing and I can see more of this beautiful country than I could ever see while riding with time constraints or riding with others, when I would often be focusing much of my attention on them.

The day after leaving Donna's, I visited with my 92-year-old stepbrother Ralph at his home in Troutville in the heart of the Blue Ridge Mountains near Roanoke. Ralph lives up in the hills, less than a mile from the famous Blue Ridge Parkway that follows the crest of the ridge as it meanders southward through Virginia and North Carolina toward eastern Tennessee. We sat outside on his veranda most of the afternoon sipping wine and admiring the beautiful panorama while we chatted for hours about old times.

I had also stopped earlier on my way across Virginia to visit the McLean House in Appomattox Court House where Robert E. Lee surrendered the Confederate Army to Ulysses S. Grant in April 1865, marking the end of the horrendous Civil War. Having visited more than a few of the Civil War battlefields on earlier trips, like Antietam, the bloodiest single day of the war, and Gettysburg, the turning point, it's a reverent experience to step inside the parlor of this remote southern farmhouse and imagine General Lee's emotions when he arrived that day to face General Grant and his staff for the final heart-wrenching surrender of the entire Confederate Army.

After leaving Ralph's, I planned to ride southwest along the Blue Ridge Parkway for several hundred miles to its end near the Tennessee state line, but one of the few low points of my trip happened to change the plan when I unknowingly rode past a rare 25 mph speed-limit sign on the otherwise 45-mph parkway, due primarily to my poor eyesight – but maybe also to day-dreaming and not paying enough attention.

The $100 federal speeding ticket I got there was for 47 mph in a 25-mile zone. The first I knew about the National Park Service police cruiser sitting tucked in behind some bushes was after I rounded the bend, and that was obviously too late. When he stopped me, the first thing I said was, "So what'd I do?"

He said, "You were doing 47 in a 25-mile zone."

Being also a little hard of hearing without my hearing aids and thinking he said 45-mile zone, which is the limit everywhere else on the parkway, I said with some resentment, "You mean to say you stopped me for a lousy two miles over the speed limit!" I was pulling my helmet off at the time so he could see that I'm not a youngster – if that would make any difference – and apparently it didn't.

He said, "You were almost double the speed limit. The limit here is 25 miles per hour," and he went on to mention about the sign "back there" that I should have seen while he pored over my license and registration. I could hardly believe it, but I took the ticket quietly then, vowing later never to ride the stinking Blue Ridge Parkway again!

I exited a short time later and followed several scenic secondary roads for the rest of the day that go in the same general direction. I steamed over it for a while, convinced that the whole deal was a speed trap, plain and simple; but I got over it, and paid the fine a month later, after getting home.

The air was brisk and cool when I left Sylva, North Carolina around 6:30 AM singing the lyrics of "Don't Fence Me In." The song became a part of my trip as I sang it often to myself during the next three weeks. I was able to put the unpleasant memory of the ticket behind me and I felt totally refreshed from a good night's sleep.

Small patches of fog were still lying in the valleys and the morning sun was beginning to break over the hilltops as I headed out through the foothills of the Great Smoky Mountains of western North Carolina into the picturesque rolling hills of eastern Tennessee. The sun was directly behind me with my shadow reaching far out in front, leading the way. Everything felt, looked, smelled and sounded fantastic, as my little Cayuse broke the early morning calm, straining only slightly for the steepest grades.

The sound of a lone single-cylinder exhaust breaking the early morning silence as it ricochets off the surrounding mountains brings with it an amazing feeling of freedom. My trusty little steed was carrying me effortlessly into the wide-open country and eventually to places far beyond the horizon.

Happiness to me is a full tank of gas, a full stomach and an empty bladder, with hundreds of miles of country roads ahead. I'd often go for as long as four and five hours before stopping for gas and a quick lunch, and I'd be singing to myself most of the way as the little bike would drift gracefully through the turns. Taking a trip like this and doing it alone is something I'd rather do than just about anything else in the world.

People would often ask, "You go on these trips alone? Don't you ever get lonesome out there, all by yourself?" My answer is always the same: I'm never alone, and I've never felt lonesome – and for some I'd add: "I can always feel God's presence."

I communicate with God and with my inner self often during these trips, about a lot of things – starting with my personal relationships, past and present, but also whatever else might come to mind. I believe that God is not only listening, but He is also watching over me, and whenever I've needed it most, His protective hand has pulled me through, like the time with the sheep – and there were many other times. It's like being on my own 24-day retreat, which is often sacrificed when I ride with others or ride with the destination as my primary objective.

It's a perfect opportunity to take a reality check on the never-ending process of striving to build and maintain a decent character: one that I can not only live with, but also be proud of and hopefully in some way be a role model and an inspiration to my children and grandchildren. It's sometimes difficult to do that while living in a world where so many seem to have lost their way, or may be in pursuit of far less venerable goals such as money, power, self-indulgence or the pointless accumulation of lots of stuff they don't really need – or will ever use.

I often get up to 80 miles per gallon for the entire day when I keep my speed down. I had been riding the

little BMW F650GS Dakar regularly for the past few
years and I had grown quite attached to it. Having
found it futile to find a decent all-weather windshield
for the bike, I asked Leif Gustafsson to make up
another, similar to the first, which had gotten smashed
when I hit the sheep on the Alaska Highway. It's still
not the panacea of windshields, but it's far better than
any of the others I've tried. This time I stood by and
watched the forming operation as Leif shaped the hot
plastic by hand; and consequently, the end product
came out a little more to my liking. At least I carry
even more of the blame this way if it turns out to be
less than what I had hoped for.

I've seldom felt the need to travel any faster than 60
along the lightly traveled byways, especially when I'm
not in a big hurry to get somewhere. I've found that
whenever I go much faster, I need to keep my eyes
peeled to the road for control and safety; and not only
do I miss out on much of the beautiful countryside that
way, but I also have much less time for the deep
thought and introspection that I often strive for. I get
better gas mileage this way too. I averaged between 72
and 73 mpg for this entire trip, which is the most I've
ever gotten on any trip with any motorcycle, and I
attribute it almost exclusively to the speed.

Whenever I plan a trip like this, using mostly back
roads, it has often taken months to plot it out so I can
thoroughly enjoy every bit of the ride. I find that in the
end it's much more enjoyable than seeing how fast I
can get there, or for the sheer thrill of riding fast. I also
try to lay it out in a way that I can enjoy the prairies,
the deserts and the farmlands as much as I do the
beautiful mountains and valleys. There's always
something of God's creation out there to see and derive

pleasure from, wherever it might be, especially when one takes the time to look around and enjoy it.

I've often thought of taking a trip across the country using the sun and shadows as my only guide, with no maps, GPS or prepared route sheets; and to do it exclusively on back-country roads. It would be like just getting on the bike and going. I believe it would be a huge challenge and a fantastic adventure, much like what the early pioneers did before there were roads. The challenge would be even greater on days with no sun. I'm sure it would take most of the summer, but what an adventure it would be! A sleeping bag and emergency food would be essential because it would be difficult to plan overnight stops with motels.

I once read that Daniel Boone often walked from his home in Kentucky through the wilds of Appalachia to Philadelphia using mostly existing trails, but he often blazed his own trails as he went. It is said that he pioneered many of the trails that still exist, like the Wilderness Trail through Cumberland Gap.

The temperature rose to 98° that day, and the late afternoon sun was directly in my eyes when I finally pulled into a motel in West Memphis, Arkansas, just beyond the Mississippi River. It turned out to be the longest day of my trip at 540 miles, almost all of which was two-lane country roads. Some of the roads that I traveled had route numbers and some didn't. I passed through many villages and small towns as I meandered across the breadth of Tennessee, much of it on roads I had never seen before, or at least I didn't remember. I gained an hour entering the Central Time Zone, which helped to put on some of the extra miles.

I often thought while riding and I've said aloud, "So many beautiful roads, so little time!" Minor errors on my route sheet contributed to at least some of the extra miles I rode that day. I would need to make impromptu changes to my route sheet whenever I came across an error, and then I would use some of the smaller roads with and without numbers, to reconnect with my original route, which often provided the opportunity to see places I would never have seen.

I re-routed myself several times that day using the sun and shadows as my guide, along with a considerable amount of dead reckoning based on the terrain. Those unplanned excursions became a major part of my enjoyment, and I would sometimes meet interesting people whenever I'd stop to ask for directions.

I prepared my route sheet at home from memory of past trips, along with several individual state maps, a Rand McNally Road Atlas and a big magnifying glass. Lately I've been using maps on the Internet as a check and balance because not all of my maps are up to date and accurate and many don't show the interesting little country roads that I often find on Internet maps. I also stumble across some of the back roads while exploring or reconnecting with my route.

Whenever I plan a trip using smaller byways that are well off the beaten path, I try to make room in my luggage for the road atlas, a few individual state maps and a magnifying glass. But since my eyesight has gotten worse and I enjoy the challenge of exploring and riding without maps anyway, I seldom carry them anymore. Whenever I did in the past, I usually wouldn't take the time to dig them out, and they would only become excess baggage.

I admit that quite often during my trips I'd say to myself, "It sure would be nice to have a map right about now." That was usually when there was no sun or shadows, and I'd be way off somewhere trying to reconnect with my planned route, or it might be while doing some ad hoc exploring. Most of my maps don't show many of the smaller roads anyway. A GPS would be ideal, except that I'm unable to read the LED screen – it also takes away the challenge of finding my way.

The blazing heat and maximum UV that day was a harbinger of many days to come. The heat was especially noticeable because I was wearing the full riding suit, top and bottom, all day every day whether I needed it or not. I didn't have room on the little bike to stow it, so I wore it for the entire trip, and sometimes the heat would become almost unbearable.

I wore only a lightweight Wickers T-shirt and under-shorts underneath to take up perspiration; and I would rinse those out in the sink almost every night. I carry a small plastic container of Tide for the purpose, and that type of fabric dries overnight.

On cool mornings I would have everything zipped up, and often wearing the jacket liner inside that I'd usually remove before lunchtime; and I'd keep the air-vent zippers open in the afternoon. As it turned out I could have done without the riding suit for the entire trip because it didn't rain from the time I left New York until the day after I arrived back home almost a month later – but who knew?

Managing the body's hydration level is a concern and a challenge on any trip, especially in the summertime; but since I was on a doctor-prescribed diuretic for congestive heart failure, my concern was even greater.

I usually tried to manage the hydration level to the low side, allowing me to travel for longer distances without stopping for nature breaks. It's not so easy to find rest areas or other places to stop in the open farm country – not like the interstates where the rest areas are spaced about an hour or less apart.

On my fifth day out, I chose Arkansas Rte 14 and followed it for more than 200 miles across the state. It's one of several scenic east-west roads through the Ozarks. Late that afternoon I turned north into the southwest corner of Missouri to find a motel in Noel, a small town off the beaten path that's a few miles from the Oklahoma state line.

The old motel I chose is along the edge of the little slow-moving Elk River. As I strolled along the dock that evening, I thought if I had brought some fishing gear I could probably catch a supper of catfish there; but I'm afraid the combination of fishing and long distance touring has its own myriad of challenges that would take a lot more planning and preparation – not to mention carrying the necessary gear. The thought of stopping to fish had occurred to me several times in the past, especially during my earlier solo adventures to Alaska where fishing would have been great in some of the lakes and streams up that way.

Finding no place nearby for a quick breakfast, I made do with a few granola bars, a handful of raisins and another of peanuts from my bag. For the first time in years I was traveling without sardines – I might have been able to find some if I dug deep enough. I often carry a coffee mug and an electric cup-heater too, with individual bags for making coffee or tea when there is no coffee maker in the room.

Granola bars work out well for lunch if it's difficult to find a fast-food place, although most towns of any size have a place to pick up a quick lunch. Sometimes it might be a small roadside stand with hamburgers and hot dogs, which makes for a nice change of pace, and I've met interesting people that way while eating lunch at a picnic table in the shade.

In the morning I located US 160 in Oswego, Kansas after traveling northeast out of Noel for about 90 miles over rural country roads. I chose Rte 160 for my main route across the country this time because it's a well-maintained and lightly-traveled scenic byway that passes through many small towns and villages as it wends its way across the heart of Middle America, much like Route 66 did many years ago. Almost the entire length has two lanes through rural countryside, with very little traffic.

I would see mostly farmers or their wives going to or from the small towns, and on the rare occasion I would get stuck behind a slow driver in a no-passing zone, they would be going less than a mile anyway, and I wasn't in that much of a hurry, so it never became a problem. I followed Rte 160 for 3 days into Cortez, Colorado, beyond the Continental Divide, enjoying much of this beautiful country along the way.

Whenever the scenery would remind me of songs that I've heard, I'd sing the lyrics as I rode: In Kansas it was: *"The waving wheat can sure smell sweet when the wind comes right behind the rain;"* – *"Home, home on the range, where the deer and the antelope play;"* and *"America, America! God shed His grace on thee, and crown thy good with brotherhood from sea to shining sea!"*

In eastern Tennessee I could sometimes imagine seeing Davy Crockett out there tracking bears; in the rolling hills of western Kansas it would be Wyatt Earp or Matt Dillon chasing outlaws; and in the Rocky Mountains it was Jedediah Smith in hand-to-hand combat with the Comanche as he struggled to survive.

Jedediah Smith (1799 – 1831) is one of my all-time heroes and a role model of sorts with whom I can sometimes relate. He once said, "I wanted to be the first to view a country on which the eyes of a white man had never gazed, and to follow the course of rivers that run through a new land." It is said that a wandering spirit was planted deep in his heart.

Jedediah Smith was considered to be one of the greatest of the "mountain men." He was once savagely attacked by a huge grizzly bear along the Cheyenne River in South Dakota where the grizzly at one point had Jedediah's head in its mouth and ripped off his scalp. He not only survived the attack but he convinced a fellow explorer to stitch his scalp back onto his head – and that was without anesthetic!

He was killed at the young age of 32 by a band of about 20 Comanche hunters while he was scouting for water for a group he had been leading along the Santa Fe Trail. It was said of Jedediah that his Bible and his rifle were his inseparable companions.

I saw thousands of acres of corn that day at various stages of growth on the prairies, from six inches tall and wilting in the sun to seven and eight feet high. Often when I would see the healthier corn, I'd sing lyrics from "Oklahoma": "*Where the corn is as high as an elephant's eye and it looks like it's climbing clear up to the sky.*"

I noticed that the growth of the corn is severely stunted in areas where the ground is very dry, and I noticed that corn and most other crops thrived best where huge watering rigs were giving it a drink every morning, which happens mostly west of the 100th meridian that runs down through the center of the Great Plains.

I saw lots of rice paddies, beans, wheat and many other crops, and I saw farmers working in the fields with tractors and other equipment. I saw rice mostly in the hot lowlands of the Mississippi River Valley – but in other areas too. I saw where the hay had already been cut and left in the fields in huge round bales.

I saw cattle grazing in the lush green fields of eastern Kansas as well as in some of the drier areas like Nevada where cattle graze on the open range, and steel cattle guards help to keep them off the highways. I saw very little green grass once I got to Nevada where the terrain tends to be much drier and the flora is considerably different from other areas.

I've heard people refer to riding across the prairies and deserts as boring. On the contrary, I can see almost everything out there as anything but boring. I can imagine every cactus, every clump of sagebrush, every blade of range grass and even the tumbleweed of each having their own individual God-given life. I think of every plant and bush out there as being unique and alive – and every bit of it is interesting to me.

The trees in the west have always been the most impressive: First the aspens of the Rocky Mountains; then the junipers and cedars in the drier areas of Utah and Nevada, followed by the ponderosa pines and Douglas firs that grow majestically throughout the Sierra Nevada Mountains from California to

Washington State and beyond; and finally the huge stately centuries-old redwoods that still thrive in the protected areas near the Pacific coastline.

The only time I got bored was when I got out onto the interstate highways where everyone seems to be in a big hurry to get somewhere, and I would often have to increase my speed to 80 mph and higher to keep up with the pack. I wouldn't see much of the scenery that way – especially when I'd be watching for fast-moving trucks and cars coming up from behind and also those ahead. I'd have to stay clear of drivers doing much stupider things than I do out there, and sometimes at very high rates of speed.

In recent years, I'd get headaches from long periods on the interstates, and the stress of it would eventually make me groggy and sleepy. I didn't mind it much when I was younger, with more strength and quicker reflexes, and when I rode the big Harley-Davidsons and Honda Gold Wings that are designed more for that type of travel – but even those feel better to me on the scenic byways and country roads.

I had ridden portions of Rte 160 several times in the past and I've always enjoyed it. It turned out to be an excellent ride this time too, although it was along this road and during this trip that I had one of the more harrowing rides of my million-plus miles of riding a motorcycle. I'm not sure exactly where or when I rode that millionth mile, but to the best of my knowledge it was somewhere on this trip.

I started my seventh day in Medicine Lodge, Kansas, making a quick gas stop in Meade where I met a guy with a nicely restored, single-cylinder BSA XT-500. We were getting gas at adjacent pumps when he asked if I belonged to a singles club. At first I thought he was referring to my marital status but he was looking at my bike at the time, and I realized he meant a club that's made up of single-cylinder motorcycle riders – so I answered that I don't.

His next question was, "How does that little BMW handle in the wind?" I said it handles fine for me just about anywhere, and I added that I've never had any real problem with it in the wind – not realizing that it would be put to an extreme test not far from there.

The wind had already been blowing quite strong out of the southwest most of way across Kansas, and I was constantly aware of it, but it was nothing like it would be a few miles west of Meade on a deserted stretch of prairie leading into southeastern Colorado where the terrain flattens out and there are very few trees or anything else to break the force of it.

I had taped my face shield earlier to hold it fully open because I wanted to ride with my glasses alone. The shield wasn't staying up on its own in the wind, and I could see much better through my glasses, without the shield. The shield stayed up when I taped it, except when the wind was strong enough to force it down in spite of two layers of tape I used to hold it up.

Eventually I rode most of the trip without my glasses, keeping the face shield fully closed. That fixes the wind problem, but without glasses, many of the road signs would be blurred. I wasn't usually that concerned about the signs, except maybe for the speed limit signs and the route numbers, so I'd try to wear the glasses whenever I could.

About 10 miles out of Meade the wind got so strong that it was picking up dirt and sand from the surrounding prairie and it was blasting the side of my face with it. It soon increased to a frightening velocity and I realized I was caught out on the open prairie in a full-blown sand storm with no shelter from it. The first thing I thought of was to stop at the edge of the road to remove the duct tape and close the face shield.

After stopping, my feet kept slipping and sliding on the sandy surface and I didn't have enough hands to hold the bike from blowing over and to work on the shield at the same time. The road was totally covered with sand. I tried to turn the bike into the wind but the sand was making the surface so slippery that my feet kept sliding out. I was miles from anywhere and there was no place to duck into or get behind.

As soon as I was able to get the face shield closed and my glasses put away, I decided to ride it out instead of sitting and struggling with it, which was no fun at all. It was a tough decision because I knew that the consequences could be much worse while riding.

After getting underway, I thought the safest speed might be between 50 and 55 mph because anything less wasn't offering enough gyroscopic action for the wheels and the wind was throwing the bike around a lot on the sand; and I figured that anything faster wouldn't leave enough weight on the road for adequate tire traction. Meanwhile, the temperature was up around 100° and it was drying me up like a prune, especially after having taken my diuretic medication.

When the wind kicked the rear wheel out about an inch the first time, I also thought about the blood-thinning medication I was on, and it reminded me that my bare thighs were exposed from the side zippers being wide open. I couldn't possibly spare a hand to zip them up, and if I stopped again, I would need both hands to hold the bike steady. I had no idea how long the storm might last, but I kept going.

My next thought was: What if the bike got hit so hard from the side that both wheels break traction at the same time? Could the wind possibly cross it up so bad that it would throw me over the high side? I was aware that any kind of spill could be serious, especially with the blood-thinning medication, but a concussion could be fatal. Of course I was aware of all these risks before I left on the trip, and I think my knuckles were turning white around that time.

I recited the Lord's Prayer as I rode, and the 23rd Psalm, some of the lines of which go: *"Yea, thou I walk through the valley of the shadow of death, I will fear no evil; for Thou art with me; Thy rod and thy staff they comfort me."* The prayers did help to calm me down a little, and I continued to ride.

It reminded me of the time many years ago when the Honda Gold Wing I was riding broke traction with both wheels together from a powerful blast of side-wind in west Texas while traveling at 75 mph or better along I-10. I was about an hour west of El Paso near the New Mexico state line. It had been very windy all day and it was pouring rain at the time. I had just passed an 18-wheeler as we both emerged from a railroad underpass.

The truck was still very close behind when a powerful gust hit me so hard from the side that both wheels broke loose, like I was on an ice pond. I could hear loud blasts of air behind me as the trucker applied his air brakes, probably thinking I had lost it. I thought so too for a moment, but I was able to regain control enough with God's help to ride it out while the bike kept turning one way and then the other. I learned quickly that skating around totally out of control at high speed gets real scary! Somehow, I managed to pull it out that time, but this time it was with a much lighter machine and a much older and more fragile bag of bones.

The rear wheel broke traction several times that day on the prairie in Kansas as the unrelenting wind and sand continued to blast from the side. I managed to cling to the handlebars for the next 150 miles through the most powerful sand storm I have ever experienced. The 21-inch front wheel never broke traction once, which was probably one of the main factors that got me through safely. The other of course was God's protective hand, and I certainly thanked Him for that.

By the time I got to Springfield, Colorado I was totally exhausted and had a wicked headache. I felt nauseous too, which was probably from the thoughts of what could happen; and maybe some of it from dehydration. In any case, it made me realize again that the Lord is my Shepherd and that it's been He who has protected me all of these years in spite of some of the disturbing situations I get myself into.

The wind died down a little by the time I gassed up in Springfield where the temperature was 102. I drank some water to ease the dehydration, but I continued to feel light-headed and nauseated for the rest of the day. By the time I reached Trinidad, my planned overnight stop, I was totally beat. It was certainly a day to remember, and yet another exciting experience to be thankful to God for my safety and well-being. I found a room at a Budget Host and slept well after 390 miles – many of which were unforgettable.

The next day was a much more relaxing day of reflection and thanksgiving as I rode through the southern foothills of the Rocky Mountains and crossed the Continental Divide at Wolf Creek Pass. I saw snow up close for the first time on the trip in spite of the extreme heat a few hundred miles back. The elevation at the pass is 10,850 feet, which in many areas is above the tree line, but Wolf Creek Pass doesn't give the same impression of high altitude as some of the other high passes farther north like Loveland, Independence and Beartooth.

Beyond the pass, I went through a few towns and more foothills on my way to Cortez where I spent the night. The road also passes the entrance to Monte Verde National Park where I remember visiting at least a few times, both alone and with my wife Lillian, but always by bike. I remembered the time 30 years ago when I camped out alone there during my first tour to Alaska when I had a somewhat disturbing encounter with a drunken Apache who had taken a liking to my bike, which I wrote about in my *Motorcycling Stories* book.

My ninth day began a little before seven, and it was a day filled with spectacular scenery. I located what the maps called County Road G about 5 miles west of Cortez, and I followed it due west across the state line into a part of Utah that's occupied predominately by Native Americans of the Ute Nation. The name of the road changes to Ismay Trading Post Road at the state line, although neither section was marked – at least I didn't see any markings from the time I left Rte 160.

I got to a T intersection in the reservation and asked a guy putting gas into a pickup truck which way to Ismay, and he answered that I was already in Ismay. I didn't see any sign of a town but his answer was enough to tell me to turn right, which my route sheet said would take me to Rte 95 and Hanksville – and it did.

Much of southeastern Utah has buttes and bluffs of all shapes and sizes, with a range of colors and shades.

Like much of Utah, the roads I traveled that day went by spectacular buttes and bluffs of many shapes and sizes, with colors ranging from light tan to golden brown and from light pink through several shades of salmon to light red. At the mid altitudes I saw mostly cedars and pines, and above the 6,000-foot level I saw aspens. It was a beautiful ride with colorful panoramas of southeastern Utah in all directions.

One of the roads went over the 7,000-foot level and afforded beautiful vistas of the countryside. I took a few photos and admired the scenery until I decided to pick up my pace a little and ride an extra 130 miles that day into Cedar City, rather than go off-course into Panguitch where I had originally planned to stop. I was due to meet my friends in Tonopah, Nevada at noon the next day, and I certainly didn't want to be late.

I pulled over and stopped somewhere in central Utah when I saw a few BMW riders alongside the road. I learned that they were from Long Island and the New York metropolitan area, and that they were in Utah for a BMW rally scheduled for that weekend in Panguitch. I mentioned where I was coming from and going to. They commented on my "funny-looking little BMW," so I proceeded to expound on its virtues, mentioning that the bike has been to Alaska and back and that it handles exceptionally well on all kinds of surfaces.

I suppose putting my overall aged, somewhat saddle-worn appearance together with mentioning Alaska and Buchanan, one of the guys said, "You wouldn't by any chance be Piet Boonstra, would you?" I answered that I was, and he said, "Wow," which I think he repeated at least once. He said he had read my book and that it had inspired him to ride to Alaska.

Being recognized on the road more than 2,000 miles from home pumped my ego, and we chatted for a while before I moved on. I reached Cedar City around 5 PM after an enjoyable 475-mile day, and I checked into a new-style Motel 6.

After a breakfast of sausage muffin with egg next door, I headed northwest towards Tonopah. An hour or so later I was in Nevada where the terrain was drier and the temperature rose steadily. It soon felt like it was well into the 90s. I stopped somewhere between Caliente and Rachel when I saw another group of riders parked alongside the road. It seemed that their main topic of conversation was how boring and tedious it was "crossing the desert," whereas I was enjoying every minute of it, even though I've been through that area at least a few times before.

Sign in Rachel, Nevada, "Next Gas 110 Miles" (Tonopah)

I ate a granola bar from my bag while gassing up at an antiquated pump along the Extraterrestrial Highway in Rachel, just outside the highly secret government facility called Area 51. I figured the snack would hold me over until lunchtime. A short while later I came very close to hitting a full-grown cow strolling down the center of the road. The critter apparently got by one of the cattle guards or through a fence somewhere, and it seemed intent on following the double-yellow line home. I didn't see it at first, and it never flinched when I flew by very close.

I learned from the desk clerk at the motel in Tonopah that my friends had checked in 15 minutes earlier. I asked the girl where she thought a couple of bikers might go for lunch, and without hesitation she directed me to a combined restaurant and bar not far from there. I figured she probably gave them the same directions a few minutes earlier.

The same two guys I met in Montana in 2004 while I was returning from Alaska were already eating lunch: Jim Bellach, from the Fresno area riding a Suzuki

DL1000 V-Strom, and John Dey from Corona, a Los Angeles suburb, riding a nicely-restored classic Honda CB1100F. With them this time was Alan Cheever from the Lake Havasu area of Arizona on a Honda XL650. During lunch I learned some of the details of Jim's plan for the next three days. He said he would be the primary host and that he would lead us from there. Both Jim and John are long-time off-road competition riders and we have a lot in common.

John, being somewhat of a protagonist of the practical jokes during my visit, announced later at the motel that, as a special treat for me, they had "fixed me up" with a woman who would be arriving at my room at 10 PM. I said, "You can't be serious!" I told him that I plan to be in bed by nine, and there had better not be a knock at my door. I thought he was probably kidding, but I wasn't totally sure.

Breakfast stop: L to R: Jim Bellach, John Dey and Alan Cheever

After we were packed and loaded in the morning, we headed north out of Tonapah and stopped at a sit-down restaurant in the desert for breakfast and additional bonding. From there we continued north through Toiyabe National Forest to US Rte 50, and west from there to Austin, Nevada where we stopped for gas.

Austin was being inundated by millions of Mormon crickets, which Jim said happens around the same time every year. The huge shield-back katydids can grow up to three inches long, and they descend on Austin around the same time every year. They often move along the ground and climb the sides of the buildings in schools.

Mormon Crickets everywhere

The "road-kill" around the gas station numbered in the hundreds and maybe even thousands. It looked like squashed bugs could become a safety problem after a while, especially for bikes. They were moving all over the ground and on anything that they could cling to.

After checking into a motel in Quincy, California, Jim noticed a soft rear tire on his bike – with a huge nail in it. He and John plugged the tire that evening, but it still had a slow leak in the morning. We stopped along the way for a can of fix-a-flat, or something similar, which worked well enough to complete our ride.

During our second full day together, on a relatively straight stretch of pavement and after stopping in Mad River for gas, John and I were horsing around and got into an acceleration test to see how well his 25-year-old 4-cylinder 1100cc Honda Classic would do against the more modern single-cylinder Austrian-designed 650 Rotax engine in my BMW Dakar.

There was no real winner, but in the process, I "did the ton" at 81, as we reached speeds of over 100 mph in a relatively short distance. It was fun, but we had to cool it quickly as we neared a series of tight turns. The result was very close, but it made the adrenalin flow and gave us something additional to talk and laugh about that evening, along with another round of John's practical jokes and many great stories of everyone's past experiences.

It was much cooler in Eureka than our first two days – certainly a pleasant change from the extreme heat. We sat outside the rooms and talked for hours while enjoying a bucket of Kentucky Fried Chicken and beer. After a few drinks, John insisted that I accompany them to a nearby strip joint where he said I would be introduced to pole dancing and I could learn first-hand about lap dancing, or whatever; but I declined and I was quite sure he was kidding.

The next day was the highlight of our three days together. We went south for 20 miles to Ferndale, a small, picturesque Victorian town; and from there we headed west on Mattole Road toward the coastline – a seldom-used, twisty blacktop road that's quite narrow with lots of tight off-camber curves and hummocks. It was a real fun ride. I saw practically no other vehicles for the entire 20 miles to the Pacific Ocean where we stopped along what Jim said is known as the "Lost Coast." He said it's also known as the longest undeveloped stretch of ocean coastline in California. I understand most of it is federal land.

After the brief stop, we continued along Mattole Road for another 20 miles to Honeydew, near the southern edge of the Humbolt Redwoods State Park – stopping only briefly at a few other interesting spots along the way.

"Lost Coast" of the Pacific Ocean along Mattole Road.

At one of those stops, we pulled over onto a grassy area along the Mattole River where a girl was drifting down the river on a float tube. John said she was carrying a case of beer for a picnic they had arranged especially for my visit. I assumed he was kidding, but he was pointing at her and waving, and she was smiling and waving back like maybe they actually knew each other, and it seemed like she was coming toward us. This time it looked much more authentic and I got suckered into believing; but when she got closer, she floated on by with a wave and a smile.

We stopped at the Country Store in Honeydew where I ordered a deli sandwich with a bottle of local-brewed ale. We enjoyed a leisurely lunch together at a picnic table in the shade. While we were there, a few other groups of bikers stopped by and John mingled through one of the larger groups, apparently telling them stories about my books, my travels and me, resulting in my getting an order from a rider from San Diego for my *Motorcycling Stories* book.

Left to right: Alan, Jim and John relaxing at lunch in the shade at Honeydew, California.

After lunch we rode through the Humboldt Redwoods State Forest, stopping to take several more photos. When we split a short while later, it was arranged that Alan would accompany me as far as Redding, probably with an overnight stop somewhere in between. As it turned out, we decided to ride straight through, and it became a long day for both of us.

After breakfast with Alan, I headed northeast alone on Rte 299, through relatively flat desert-like terrain towards eastern Oregon. It was an enjoyable and relaxing ride with no traffic. Several minutes would go by before I would see a vehicle in either direction. I saw Mt. Shasta and the beautiful Cascade Range many miles to my left – an impressive sight. I spent the time reminiscing the visit and laughing a lot.

The time I spent with the three guys was certainly the highlight of my trip, especially the exciting twisty ride along Mattole Road to the coastline, our lunch in Honeydew and the stop in the redwood forest. They're great fun to be with and I hoped they would come east soon so I could return the favor.

The first town of any size I came to after 335 miles was Burns, Oregon where I stopped for the night. It struck me as a nice town – mostly because it was relatively clean with wide streets and handsome, well-kept homes. I checked into a Days Inn and chatted for a while with the female manager before finding a place for dinner not far from there.

I had originally anticipated an easy 375-mile day from there to Carey, Idaho; but finding no motel in Carey, I pressed on for Blackfoot, another 100 miles, figuring logically that it would take about two hours. But as fate would have it, I ran into road construction when I was about halfway to Blackfoot, and that shattered my two-hour estimate.

I didn't see the warning sign near the start of the first construction area, and I flew unexpected off a 4-inch drop onto soft, deep dirt at 70 mph. Fortunately I was riding the Dakar, and I rode it out safely. Later, as I was following a pilot car through another construction area near the entrance to Craters of the Moon, my wheels dropped into a deep rut, and the bike squirreled around a lot, but the Dakar came through again.

Pilot cars were used in both places. Together the two construction areas cost me more than an hour. I had to wait each time for the pilot car to come from the other end and then follow it slowly through the work area whiles sandwiched between a long string of cars, trucks and RVs. I eventually got to Blackfoot around 6:00 and checked into a Super 8.

The decision to go all the way to Blackfoot put me ahead of my planned schedule and out of synch with my original plan for motels, so I took out the map of the western states that John insisted I take before leaving, and the magnifying glass that Jim insisted I take, and I laid out an extra loop through an area of Idaho, Utah and Wyoming that I had never seen.

The impromptu ride took me through many of the potato farms of southeastern Idaho where watering rigs were being used. They look so beautiful with huge sprays in all directions in the morning sunlight. I assumed the water was coming from the nearby Snake River that I crossed at least a few times that morning.

I went south from Idaho along the west side of Bear Lake into the northeast corner of Utah – also skirting the edge of the Wasatch-Cache National Forest. From there I went through Logan Canyon and east into the southwest corner of Wyoming. I had a few close calls during the day's ride. One was in a small town in Idaho where I found myself headed in the wrong direction on a one-way street. The other was in Logan Canyon where there was sand in the pavement halfway around a turn. They were both close, but the sand was the closest to my having a mishap.

I stopped for lunch at a privately owned fast-food place that I found in Kemmerer, Wyoming. I ordered a taco salad with lemonade and a senior discount. The girl behind the counter asked if I was 65. I laughed and thanked her for the complement and told her I was 81. She couldn't believe it and called a few of her friends out of the kitchen to guess my age – none were close.

I had hoped to make Manila, Utah my overnight stop after a long, hot 400-mile day, but the only two small motels I found had no vacancies. I was exhausted from the heat and the long ride when the woman at the second motel said the nearest one might be in Vernal, but she said they too were probably full because of some kind of work going on in the area by Haliburton.

She said that overflow motel business was being felt for a hundred-mile radius, and it was unlikely I would find a room there either. The next town in the direction I was headed was Craig, Colorado, 120 miles east of Vernal, but there was a possibility they also might be affected. It was an additional three-hour ride to Craig, which would have taken me into the night hours and I was already too tired to ride safely.

I had also been running with a blown headlight bulb for most of the trip and this was the first time I might need it. It was almost 5 PM when I suggested to the woman that I should be able to make it into Vernal in an hour. She shook her head and said, "That's highly unlikely. It's 67 miles and the road goes through the mountains with switchback turns most of the way." She added that it was also patrolled, and that there were many deer. I've been over the road before.

I figured I'd give it a try anyway. Needless to say, I seriously wore rubber from the sides of the tires for the first time since leaving home; but it paid off because I got there just before six and got the very last room at a Days Inn. The next day I rode 160 miles across desert-like terrain into Steamboat Springs, Colorado, followed by a 100-mile ride through the foothills of the Rockies to Dillon where I got a room at a Super 8.

Early the next morning I rode 18 miles up the old section of US Rte 6 to Loveland Pass, rather than go through the Eisenhower Tunnel. I had tried on three previous occasions to reach the pass, but each time I was turned back and never made it. On my first try, in the early 1980s, there was far too much snow and the road was closed; the next time there was a forest fire on the mountain and all traffic was being detoured through the tunnel; and on my third try, a truck was jack-knifed across the road near the summit, and the road was far too narrow for cars and trucks to turn around. The traffic jam was a nightmare. Fortunately I was able to make a U-turn and detour around again.

I made it this time, but I had to wait for almost an hour for the morning fog to clear enough to see anything. The temperature was only 35° at the summit – the coldest of anywhere on my trip. Not long after getting onto I-70, I exited near Central City and had a nice ride down through another canyon to Boulder where I had been invited to visit with Chris and Erin Ratay. Chris and Erin are in the Guinness Book of Records for the "Longest Motorcycle Ride by a Team" for having ridden their two BMW F650GSs around the world together between May 1999 and August 2003. During their trip they visited 50 countries on 6 continents and went though 86 borders, for a total of 101,322 miles.

I had no trouble finding the street they live on, but I had a little difficulty with the house number because of my poor eyesight; Erin heard the bike and came out to guide me the rest of the way into their garage. I arrived just in time to get invited to a company picnic that was arranged with Chris' fellow real estate entrepreneurs and their families that was being held on the lawn of a local park.

We broke away from the picnic early because they had invited friends over for a backyard cookout to coincide with my visit. Later at their home I met Chris and Spice Jones, a friendly young couple who are also riders of some renown. I learned that Chris Jones was signed up to ride the upcoming Paris-Dakar desert race in Africa with a KTM 650RR, and that Spice was psyched about the prospect of taking an adventurous motorcycle tour across Asia with Erin and a few other famous women riders. They were not free to discuss the details that were still being worked out.

Two other riders, Steve and Paul, joined us, and we spent most of the evening eating and talking about motorcycling. They are all experienced off-road riders, and it was a pleasure to spend time with them. When I left the next morning, it was with a genuine admiration for Chris and Erin as the kind of couple that I'm proud to know and proud to call my friends. They graciously invited me into their home and into their own circle of friends while treating me as their honored guest.

I headed out directly into the bright morning sunlight and failed to see several signs, which has become a common problem for me lately – especially traveling east into the early morning sun. I hadn't intended to use I-70 until I got beyond the interchange east of Denver, but being unable to read the signs, I found myself on I-25 heading north directly into the huge interchange, in the midst of morning rush-hour traffic headed into Denver. If I had blundered onto I-25 going south rather than north, I'd probably have stayed with it since I was headed southeast anyway; but after a few lucky guesses, I was able to bumble my way onto I-70 heading east, which is what I originally intended to use as far as Limon, Colorado anyway.

I rarely ride the interstates any more, but when I feel a
need to, I can usually expect problems in heavy traffic
around the big interchanges where everyone is driving
fast and jockeying for position for the highway splits –
which doesn't bode well for anyone with poor eyesight
and not sure of which lane he needs to be in.

The route sheet I made up at home said I should make
a left turn in Kit Carson and go 23 miles to the next
turn. I made what I thought was the correct first turn
and went at least 45 miles across the prairie without
ever seeing another place to turn. I thought it sure
would be nice to have a map right about now. I spotted
a farmhouse with someone cutting grass out front, so I
pulled into the driveway to ask for directions.

It didn't take long to see that the grass cutter was a
healthy-looking farm girl in a bikini that might have fit
well last year but she outgrew it – and then some. She
grabbed a blouse or something from the seat of the
mower to cover the exposed areas, and walked toward
me smiling. I learned that I was definitely on the
wrong road, but her shy smile and friendly demeanor
made it another memorable moment of my trip; and it
reminded me that you meet some of the nicest people
along the way. Her directions said I had to return all
the way to Kit Carson for the road I was looking for.

A few of the mistakes I made on the trip could have
had much more dire consequences, like when a car in
one town and a pickup truck in another almost hit me
while I was making lane changes without signaling or
looking first. I would also occasionally go through red
lights and stop signs that I didn't see. The other drivers
were usually in a much bigger hurry than I was, but the
fault would be mine because I would often be over-
tired and not paying enough attention.

I called it a day in Scott City, Kansas after only about 300 miles, which was 120 miles short of my goal for that day. It was due mainly to the route sheet error – but also to a time zone change that I hadn't figured into my day's plan. I didn't have much of a choice of motels in Scott City and I eventually settled on sharing a crummy room with a bunch of dead crickets.

Around noon the next day I stopped in the small town of Beloit, Kansas to inquire about US Rte 36, a road I had been looking for and thought I might have passed. The road I was on was very lightly traveled and it went straight through the town, like in many small towns on the prairie. I parked in front of a Case-International tractor dealer and walked inside to ask for directions. There was no one around so I called out, "Anybody here?" No one answered and I repeated it a few times. My voice echoed inside the building. There were many huge farm tractors and pickup trucks inside, and at least three offices, but there was not a soul around. It looked like someone could walk off with the place.

I went next door to an open hardware store and called out again: "Anybody here?" There was no one there either. I walked across the deserted street to a gas station that I found to be closed and locked. I stood for a minute and looked around. Nothing was moving anywhere, and I saw no one. There was just dead silence. I was beginning to get an eerie feeling that maybe there was no one in the entire town – like on the old TV series *The Twilight Zone.*

I went back to the bike, got on, and drove off slowly, looking into every yard for someone to ask. As I was about to leave the north end of the town, I saw a diner with at least 15 to 20 pickup trucks parked outside. The place was packed. I parked the bike and went inside.

The loud din of voices that I met suddenly fell silent as everyone turned to look at me. I said, "Could anyone please tell me where I could find US Rte 36?"

After a brief pause, I heard a gruff male voice say, "Up the road about 12 miles."

I said thanks, and I added: "Does everyone in this town go to lunch at the same time? I couldn't find a soul anywhere." I left while they were all laughing.

Shortly after leaving town I noticed a car quite close behind me with his left-turn indicator blinking. I thought he was about to make a left turn, or maybe he intended to pass, but he didn't do either. He got even closer behind me with the light still blinking. I didn't see any place to turn and I thought he probably doesn't realize it's on. Then I realized it was mine that was on! So I turned it off and his went off.

When he pulled out and passed me, accelerating like he was in a hurry, I noticed the word "Sheriff" painted on the side. I guess I was lucky I didn't get a ticket, or at least get stopped and checked out. I wondered if he was parked somewhere in town watching everything I did, or maybe he was in the diner. I got up the road about four miles and saw him tucked in behind some bushes. I threw him a big wave. Quite often on the trip I'd ride for miles with my turn indicator blinking, like on the Alaskan trip when Jim Hoellerich would tell me to turn it off practically every time we made a turn – for a while anyway.

I checked into a Super 8 in Chillicothe, Missouri late that afternoon after what seemed like an exceptionally long 540-mile day – all of it on two-lane country roads. It was in fact one of my longest days of the trip.

I continued to follow US 36 in the morning, out of Chillicothe. It was a rough 4-lane-divided highway for much of the next 100 miles. I turned north on US 24 just before Hannibal and crossed the Mississippi River into Quincy, Illinois. I missed one of the many turns that US 24 makes in Quincy, and I found myself leaving town on Rte 104. I stopped at a custom bike shop to ask, "How can I get back to US 24 East?"

The middle-aged proprietor looked at me strangely and said, "I don't think you want that road. Where are you headed?"

"New York," I said.

He said with a strange look, "Not on 24 East, I hope."

"Why? What's wrong with it?"

He said, "It's rough. You don't want that road."

"What do you mean by rough? Does it go through towns with a lot of congestion and traffic lights?"

"No." he said, "It's all hummocks and potholes and it's narrow. No one ever uses that road."

I asked if there were small farms with cornfields and pastures along the way and he answered, "There's a lot of that, all right."

I said, "That's the road I'm looking for. It's not a problem. The bike has good suspension."

"You'll need it!" He said and he sounded serious.

He was right about the roughness. The rear mudguard snapped clear off, probably from one of the many potholes that I didn't see. By the time I got to Indiana I was sore all over, but I certainly saw a lot of corn and beans – mostly corn, and I wasn't singing the lyrics from "Oklahoma" at the time. It was an interesting ride though. I didn't find much of a choice of motels in Attica where I planned to stop, but I eventually found a small one in the farmland a few miles east of town.

The next day was a short ride to Montgomery, Ohio where I planned to visit with Walt Maerki, who was a US Navy dive-bomber pilot during WWII. He flew in the same squadron with my brother Dirk, who lost his life in the South Pacific while serving as a tail gunner.

A few years earlier, while I was authoring a labor-of-love biography of my brother entitled, "Never to be Forgotten." I was unable to find information about which aircraft carriers and small islands Dirk flew from during the last six months of his life. The war was moving along swiftly at the time and his squadron moved around a lot – both aboard aircraft carriers and island hopping where they used tiny airfields captured from the Japanese – or were built hurriedly by the Seabees.

I had seen the name WG Maerki on a condolence letter that was sent to my mother after Dirk was killed in January 1944. I was sure that this man, who was the Senior Naval Aviator of the squadron at the time of Dirk's death, could fill me in on the details, but I had very little hope of ever finding him – that is until I thought of the Internet and Google.

I thought to myself, I'll bet I can find this guy if he's still around. So I entered the name WG Maerki into the White Pages on my computer, using the entire country as the search location. The name Walter G. Maerki popped up immediately with a Cincinnati address and phone number. It was late at night and I figured if it were the same man, he would be in his mid 80s by that time and would probably have turned in for the night, so I waited until morning.

My hand was trembling when I dialed the number. A woman's voice answered, "Hello?" I was so choked up with emotion that I had difficulty with the words, but I asked if Walter Maerki lived there.

"Yes he does," she said. "Hold on and I'll get him for you."

I said, "No, wait please! Was he a Navy dive-bomber pilot during World War II?" I was barely able to get the words out through the emotion.

"Yes he was. Here he is," and she handed the phone to him. I was almost unable to talk, and it took great effort to get the words out; but yes, he was the same person. We eventually talked for a long while and we talked several times by phone and by e-mail during the next month. I got the information I needed, and I sent him a copy of the book as soon as I finished it and self-published it.

Not long after our first talk, Walt lost his beloved wife. I had also recently lost my mother, my wife and my oldest daughter in a short seven-year period, so I was familiar with his pain, and I wrote a long condolence email to him. Soon afterward he invited me to come to his home in Ohio so I could meet him and his family. Since I was planning this trip at the time, I suggested that I could stop for a brief visit while passing through.

I used mostly I-74 to get from Attica to Montgomery, a Cincinnati suburb. I arrived around noon and had no problem finding his address. Soon after we met, he called his daughter Chris to join us. She was about to leave with her family for a July 4th holiday weekend, but she stopped by for a brief visit and the three of us talked – mostly stories about my travels. Her family was waiting, and she had to leave after only about a half-hour, but Walt and I continued to talk for the rest of the afternoon and into the evening.

After a great breakfast of bacon and eggs that Walt prepared and served in his kitchen, I was on my way to AMA headquarters in Pickerington, east of Columbus, to visit briefly with a few members of the staff, after which I put on a few hundred miles to bring my total mileage for the day to 380, leaving an easy 330 miles for my last day. My average daily mileage for this trip was about 375, with a 24-day total of 9,000 miles.

Three

High Plains Drifter

June 13 – July 10, 2008

In spite of the extreme heat I endured most of the time on the trip to California in 2006 and the heavy riding suit that I wore, the effect the trip had on my body was minimal. I took a trip two years later with similar conditions and roughly the same length, but the way my body coped with it is yet another story.

This trip brought with it many physical and medical challenges that needed to be addressed and managed while I was on the road, as well as after I got home, which probably isn't surprising because I was 83 this time. Another difference was with the bike that I rode – a 650cc Suzuki V-Strom, whereas both earlier trips were taken with a 650 BMW Dakar, which is a far superior motorcycle for its ergonomics, suspension, handling and overall riding comfort.

I bought the V-Strom in December 2007 and didn't ride it much during the first winter, but I noticed the seat height and the position of the foot pegs didn't fit my large frame very well, and the suspension was a lot stiffer. It made me wonder if I could ever get a comfortable long distance ride with it. The seat was far too low and the foot pegs were too high and too far forward, putting me in a cruiser position with my knees at almost the same level as my tailbone. That position puts the entire weight of my torso and part of the weight of my thighs onto the tailbone – definitely not a good position for my type of riding. I tested the bike to try and determine what changes would need to be made, but eventually I decided to wait until after my annual trip to Daytona Bike Week, before making any final decisions on modifications.

When I left for Daytona around the 1st of March, I was using a gel-filled "butt pad" on the seat that raised the sitting position slightly and made it a little more comfortable for my tailbone. But after a few hours, the pad, or its position, cut off circulation to my privates and everything went numb before the end of the first day. Fortunately it returned to normal by morning, so I continued, but I rode without the pad for the rest of the trip; and after a while the cruiser position and the small stiff seat became quite uncomfortable.

Overall fatigue became a factor on the third day from struggling with wind currents rebounding off the trucks along I-95 in Georgia. Traffic was heavy and running at 80 mph with the wind ricocheting off the sides of the trucks and hitting me from all angles. It was throwing me all over the road, and making it a constant struggle to maintain control. I was totally exhausted by the time I got to Florida. The wind bothered me far more with this bike than it did with the Dakar.

I compiled a list of things to be fixed, including an accessory touring seat to replace the original; a set of foot pegs that were lower and set farther back; handlebar risers to put the bars in a more comfortable position; and a California Scientific windshield for my weather protection. The changes helped to improve the overall ergonomics, the sitting position, the handling and the riding comfort in bad weather, although the touring seat was still not nearly as comfortable as what I would like for the many hours I spend on it during the longer trips, and there was nothing I could do for the suspension. Those two remaining problems would eventually take their toll on the arthritis and stenosis in my lumbar spine. The handling was also not nearly as confident as the Dakar, especially on loose gravel; but I was ready to try it on a 7,000-mile trip.

I was aware that as I got older I would have to live with an ever-increasing level of pain and fatigue, but unless I was able to make it comfortable enough, and handle well enough, it would hinder my ability to continue riding. One positive note about the Suzuki is that it's definitely the most-reliable motorcycle I have ever owned. As of this writing I've put over 100,000 miles on it in a little over three years, and I've done nothing to it other than the normal maintenance, like changing the oil, filters, plugs, tires, chains, sprockets and brake pads – and that's about it. It's never needed a single repair of any kind or even a valve adjustment during that time.

Before leaving on this 2008 trip, I read an editorial in the American Motorcyclist Magazine entitled, *Group Dynamics,* which asserted that motorcycling today is basically a group activity and that the *Then Came Bronson* stereotype simply doesn't exist. I strongly disagree because traveling alone is one of the things I enjoy most in life; and although this trip might not be quite the same as Bronson's, especially because I don't sojourn, I still had several interesting encounters with strangers along the way that reminded me of the series and of the article.

For those unfamiliar with this short-lived 1969-1970 TV series, it was about an ex-newspaperman who, after the loss of a close friend, became a nomadic vagabond motorcyclist, searching for the meaning of life and experiencing whatever life had to offer. During his travels on a Harley Davidson Sportster, he shared his values with people he met along the way and he would lend a hand whenever he could – much like the Lone Ranger did many decades before him.

My plan for this trip was to meet Jim Bellach, John Dey and Alan Cheever for a ride together in the Rocky Mountains, starting in Albuquerque, New Mexico and ending in Red Lodge, Montana five days later. Our plan was to take in some of the more beautiful areas of the Rocky Mountains, including a few high passes.

I left home in a light rain that lasted for about an hour, after which I dealt with wet roads for another hour before it began to clear and the roads dried up. I was allowing 17 days to get to Albuquerque, so it's clear I was taking my time and hoping to enjoy whatever I might find along the way.

The rain stopped around 10 o'clock and the sun began to break through an hour later. The temperature rose quickly into the 90s and it got very warm and humid. I stopped for lunch at the same McDonald's in Pine Grove, Pennsylvania where I've stopped several times before, and I removed a lot of the outer clothing and rain boots before going in for lunch. For the rest of the day I rode with my full riding suit over a polyester T-shirt and under-shorts, much like I did for the entire

California trip in 2006. I already felt half-wiped-out at lunchtime, and I didn't quite know why.

The nicest scenery I saw in the morning was along Mountain Rd west of Palmerton, followed by a series of farm roads that I've ridden several times in the past that lead to and over a high ridge and through Hawk Mountain Bird Sanctuary. Later in the day, I enjoyed riding along Rte 997, which meanders around much of south-central Pennsylvania and through the picturesque corn and hay fields of Amish country where I saw horse-drawn buggies and well-kept dairy farms.

My eyes got blurry around mid-day and started to hurt, which I thought might be at least partially due to the glare of the sun – and maybe also from eye strain. My eyesight would get worse as the day wore on, and each day it got worse than the day before. By the time I checked into the Motel 6 in Hagerstown, Maryland, I clocked only 312 miles and I was totally exhausted. I suspected that my heart was acting up, and I wasn't quite sure what it was from, other than exhaustion and maybe the heat.

I realized after checking in that the rhythm was irregular and the pulse rate was about double what it should be – an indication that my atrial fib was acting up. In the past I went to the emergency room whenever it's gotten this bad and had it brought back with cardioversion, mostly using drugs, but once it needed electrocardioversion, which is when it's brought back by electric shock. The irregular beat usually happens with me for a number of reasons, but I thought this time it might be from a combination of exhaustion, dehydration and possibly from the diuretic I was taking for my congestive heart failure – one of the tougher medications to manage on the road.

I wondered if I should turn back for treatment or continue at least another day to my daughter's home in Virginia. I was about halfway between the two places, and I assumed that as I got deeper into the trip I would get more and more exhausted, and probably have more dehydration problems, which I thought could make the condition worse.

I had discussed with my primary doctor not taking the diuretic during the trip, but he agreed only that I could cut the dose in half; but whenever I could, I should take the full dose. I soon learned that half-a-dose while riding in the extreme heat was still too much for the condition, especially since I was limiting the amount of water I drank because I could never find a place to stop and let it out along the roads that I traveled.

I thought if I were lucky, I could correct the arrhythmia on my own; so before turning in, I tried doubling up on two of my heart meds that have helped in the past to bring it back. I was determined to keep going, and I had no intention of turning back.

The second day began with a painful reminder that I should have taken the time before leaving to get a steroid injection in my spine to control the pain from the arthritis and stenosis, which got progressively worse in the past few years. The seat, along with sleeping on different mattresses every night aggravated the problem to a point where the pain would become very intense at times – especially during the first hour in the morning. Each day it took a little longer to get the bike loaded and get on the road. The pain level on a scale of one-to-ten would be at least a seven when I got out of bed, and it would usually drop to around a five for the rest of the day.

The good news was that the rhythm was not as bad in the morning as it was the night before, and the pulse rate slowed considerably; it was still higher than normal, and the beat was still just as irregular as the night before. But the improvement was enough for me to decide to continue to at least my daughter's home in Virginia and see how it goes from there.

The irregular beat and faster pulse rate actually stayed with me for the entire trip, and I never knew if it might become an even greater problem – or what the prognosis was for my continuing on the trip. I was aware that I would have to keep checking on it and manage the hydration level and the other issues.

It wasn't until a month after I returned home that I learned at my next regular cardiologist check-up that the atrial fib had become chronic, which means that my normal rhythm would never return. I didn't ask, and I've wondered since, if it would have made a difference if I had turned back and gotten a cardioversion when it was irregular; but one of my daily supplications is, "Let me not whimper about things over which I have no control, or things that are already behind me!"

The highlight of my second day was my ride along Virginia Rte 231, with its green rolling pastures, horse farms and beautiful mountains in the background. I was determined to not let the physical problems affect the pleasure of my ride. I got to my daughter's in Prince George at 3 PM after a very nice 335-mile day.

I revised the plan slightly for the third day to make it a little easier and more relaxing. I started late, finished early and planned only 250 miles for the day, which took me to Christiansburg in the beautiful Shenandoah Valley. It was a scenic ride across Virginia and over the Blue Ridge – the highlights being Rte 40 from

Rocky Mount to Woolwine, followed by Rte 8 up and over the Blue Ridge Mountains into Christiansburg.

I checked into a Knights Inn around 2 PM, which was just about the crummiest motel of the entire trip. The mattress certainly didn't do my back any good. The temperature rose into the high 90s by the time I got there; but the ride was outstanding, and I felt a little better physically from having made the day shorter.

I had been looking forward to riding a few sections of Virginia Rte 42 in a valley west of the Shenandoah in the heart of Appalachia. Rte 42 is known for most of its length as Old Bluegrass Road. It has been one of my favorites for many years. I had difficulty finding the section of it that I was looking for near Newport, which I vaguely remember having ridden. Nothing in the area looked familiar. I tried following a narrow twisty road off the main road, thinking it might have been it, but it petered out to gravel after about 10 miles – so I came back to US 460 to ask for help finding it.

Virginia Rte 42, Old Bluegrass Road

I asked an older gent at a gas station and he said, "Oh, they did away with that section of Rte 42 when they brought this new highway through" – meaning US 460. He explained how I could hook up with it about 25 miles south of there. His directions took me to near where it goes through Bland, an area I remember well. I've used a motel at the I-77 intersection near Bland several times. I also passed through several smaller towns that I remembered from the old days.

I got to Saltville and looked for Allison Gap Road, which I've taken at least once before. I planned on taking it southwest this time in the general direction of Tennessee. I spotted a guy loading a pickup truck alongside the road, so I stopped to ask him for directions. He looked at me somewhat strangely and said, "Allison Gap Road? Where do you want to go?"

I said, "No place in particular, I'm just riding around and thought I'd like to go that way." I was reluctant to say where I was headed because I suspected the kind of response I would get.

He said gruffly, "There's nothing up in there."

Not knowing quite what to say next to get him to tell me how to find the road, I said, "It heads out towards Mendota, right?" – a small town I remembered in that direction.

He answered emphatically, "That's not the way to Mendota. For Mendota you take this road here, and you go…" and he proceeded to give me directions for a totally different way.

"Thanks, but I'd rather use Allison Gap Road."

By this time he was a little annoyed and asked gruffly, "Where are you coming from?"

"New York," I said, not knowing quite what else to say or what might come next.

He stared at me for a moment with a puzzled look and went back to loading his truck, shaking his head in obvious frustration.

I eventually found the road on my own. It took me into the hills and though a series of twists and turns before emerging in a picturesque, well-manicured valley with several nice country homes and farmhouses that looked familiar, and I remembered having been through there before. If it was the road that I remembered, I was on course, and I was quite sure it would come out on US 58 in Hilton.

I came upon a minivan stopped in the middle of the road, so I thought I'd stop and ask, just to make sure. The driver of the van, a middle-aged woman, was talking with a younger woman standing alongside the van. After stopping, I directed the question at the older woman, "Could you possibly tell me where this road comes out?"

"Where do you want to go?" she asked quickly.

I said, "No place in particular. I'm just riding around."

"Where were you headed when you stopped?"

"Well, I was headed generally southwest, but I can tell from my shadow that I'm going in the right direction. I was just wondering where the road might come out."

I was trying to avoid a similar line of questioning like I just went through with the guy. It seems as though no one wants to give information, without getting some first.

"Where are you coming from?" she persisted.

I thought here we go again! I answered, "Upstate New York."

The two women looked at each other and laughed and then she said, "You mean you're from upstate New York and you're down here on this little country road in Virginia just taking a ride?"

I said, "Yes Ma'am. This is a beautiful part of the country. I just love it down here."

"Do you have any destination in mind?"

After a brief pause I said, "Well yes! I had promised some friends from California that I'd meet them in Albuquerque on the 30th, but I have more than two weeks to get there, so I've been enjoying the scenery along the way."

"Albuquerque, New Mexico?" The older woman was finding the whole thing quite fascinating, so I thought I'd spice it up more for her. I had my helmet on when I said, "You haven't heard the most unusual part."

"And what is that?" she said.

"I'm 83 years old."

"No!!"

"Yes Ma'am, I'm 83."

She said, "Take off your helmet. I have to get a picture," as she reached for a professional-looking camera from the seat next to her and started snapping pictures. She took a note pad from her purse and began asking questions and taking notes.

After answering a few of her questions, I said, "What do you plan to do with those notes?"

"I'm going to write a story about you!" she said.

I took out one of my cards that advertise two of my books on the back, and says I was *AMA Road Rider of the Year 2002,* among other things. I handed the card to her and asked if she would please send me a copy of her story when she finishes.

She seemed even more fascinated by my card and asked if I would come with her to her home. She said that she'd, "mix up a batch of mint juleps or something and we can continue the interview there."

I thought I was probably getting myself in far deeper than I had anticipated, and I didn't have the slightest idea where I might find a motel that night if I spent a few hours with this nice lady. I thought about the *Then Came Bronson* character and assumed that he would have gone with her in a heartbeat – but he wasn't 83, and I did have other plans.

We had been talking for several minutes and I noticed a car behind her, waiting to pass, so I said, "I should really move on so this guy can get through." Of course I was trying to escape!

She said, "This is only a little country road and he can wait." But I put my helmet on, restarted the bike and got myself out of there as quickly as I could with an apology, a smile and a friendly wave.

I never heard from the woman again. Maybe another time, another place; but things were moving much too fast for this old man, and I thought retreat at that point was the better part of valor – so I aborted what was one of the more interesting encounters of the trip. I had put more than a dozen of those cards in my wallet before I left home, and I had none left when I got back. They all went to interesting people that I met and chatted with along the way.

The road came out in Hilton like I thought, and I continued southwest along several other unfamiliar back roads toward Tennessee. I got myself turned around a few times on narrow unnumbered roads while trying to follow the route sheet I had prepared. For the most part I used the sun and shadows as a guide as I continued to head southwest without too much concern for how long it was taking.

I vowed to carry a compass after getting turned around a few more times, especially for cloudy days. I actually had one buried deep in my overnight case, but it would have been too much of a hassle to dig it out. I wondered how Daniel Boone made out when he trekked through much of the same area of Appalachia on foot in the 18th Century, long before there were roads – I wonder if he carried a compass.

Many of the roads I traveled that day had neither numbers nor names – at least I didn't see any. I made several in-course corrections and doubled back a few times, which amounted to about 100 miles more than I planned for the day. After reaching Tennessee on the back roads, I used mostly Rtes 33, 61 and 62 south of Cumberland Gap on my way west. I was familiar with those. I included them this time because I remembered they were excellent scenic bike roads.

I covered a total of 470 miles in 11 hours. Considering the trouble I had with my heart during the first few days, I thought it was a good day, although it was a long day for me. I checked into a motel in Cookeville where I originally planned to stop. I skipped my diuretic altogether because it was too late to take it when I got in at 5:30, and still have time for it to run its course before bedtime. I was exhausted, but I enjoyed every minute of the day.

Scene along Tennessee Rte 33, taken during an earlier trip.

I was plagued even more the next day with an inability to follow my route sheet. I eventually decided to "wing it" for most of the day on whatever numbered two-lane roads might be going in the direction I wanted to go; although I headed due north out of Cookeville in the morning to find Rte 52, which I remembered from years past as a scenic two-lane road near the Kentucky state line. After finding it, I followed it west for about an hour before trending southwest again on mostly numbered roads.

The northern swing was designed mainly to stay clear of Murfreesboro and Nashville, and I thought it would be a more scenic ride than going south of Nashville. The roads I chose later in the day were not nearly as well marked, and I was often unable to locate the route markings, especially in towns where my main concern would be to see the traffic lights and stop signs, and to stay clear of other vehicles.

I reached a T-intersection near the center of Holly Springs, Mississippi where I couldn't find any route-number markings to show which way the highway went from there. I asked at a nearby gas station and learned that the route markings end at the east side of town and start over again at the west side from a different street. No wonder I had so much difficulty in Tennessee where I kept losing the route almost every time I went through a town. I figured maybe they were doing the same thing there.

Holly Springs was my planned overnight stop. I got there with a total mileage for the day not far from what I had planned, in spite of the many impromptu changes I made during the day. I felt I had done well though, and I saw lots of nice scenery and had relatively light traffic all day – and there was no need to rush. The temperature was almost 100° by the time I found a suitable motel around 3:30 on the far side of town. The place must have changed hands recently because the doormats and other accoutrements in the lobby still bore the logos of a Holiday Inn Express, and the place was now called Magnolia Inn.

I crossed the Mississippi River into Arkansas not long after having a sausage muffin with egg and cheese at a nearby McDonald's. I saw a lot of rice paddies along the river, some of which were as far as the eye could see. After crossing an old steel truss bridge along US 49, I ran into some difficulty with my route sheet again in Arkansas, and decided that since I had brought a road atlas and a magnifying glass, I would use them every night from now on, to double-check the next day's route and correct whatever discrepancies I find.

I came close to running out of gas that morning while sightseeing through cotton fields in eastern Arkansas. When I spotted an entry ramp for I-40, I got onto the interstate to look for gas. As soon as I spotted a station,

I got off, got the gas and managed to reconnect with my planned route about an hour later by heading west and feeling my way across 30 to 40 miles of back roads through a lot of cotton fields.

I reached Conway before noon, as I had planned, and I checked into a motel there. After lunch, I got directions for Bigelow, about 15 miles west, for a brief visit with my nephew Paul and his family. I wasn't carrying his phone number, and I had Internet directions on how to find his house. Unfortunately, he lived on one of those roads that have only a name, and the number that I had for it was only used on the Internet maps, and was meaningless unless I was traveling with a GPS. The local people know the road by its name, and no one recognized the number.

I found the general store in Bigelow and they happened to know Paul and coincidentally his phone number, so the girl called him for me. Paul came out with his pickup to lead me back to his place where I spent the afternoon visiting with him and his very nice family. The temperature meanwhile rose to over 100° in Conway by the time I got back to the motel.

My original plan was to head east to Birmingham, Alabama in the morning to visit the Barber Motorcycle Museum, followed by a leisurely ride north on the Natchez Trace Parkway to find and ride some of the nicer Kentucky parkways before heading more directly toward Albuquerque. The Weather Channel changed my plan again when it reported that Hurricane Edouard was headed for the Birmingham area.

Temperatures in the entire southeast, and as far west as Texas, were expected to be between 95 and 106° for at least the next week. I wasn't sure that my already ailing old body could handle the extreme heat for that long, so I decided to abort the route sheet altogether, at least for a while, and plan my days based on the daily forecast that I would get from the TV each night.

My first major change was to head due north from Conway into the Ozarks, and keep going north until I found cooler weather, even if it took me into Canada. I would decide on where I was going each day as I went along. It's one of the benefits of traveling alone with time to spare and a lust for adventure. I believe this is also what the Bronson character did.

I had a very enjoyable ride the next day following Arkansas Rte 9 through the heart of the Ozarks, and later Rte 19 in Missouri. I found both to be nice bike roads with scenic two-lane blacktop and gently winding curves through the hill country. I stopped to chat with the indigenous mountain folk as I traveled, which I got a great deal of enjoyment from. One guy I met at a gas stop reminded me of Leroy Winters, an enduro champion I knew from the 1960s, who once lived less than 100 miles west of there, in Fort Smith. I visited with Leroy on an earlier trip.

Around midday I spotted a small roadside hamburger stand as I was passing through one of the smaller towns. I made a quick U-turn and ordered a hamburger and fries with a big cup of freshly made lemonade that came highly recommended by the friendly young girl at the window. She said she made it herself. I sat alone in the shade of a huge oak tree and enjoyed my lunch in the relative coolness of the spot. I even felt a slight breeze occasionally.

Most of the day I was able to maintain a steady 50 to 55 mph, which was an ideal speed for me to see the countryside and enjoy the ride, especially along the byways. The temperature reached the high 90s before I stopped at a Super 8 near Cuba, Missouri.

I checked in at 1:30, after a 325-mile, 7-hour day. Part of my new strategy was to start earlier, finish earlier and ride for only 7 to 8 hours, which enabled me to manage my meds better. I would take my diuretic pill when I checked in, and it would run its course before I turned in for the night. Consequently, I wouldn't be bothered during the day with the urgency to find a place to stop. I also got into the motel before the hottest part of the day and before the thunderstorms moved in. It was also before my eyes would start to hurt from the glare of the afternoon sun.

The forecast for the next several days was for more of the same – hot and humid with late afternoon storms. I didn't get caught in a single storm, or even a shower, since leaving New York. A few times I got sprinkled on at the outer fringes of a thunderstorm, but I never got wet on the entire trip.

I stopped for gas and lunch at a Casey's General Store in Mexico, Missouri. Casey's is a chain of combination gas station and convenience store that are plentiful in the Midwest, and I stopped at several during the trip. The only trouble with Casey's for lunch is that there is no place to sit, inside or outside, so I would usually eat my lunch standing outside. I chose chicken nuggets this time, which came hot in a big insulated cup. They were very good – must have weighed almost a pound. I thought of taking half with me for later, but I had no place to carry them. I was stuffed before I could finish the whole container with a bottle of juice.

*I remembered Mexico from 1988 with Bud Peck. It was
the place where he was able to locate a BMW dealer at
the guy's home to replace a broken headlight lens that
had gotten hit by a stone or lump of coal thrown up from
the rear tire of my Gold Wing somewhere in West
Virginia earlier on our trip together.*

While I was traveling the rest of the way through
Missouri and into south-central Iowa, I had to take a
few long detours around some recent flooding – mostly
in Iowa. But detours are often more interesting than the
main routes, and I was in no hurry. I thought it was an
excellent ride that day through America's breadbasket.

I stopped at a beautiful inn that I spotted along Rte 2 in
Iowa, after traveling 380 miles. I was reluctant at first
to approach the Mt. Ayr Inn because I was concerned
that the rate might be at least a hundred bucks; but a
storm was closing in, and it was the only place around.
Surprisingly, it cost only a little over $60, which I
figured would be the norm for most lodging west of
the Mississippi anyway. It was a beautiful place, and it
included breakfast.

I had dinner that night at *Peggy Sue's*, a small place in
town that was decorated like something out of the
1950s. They even used the actual front end of a 1957
Chevy for the marquee over the front entrance. I asked
the middle-aged, female desk clerk at the inn, "Where
would an old guy riding a motorcycle enjoy having
dinner?" – and she recommended it. The food was
good, and I enjoyed the miscellaneous memorabilia
and photos that hung from the walls.

The daytime temperature seemed to be easing a bit
each day and the TV forecast showed less afternoon
storms west of there, so I thought maybe I had gone far
enough north. I laid out a route that night that would

take me west into Nebraska. I had always liked the high plains and prairies of Nebraska, and the weather was looking better in that direction.

I took this photo during a bike trip through Nebraska in 1984.

The plan changed again in the morning when I woke up and it was still raining and windy. I checked the Weather Channel again and learned that a deluge was raging just west of there, with as much as six inches of rain having fallen overnight, and it was still coming down. I rechecked the maps and saw that US 34, a two-lane highway that runs through much of the west, was less than 30 miles north of there and running parallel. According to the weather maps it was just outside the heaviest rainfall and flooding; so I decided to leave an hour later and head north to pick up US 34, and I'd use that to get into Nebraska.

I left around 7:30, just after the last drops had fallen. I saw temporary signs on US 34 indicating that traffic was being detoured there from Rte 2. It was certainly a nice way to get across Iowa, and I remember thinking, as I often do, 'so many beautiful roads – so little time.'

When I got near the state line where Rte 34 crosses the Missouri River, there was a sign that said the bridge was out and traffic was being detoured 30 miles back to Rte 2 to cross the river.

Not long after entering Nebraska, I spotted a Motel 6 just short of Grand Island, so I called it a day at 1:45, after 330 miles. The choice of places to eat was slim, with only Grandma's Truck Stop located in a nearby truck terminal. Eating there rather than riding a few extra miles up the road turned out to be a disaster for me. I ordered the chopped beefsteak with brown gravy and caramelized onions, and I got a severe intestinal upset from it, with nausea and diarrhea that sapped just about all of my remaining strength.

In spite of still feeling very weak when I left in the morning, I managed to get on the road by 6:20. I skipped breakfast because I wasn't about to eat at Grandma's again, and I didn't find a place until almost 20 miles out where I stopped at a Casey's look-alike with inside seating, unlike Casey's. I rarely found anything to sit on at Casey's, even outside, except the bike, and I welcomed a break from the seat. My need to sit that day for the brief rest was even greater. The ready-made sausage and egg sandwich tasted good, in spite of my having been sick the night before.

I was still very weak when I stopped a few hours later at another Casey's look-alike for gas and lunch. I stopped the bike at the pump, turned off the key, and pushed the kickstand down – but without making sure it was all the way down. When I went to lean it over onto the stand, I realized too late that it wasn't all the way down, and much of my weight was in that direction to get off. There was no way I had enough strength left to keep it from going all the way to the ground, with me still half on it. It threw me out onto the tarmac, and I landed hard on my side. As I lay there feeling helpless and maybe a little stupid, I said aloud, "I'm getting too old for this crap!" I managed to get myself up and I thanked the two aging cowboys who rushed over to pick the machine up.

Of course they noticed the New York plate and remarked on it. I thanked them profusely and said I'm glad I didn't drop it somewhere out on the prairie, because I'd never be able to pick it up by myself. I added, "It probably doesn't look like it to you fellows, but I've been at this thing for 62 years, and I suppose one of these days I'll get it right." I ordered a chicken fajita sandwich with orange juice, and sat at an inside table for a long while before heading back out.

Rte 2 in Nebraska runs alongside busy railroad tracks for well over a hundred miles. While riding, I counted more than 25 trains heading east, with up to 150 fully loaded coal cars in each train. The trains were running less than 10 minutes apart, with up to four diesel-electric engines pulling each one. Some of the longer trains had two additional engines pushing. I didn't see any trains pulling empties in the other direction, and I wondered what they did with all the empties.

When I came through that area 20 years ago on a big Harley, wheat was the predominant crop in Nebraska. This time it seemed to be corn, and I wondered how much of it was used for making ethanol for fuel. I rode a total of 345 miles before checking into a Super 8 in Chadron at 12:20 Mountain Time. I used the extra time-zone hour to rest up.

Chadron is a typical western town located near the northwest corner of Nebraska. I was getting quite far north, but it was hot there too. I learned from the desk clerk that my room was the last in the place because of some kind of special event going on in town that weekend. I decided to rent the room for two nights because I intended to go into South Dakota the next day and return the same night, after which I'd think about starting to head in the general direction of Albuquerque again.

The next day I had a nice ride into the Black Hills of South Dakota and through Custer State Park. I also rode the Needles Highway that I remembered riding with Bud Peck in 1988 during a heavy thundershower, sandwiched between giant motor homes, which made it more of an ordeal than a pleasure. This time the highway had no traffic at all, and I enjoyed the twisty ride between all the giant granite needles much more.

I saw a minimum of motor homes on this entire trip, probably because of the high gas prices. The most beautiful scenery of the day was along Rte 87 in Custer State Park. A thundershower passed through less than an hour before I got there and many of the roads were still wet in spots; but it was a great ride. The roads from Chadron to and from the Black Hills went across about 50 miles of deserted and relatively dry high plains each way, with long, clear vistas in every direction – and no traffic. I used different routes up and back. It was one of my most enjoyable days for riding – maybe because I took time for sightseeing.

I had gotten gas that morning in Chadron and didn't get off the bike until six hours later when I pulled back into the same gas station after a 290-mile day. During the return trip, I rode a section of Rte 71 that was under construction, with loose gravel for about a mile. I noticed that the Suzuki doesn't track nearly as well through gravel as the Dakar did on the Alaska trip four years ago. I think the good handling of the BMW was due in large part to the 21-inch front wheel. Both bikes are in the dual sport category, but the Dakar leans much more toward being a dirt bike, whereas the V-Strom is more of a road machine – but the Dakar is also more comfortable on the road.

I tried wearing sunglasses that afternoon for the first time on the trip and although it cut down considerably on the discomfort from the glare, it also cut down on my ability to see – so it's the last time I wore them.

I still had almost a week to get to Albuquerque, and I toyed with the idea of heading west into Wyoming. From there I thought I might even go to Glacier Park in northern Montana, or even Yellowstone and the Grand Tetons; or possibly even as far west as Oregon. But in each of those cases I would have to use the super-slab to make it to Albuquerque on time, which I didn't like the idea of doing. The weather forecast across Wyoming wasn't the greatest either, so I dropped the idea of going that far west.

I then thought about heading for somewhere closer to Albuquerque, and I came up with the idea of visiting the Chester W. Nimitz museum in Fredericksburg, Texas again if the weather was cooler there by now. I already saw the museum, but as a WWII Navy veteran I thought I might like to see it again, like a pilgrimage. I could possibly retrace the historic Chisholm Trail on my way – the overland route for cattle drives that ran from what was once known as Red River Station, Texas through Oklahoma to the railheads in Kansas.

It seemed reasonable, so for starters I put together an impromptu route to take me across some scenic high plains for the first 375 miles to McCook in southern Nebraska. There was no traffic at all when I headed out, and traffic was still light after crossing the Platte River, with the exception of a few minor construction delays.

I passed through Ogallala, which reminded me of my favorite mini-series *Lonesome Dove;* and I wondered how they were able to lead a huge herd of cattle from south Texas across the expanse of Texas, Oklahoma and Kansas in the 1800s, with practically no landmarks to go by, or rivers to follow, and then somehow miraculously come out in a tiny place like Ogallala, Nebraska. I suppose some of the major cattle routes like the Chisholm Trail had some kind of marking; but I've always thought it was amazing how people found their way across a thousand miles of prairies with limited navigational techniques and no instruments.

Famous frontiersmen like Kit Carson, Daniel Boone and Jedediah Smith were able to find their way across huge expanses of nothingness and come out exactly where they wanted to be – and probably without a compass or a map of any kind. Jedediah often did his thing in the mountains, which might have been a little easier because of natural landmarks; but it's always been a mystery to me how they did it on the open prairies. I think Kit Carson was one of the best. I once stopped at his museum in Taos, New Mexico.

The temperature was well into the 90s when I got to McCook at 1:30. I was overheated and exhausted, and it reminded me of the problems I had with my heart earlier on the trip. I had been running at 65 and 70 mph against a dry headwind all day, and it complicated my efforts to manage my hydration level – it also dropped my gas mileage drastically.

Some of the terrain I went across that day was flat as a tabletop for as far as I could see, and some of it was gently rolling prairie. Most of it was still green in spite of the heat. Traffic was exceptionally light, which was the best part. I saw cattle grazing in some of the areas, and I saw corn and wheat growing in others. Later, a lot of the land was covered with a kind of range grass, scorched dry by the sun.

I checked the Weather Channel that night and learned that Dallas and other parts of Texas were still due to get several 106-degree days that I really didn't need. I took out the maps again and put together yet another route that would take me west into Fort Collins, Colorado, even though the temperature in Denver had been reported to be over 90° for something like 27 consecutive days, but I figured I'd keep going west into the mountains where it should be a little cooler at the higher elevations.

The temperature was 72° when I left McCook at first light, and it rose quickly into the 90s on the prairie. I stopped for the day at 12:30 in Fort Collins where it had been predicted to be over 100° by mid-afternoon. Fort Collins is a relatively clean college town and the home of Colorado State University. After scouting around for a motel, I located a string of inexpensive places on College Ave at the north end of town. I rented a room and unloaded my gear before heading out for lunch at a Denny's I spotted on my way in.

During the previous week I had been strapping my heavy jacket on the back of the bike no later than 11 AM, and I would ride with a light cotton jacket for the rest of the day. I wore the bottoms of the riding-suit all day because they didn't bother me nearly as much. I thought I might be dehydrating faster in the hot dry wind from not wearing the weatherproof jacket.

After leaving the room for the last time in the morning and locking the door-key inside, I realized that I didn't have my gloves, and I thought maybe I left them in the room. It was before six and a sign on the office said it would open at seven, so I located a Home Depot, but they too opened at seven. I returned to the motel to wait, and when I didn't find the gloves in the room, I went back to Home Depot to buy a pair. Their largest size was barely big enough to get my hands into and certainly wouldn't fit with glove liners; but they would have to do – so I bought a pair and left.

I finally got on the road by 7:15, having lost a little over an hour to the glove problem. Later on the trip, Jim Bellach graciously gave me a practically new pair of gauntlet motorcycle gloves to replace the gloves I lost. He insisted that I take them. Now that's a friend!

I started up through the beautiful Poudre Canyon (pronounced *Pooder* by locals), and as I leaned into one of the first turns, clocking about 60, I met five Hereford steers standing in the middle of the road. I was halfway around the bend and it was impossible for me to stop or to hit the brakes hard. I was still doing about 40 mph with my foot on the brake while I was threading the needle through the herd.

About 12 miles farther up the canyon, I came around another bend where there was a sports car lying upside-down in the middle of the road. It was still steaming from something that probably spilled on the hot exhaust. The roof was crushed to almost the level of the hood. I'm quite sure the occupants were still inside, as it lay there upside-down. It happened in front of a popular restaurant, serving Sunday brunch. There were at least a dozen people standing around looking at it, helplessly. I assumed they were waiting for the rescue vehicle, so I didn't stop. It must have happened a minute or so before I got there. Other than the Herefords and the overturned sports car, there was practically no one on the road that morning, and I enjoyed the nice cool ride.

I followed Rte 14 up through the canyon for about 40 miles as it wound its way alongside the Cache la Poudre River toward the Continental Divide. Much of the ride was spectacular, especially where the river has carved its way through the rocks, leaving huge craggy walls and glacial debris. Being a Sunday morning with very few cars on the road contributed to making it an excellent ride. I saw cars parked in a few places along the highway where I assumed people came for the activities along the river, like rafting. I went over Cameron Pass and Rabbit Ears Pass before reaching Steamboat Springs on the far side of the divide where the town was packed with vacationers and weekenders.

The heat returned as I continued west along US 40 through some hilly desert-like terrain for another 160 miles west of the Rocky Mountains. I stopped for gas in Dinosaur where I paid the highest price per gallon of any place on the trip. Overall, gas prices had been coming down during my trip. The lowest price I paid was in Ohio on my way home.

I went as far west as Vernal, Utah, 350 miles from Fort Collins. I found a huge new Motel 6 there. I've heard that a French company took over the chain in recent years and that they're building a totally different class of motel. I was originally quoted $83 for a single room, which is a lot for a Motel 6, but my AARP discount brought it down to around $66. It was one of the nicest rooms of the trip, with an excellent mattress and a first-class bathroom. There was a Golden Corral next door where I could walk for my dinner.

I had worked myself into somewhat of a box relative to my arrival time in Albuquerque. No matter where I chose to go from Vernal, it seemed that I would be either a day early or a day late. I opted for the early side and figured I could take short side trips each day to fill in the gaps. If I still got to Albuquerque early I could get the rest my body needed. I headed east from Vernal over the same road I came in on, and I turned south on Rte 64 in Dinosaur toward Rangley.

In Rangley I chose Rte 139 for Grand Junction, which was a beautiful ride for the next 75 miles. The road goes over Douglas Pass (8,268 ft) with several scenic pullouts that offer spectacular panoramas of Grand Valley of the Colorado River, 25 miles away; Colorado National Monument, 30 miles away; and the La Sal Mountains in Utah, 70 miles away. Needless to say, I was pleasantly surprised, and I stopped at a few of the lookout points to admire the scenery.

When I got to Montrose I decided to stop there for one of the many motels, in spite of it being early in the day. I thought I would put together a side trip for an afternoon ride into the mountains toward Gunnison. I also remembered that motels in Montrose are far less expensive than they would be in Durango. I found a beautiful first-class room in a privately owned motel for $65, and I checked in at 11:30. I figured I probably would have paid at least $100 in Durango for the same class of motel. They had a nice pool and other perks that I didn't use.

The first thing I did was put together a 140-mile loop that took me to Blue Mesa Reservoir, near Gunnison, followed by a ride along the north rim of the Black Canyon of the Gunnison that was truly spectacular. I had never been that way, and I regretted not knowing about it early enough to plan it into the route that I had put together for the ride with the guys.

I learned that the Gunnison River drops an average of 43 feet per mile throughout its length, making it one of the steepest mountain descents of any river in North America. I found that in Wikipedia.org. Black Canyon is so named for the steepness of its walls, which make it difficult for sunlight to reach very far down into the canyon. As a result, the craggy, vertical walls are almost always in shadow, causing them to appear black, hence the name Black Canyon. At its narrowest point, at river level, the canyon is only 40 feet wide. The road I was on skirts very close to the edge of the canyon in a few places.

I got back to the room at 2:30 with a total mileage for the day at 350. On my way back, I spotted a Suzuki dealer at the edge of town and stopped to pick up a spare can of chain lube. After a brief rest at the motel I chose a nearby Denny's for dinner.

Day 16 started with the temperature at 61°. It was the first time on the trip that I slept past 5 o'clock – which I attributed to the great mattress. It was almost six when I finally woke up. I managed to pack, attend to all my meds and toilet, load the bike, eat at a nearby McDonald's, and be out of town in an hour flat – possibly a record for an octogenarian. The temperature dropped at least 15 degrees by the time I passed through Ouray on my way up into the mountains.

US Rte 550 between Ouray and Silverton is still one of the most spectacular rides in the country. I first used it in 1977, on my first trip to Alaska. The 25-mile section that goes over Red Mountain Pass (11,018 ft) and into Silverton is often referred to as the "Million Dollar Highway." Traveling south, like I was doing, put me on the outside of most of the perilous turns where it's apparent the cliff drops off abruptly as much as a thousand feet from the edge of the traffic lane.

Many of the drops start within a few inches of the white line that denotes the edge of the lane, and there are no guardrails. Needless to say I didn't ride very close to the edge, and a few times I probably had white knuckles. After passing close to Silverton, US 550 continues south toward Albuquerque, going over Coal Bank Pass (10,640 ft) and Molas Pass (10,910 ft) on its way to Durango.

I was rolling easily into Durango, doing about 60 on a fairly straight stretch of road, enjoying the sights, when a railroad-crossing signal began to flash red and a big striped bar dropped across the traffic lanes. I was daydreaming and didn't see it soon enough, and I couldn't possibly get through before the bar would be all the way down. When I finally saw it, I hit both brakes as hard as I dared, trying to keep the bike from going sideways. The tires screeched loudly and I could see that it was already too late to fit under the bar without hitting it – and probably knocking me clear off the bike. I released the brakes enough to make an in-course correction and miss the end of the bar; but I had to hit them again quickly to keep from going onto the tracks. The end of the bar brushed my arm on the way by, and when the bike finally stopped, the front wheel was only inches from the rails.

I began to backpedal as fast as I could, to give the train enough room to get by without hitting my front wheel. I glanced to my left while I was peddling, to see how close it was, and I noticed it was a guy on something that looked like an oversized golf cart, riding the rails. My thoughts at the time were not kind ones as he stared straight ahead, poker-faced, and he motored right on by, like he never even saw me.

I got gas in Durango and continued to follow Rte 550 toward Albuquerque. I didn't remember ever having been on that section of 550 before. I thought if I came across something that looked halfway interesting, I'd take a side trip. I still had plenty of time to spare. Meanwhile the temperature had begun to rise again and it was already getting very hot.

I stopped for lunch at an Arby's that I spotted in one of the towns, and I ordered a Philly Beef and Swiss with orange juice. It wasn't anything special, but at least it was different from the usual McDonald's – although it's just another fast-food place. The terrain in the area was the high-plains type, although it looked more like high desert. The ground was much drier and the flora was different. I crossed the Continental Divide, but I didn't see a sign for it. Much of that part of Rte 550 is above the 7,000-foot level for its last 150 miles to US 285 in New Mexico.

I arrived in Albuquerque at 2:15 on the 29th, a day earlier than I planned, having traveled 340 miles the last day. My odometer showed a total mileage from home of 5,500 miles. I could have almost gone across the country and back in that distance. My average figured out to be a little less than 350 miles per day. The chain didn't need any adjustment since I left home, and the engine didn't need oil. I would always take the time each afternoon to lube the chain and check the oil; otherwise, the bike remained essentially maintenance-free.

 I waited an hour for a room to be cleaned at the La Quinta where we had reservations for three first-floor rooms, hopefully adjacent, beginning the following night. I took a ride in the heat while waiting for the room. I stopped for a milk shake at an ice cream place during the ride. The temperature reached the mid 90s that day. I was not particularly impressed with the city at first glance – I'm definitely not a city person.

Fred Lederer and his wife Elizabeth stopped by in a car for a brief visit. John had told him that I'd be there a day early, and I had never met him. I learned from Fred that he would be riding with us for at least a day. I also learned from talking with him that he was once a motorcycle cop in Suffolk County, New York. It wasn't surprising to learn that we both knew Gene Baron, the long-time owner of the Suffolk County Harley Davidson dealership. I first met Gene in 1947 when he worked as a mechanic at Jack Tracey's Harley Davidson dealership in Yonkers where I bought and quickly crashed my first motorcycle in front of the store. Gene was an avid enduro rider in the early days, with sidecars as well as solo bikes. In later years he rode vintage board track races well into his sixties and maybe even seventies at Davenport, Iowa.

Fred rides a Harley Road King and Elizabeth rides a Harley 880 Sportster. He confirmed that John Dey and Alan Cheever would be arriving from California the following afternoon with a rental truck and three bikes: John's new Kawasaki 650 Versys, Alan's Kawasaki 1000 Concours and a Honda 650 XL that John planned to give to his brother Tom, who would be arriving by

air from Joplin, Missouri that same afternoon. Jim
Bellach was riding in alone from Fresno, California,
and would meet us in Chama, New Mexico during the
first day of our ride.

After having breakfast in the lobby the next morning, I
took a ride around the city and ventured a short
distance into the desert. I still wasn't impressed with
the area, and I concluded that I wouldn't want to live
there. It's certainly a lot different from the Northeast
and it seemed almost foreign to me. John and Alan
arrived with the rental truck around 1 PM and
unloaded the bikes at the motel. Fred came soon
afterward to accompany John to the rental place to
return the truck and pick up Tom at the airport.

Meanwhile Alan, after having driven the truck much of
the night, went to his room for a much-needed rest.
Unfortunately Tom's plane was four hours late getting
in. John called at 7 PM to suggest that Alan and I go to
dinner without them. After trying unsuccessfully to
wake Alan by pounding on his door, I walked to
Denny's next door to eat alone, after which I came
back and went to bed.

I met Tom in the morning, and he confirmed that he
and Fred would accompany us for only the first day –
and that Jim would be getting to Chama between noon
and 2 PM. My route sheet said we'd meet him at noon,
and John also told him noon, but I had given Jim a
pessimistic guess of our not reaching Chama until 2
PM. My guess was based on the group having a sit-
down breakfast in Albuquerque, and probably not
getting underway before at least 9:30.

I was packed and loaded and ready to leave for
breakfast when John appeared at 6:15, bright-eyed and

bushy-tailed, saying that he hadn't slept well but he's ready to go – and he said he'd prefer that we avail ourselves of the complementary breakfast at the motel rather than wasting time at a sit-down breakfast. So after everyone was packed and loaded, and we had a quick breakfast in the lobby, we were on the road by 7:15. I figured that would probably get us to Chama by noon as John and the route sheet originally said – and Jim would be shooting for two o'clock.

A few of the group needed to top off on gas, so Fred, knowing the area, led us to a gas station a few blocks away. We skipped a section of Old Rte 66 that I had planned to use, after Fred advised against it because of road construction and detours. Skipping the section made us even earlier, and we headed directly for Tres Piedras along US 285. I planned on stopping in Tres Piedras for gas, but when we got there, there were no gas stations; and Tom's Honda dual sport, with its small tank, was about to run out – even after using the spare gallon he carried on the back.

I cut the pace considerably to conserve on Tom's gas, and we still got into Chama by noon as the original plan said. We filled up and figured we'd wait for Jim. We were quite sure he wouldn't be there before two, but this was still not a problem because I had planned a short ride for the afternoon.

After a leisurely hamburger lunch at one of the town's biggest and most-conspicuous saloons on the main drag, with the bikes parked conspicuously out front, Jim still hadn't shown. As we stood outside on the porch at 2 PM, there he came – right on time, loaded down with a full complement of camping gear that he probably used on his way out. There was lots of waving, shouting and even a few good-natured single-finger salutes from the raucous gallery on the porch of the saloon, after which Jim settled in and ordered a hamburger with the appropriate beverage. We watched him eat it at a table on the porch, which I'm sure made him nervous, but that's all part of the game.

The six of us headed toward Antonito, Colorado along Rte 17, a ride that I once considered to be one of the most beautiful in the country – and it still is. The road climbs steadily through a broad valley of rolling green meadows while a small steam train chugs its way up through the same valley, belching smoke and steam as it climbs towards Cumbres Pass (10,020 ft), the highest mountain pass reached by rail in the United States. Both the road and the train scale the pass before splitting; and the road continues to climb over La Manga Pass (10,230 ft) towards the Colorado state line. It was a little cooler at the higher altitudes, but being an exceptionally hot day, it didn't cool down by much. We got to our overnight stopover in Alamosa, Colorado at 3:30, after 275 scenic miles.

We chose an old, inexpensive motel where we could park in front of the rooms. We actually inspected the rooms before checking in because the place looked so rundown, and it barely passed the inspection. I chose to occupy a room alone to facilitate managing my meds and biological idiosyncrasies, one of which was that I need a full-night rest, and I expected late-night activity in the parking lot.

I think it was Alan, Fred and Tom who walked next-door to a KFC around six for a ton of fried chicken with all the trimmings – coleslaw, mashed potatoes, baked beans, gravy, dinner rolls, et al. I don't know who paid for it, but they wouldn't accept money from anyone. We all ate our fill, and there was a lot left over, which we talked about possibly having for breakfast the next morning.

I turned in around nine while the others were just getting warmed up for a much longer evening, with after-dinner brandies and loud discussions about world politics, or whatever, for at least another hour – before Jim hit the showers, literally, and he came away with a bruised elbow that he got from the fall. I understand he took the shower curtain and rod with him when he went down, and he blamed it all on space aliens.

I heard all about it in the morning when I hustled them out at six. I don't know how much of it was true. Suffice it to say there were a few hangovers and I'm not sure we'd be invited back to the grubby motel anytime soon. I was glad that I chose a room alone. We didn't eat the leftover chicken for breakfast after all. I think Fred might have taken it with him when he left, which would suggest that he might have been the one that bought it. In any case, we all went together to a nearby McDonald's for breakfast.

Fred and Tom, who had planned to be with us for only the one day, headed home in different directions – Fred toward Albuquerque on his Harley, and Tom went east across the prairie on his newly-acquired 650XL toward his home in eastern Kansas. The rest of us headed north into the mountains around 7:30, which was extraordinarily early under the circumstances. Jim got his ton of gear together and loaded it onto the bike in record time, without his famous "Jimmy Dance" that he sometimes does.

We headed northwest from Alamosa on US 285 and north toward Slumgullian Pass along Rte 149. The scenery on the twisty ride up through the valley was spectacular, with hillsides like huge blankets of gray-green velvet. We went by Wagon Wheel Gap and the town of Creede as we continued our climb toward Slumgullion Pass (11,361 ft), one of the highest points we reached on our trip.

Jim and John spotted several Rocky Mountain bighorn sheep not far from the road, which of course I couldn't see, even though we stopped for a better look. Jim said there were seven, less than 150 yards from the road, but I still couldn't see them, even though everyone else could. He said they trotted off looking like a typical Dodge truck commercial.

Before reaching the pass we went by the headwaters of the Rio Grande River where many mountain streams and springs come together in a huge marshy area to form the famous river that flows almost 2,000 miles to the Gulf of Mexico, much of it forming the long border between Texas and Mexico.

We stopped for gas in Lake City at a small station that wasn't set up for credit cards at the pump, but it was okay to pump the gas first and then pay. The four of us used two pumps. I was alone at one while the others used a single pump on the other island. Alan first tried to use the high-test pump there, but it wasn't turned on, so he used the same pump as Jim and John.

They didn't reset the meter between fill-ups, making the total cost for the three of them around $30. Meanwhile I finished and went in to pay my $9.50, after which John paid the combined total from their pump. After we left the gas station, the girl attendant apparently thought one or more of us hadn't paid for gas, so she called the police.

By heading north, we could only possibly be headed for US 50, about 45 miles from Lake City, so they waited for us there; and as soon as we pulled into a small scenic turnout area near the US 50 intersection, a Colorado state highway patrolman in a marked cruiser and a national park cop in an SUV came charging over with their red lights spinning. We were detained for at least 45 minutes while the trooper checked out our papers and proceeded to try and resolve the problem with the girl on the other end of a telephone line.

I think it was John who finally broke the logjam when he suggested to the trooper that he do the simple arithmetic, which is that we're traveling together and if one bike takes $9.50 to fill, wouldn't the other three together take roughly three times that amount, like around $30? The trooper understood, but apparently the girl on the other end of the phone was having difficulty with it. It eventually got resolved. During most of this time I chatted with the friendly NPS guy, and I gave him one of my cards. We were finally on our way, and I don't think we ever got an apology.

We stopped in Gunnison for lunch. After not seeing a Burger King, Wendy's or McDonald's, we settled for a Sonic Burger, which everyone agreed was a dud; and Jim was charged 30 cents for a cup of tap water that didn't set well with him at all.

After lunch we went over Monarch Pass (11,312 ft) where Jim and John pushed the limit a bit along the 4-lane stretch of road on the climb to the top. At Poncha Springs we turned north on Rte 285 and rode along the headwaters of the Arkansas River towards Leadville. We saw white-water rafting and several 14,000-foot peaks looming to our left during the ride.

When we got to Leadville around 2:30, there was a celebration going on, including a parade. We still had 30 miles to go for our planned stopover in Dillon, but we had already covered 300 miles and I was getting very tired. I think the altitude was also probably affecting my congestive heart failure because I seemed to be a little short of breath. It was probably a little more than I should have planned for the day, especially since we had just reunited – I should have known there would be much celebrating the previous night.

I was anxious to get to the stopover to take some of my meds, and I thought that Jim also looked like he needed a break. I didn't realize it at the time, but he spotted one of his favorite-type roach coaches parked in the pull-off area. We stopped in the same area for a riders' meeting where it was agreed that since we only had 30 miles to go, we should tough it out and keep going – which I suspect was to Jim's utter dismay. He didn't even get to stop for a quick taco. He said later that the guy had the complete menu – tongue tacos, brains tacos, tripas (intestines), goat, you name it – and he missed out on all of that.

After reaching the Super 8 in Dillon, we learned that there were no vacancies due to a special event going on in town, or nearby, which probably had all of the motels and hotels in the entire area full, and probably had something to do with the parade in Leadville. The desk clerk suggested that the closest rooms might be in Denver, 70 miles east. I was in no condition to ride another hour-plus to Denver or anywhere else; and it would screw up my planning big-time.

Other than being exhausted, my eyes had gotten so blurry that I could barely see, and I thought Jim also looked tired. After calling around town from the desk phone, Jim was able to locate a couple of rooms at a nearby Quality Inn. When we got there, we learned that their special-event room rates started at $165 for a single.

We agreed that we were fortunate to find any rooms at all, so John and I each took singles while Jim and Alan shared a double. It was the most expensive night of my trip, and probably theirs as well; but I figured if I were to spread the extra cost of the room over the entire trip, it would only raise my average by about four dollars a night, which wouldn't break the bank – in spite of my inborn Frisian frugality.

Our third day together, and my 20th, was short on miles but exceptionally long on beauty. The highlights of the day were Loveland Pass (11,990 ft), another of the highest points of our ride, and US Rte 34 through Rocky Mountain National Park where there's a sign that marks a short piece of the road, close to Fall River Pass, to be at 12,183 feet, the highest point we reached on our ride.

When we entered the west end of the park, I whipped out my 25-year old "Golden Age Passport" card for the young attendant at the tollgate. He looked at it and smiled, and said, "Wow, I've never seen one like this!" It was a thin wallet card that had gotten pretty well dog-eared during the many years that I carried it. Most of the print was worn off, including a portion of the "Golden Age" logo. He said, "They don't make 'em like this anymore. Would you like a new card?"

I said reluctantly, "If it doesn't take too long."

He said, "It'll take about 30 seconds," and so now I have a brand new heavy plastic card that says, "Senior Pass" on it, and it doesn't say "Golden Age" anywhere on the card. I suppose it wasn't politically correct. I can personally attest to the fact that the years are not all golden. He kept my old card that Jim suggested later I should have hung onto as a keepsake.

After our spectacular ride through the national park, we exited and rode through Estes Park where the town was packed with "Yuppie types." We followed Big Thompson Canyon as we continued to descend from the higher elevations into Loveland. The temperature there was in the high 90s. After a quick lunch, we got directions on how to bypass Fort Collins and find US Rte 287 north of town. I felt several huge drops of rain from a shower that we skirted while on the bypass. The temperature also dropped sharply, but we stayed dry.

As soon as the three guys reached US 287, they were gone – on the nice, smooth and slightly curvy 2-lane blacktop. It was an excellent bike road to get out some of their frustrations on after riding at lower speeds in the park for so long. And we had agreed earlier there'll be times when "I ride my ride; you ride yours," which helps to keep peace in the family.

The next time I saw them, Alan and John were talking with a biker gal who had stopped – probably for a break from the little Ninja she was riding. Jim was nowhere in sight. Making a quick assessment of the situation, I chose to pull in a few hundred feet up the road and wait. John told stories later that he and Alan popped open refreshments while waiting for Jim, and they declined to share it with her after learning that she was underage. Give me a break! When Jim returned from his nature break they told him a different story – one that Jim didn't believe either. I did see them talking with a girl, and I saw her leave, but that's all I know for sure. Good on the gal for leaving!

The traffic dwindled to almost nothing on the high plains soon after we left the Fort Collins area for Laramie, Wyoming, about 40 miles farther north. We called it a day after checking into the Gaslight Motel on the north end of Laramie. It was a nice place, with lots of cowboy memorabilia and other decorations in the lobby. After chatting with the owner, we concluded that they have a sense of humor and probably cater to bikers. We rode about 250 miles that day, and sat outside the rooms for a long while, talking. We had a big pizza brought in to have with the beer.

It was cool when we got back out onto the high plains in the morning. The first town we came to while heading north was Medicine Bow where the TV series *The Virginian* and a few western movies were filmed. We stopped for a few minutes to look around – seems like a quiet town with next to nothing going on. It looked like practically no one lives there.

We stopped at a McDonald's on the outskirts of Casper for a second breakfast, just before lunchtime. John suggested I try the McGriddle with bacon instead of my usual sausage muffin with egg. I thought it taste fine, but I prefer sausage and I like the egg with it for extra protein. I tried it again later on the trip with sausage; but I concluded that I'd stick with the sausage and egg on the muffin – the pancake syrup makes it a sticky mess, and there is far too much sugar.

Soon after leaving Medicine Bow on one of the longer and straighter stretches of road, John gave a signal that he wanted to test the acceleration of his new Kawasaki Versys against the Suzuki V-Strom, both with 650cc twin-cylinder engines. We spun the throttles wide open in 6th gear while already running around 75 mph. It wasn't surprising that the Versys easily out-accelerated the V-Strom. Mine topped out at 100, while John's speed increased to at least 105 before he cut back. About that time, Jim humbled both of us when he flew by doing around 115 with his 1000cc V-Strom. We learned later that the road is heavily patrolled.

If all things had been equal, the acceleration between the two bikes might have been closer, but I was pushing a lot more wind with the larger windshield, and I was toting a lot more luggage, not to mention more body weight, although Motorcyclist Magazine named the Versys to be the Motorcycle of the Year.

The scenic highlight of the day was our ride from Shoshone to Thermopolis through the beautiful Wind River Canyon near the confluence of the Wind River and the Big Horn River. I saw several people rafting, which is apparently one of the favorite recreational activities in that part of Wyoming.

Jim spotted antelope, golden eagles and even a badger. We stopped and Jim tried to get a closer look at the badger by chasing it through some high grass, but he couldn't get close enough. It's a good thing he didn't corner the critter, because they can be quite mean. We checked into a motel in Thermopolis early, after a 230-mile day. After dinner we visited the shoreline of the Big Horn River and sat for a while at the riverbank before heading back to the motel where we sat outside the rooms and talked until it was time to turn in.

We passed the famous mineral hot springs on our way out of town while heading north toward Cody. It was my 22nd day on the road and our fifth and last together. I chose Rte 789 that follows the valley of the Big Horn River and passes fields of alfalfa, sugar beets, beans and barley. Alan said he saw a huge Coors icon on one of the larger silos. We stopped to check the map in Worland and realized that leaving town on Rte 120, rather than Rte 789, would have been shorter, but the scenery is better the way we went, so we continued on Rte 789 and later took Rte 14 west into Cody where the mountains loomed as we approached.

We stopped for breakfast at a McDonald's in Cody before getting onto Rte 120 and starting the long climb into the mountains toward Beartooth Pass. After about fifteen miles, we turned onto the Chief Joseph Scenic Highway, which continues to climb northwest toward Dead Indian Pass at the 8,048-foot level. We pulled over into the parking area at the pass to take in the beautiful panorama and read the plaques.

One of the plaques explained that the ridge was the last significant barrier for more than 600 Nez Perce Indians and their 2,000 horses as they fled the pursuing U.S. Calvary after the Battle of the Big Hole a month earlier, during the Nez Perce War of 1877. The Nez Perce knew that the Army did not intend to leave survivors, so for them it was a flight for their lives.

After reaching US 212, we turned northeast and continued to climb toward the famous Beartooth Pass (10,947 ft). I had been over the pass several times, but it was a first for the rest of the group. We passed beautiful alpine meadows with snowfields, flowers and spectacular vistas, while snowcapped peaks loomed to our left. It is one of the highest and most rugged areas in the lower 48 states, with 20 peaks reaching over 12,000 feet. Charles Kuralt, in his book *On the Road,* called the Beartooth Highway "the most beautiful drive in America," and he will certainly get no argument from any of us.

Jim and Piet standing while John is kneeling with a big Ta-daaa.
Alan took the picture at Beartooth Pass.

After parking the bikes, we shared a tin of sardines in what Jim proclaimed to be a ritual in commemoration of my many motorcycle tours throughout North America; of our trip together; and of our fellowship. I brought a fork from McDonald's for the occasion and Jim had his flask with him – so we capped the whole deal with a nip of celebratory brandy in what Jim referred to as a "communion." I learned later that he saved the lid as a keepsake, and he buried the can and the fork at the site, which he said was a sign of camaraderie – but it was mainly to avoid littering.

The ride down the north side of the mountain is an equally spectacular experience. The road drops sharply as it clings to the edge of the mountain and winds downhill for miles, much of it from well above the timberline. In May 2005, melting snow and heavy rains sent mud and rock slides across several sections of switchbacks, causing the highway to be closed for repairs for five months until October 2005. We stopped a few times for photos on our way down to Red Lodge, Montana where we stumbled onto the Rockin' J Restaurant where we stopped to eat. The place looks from the outside like a Subway, but it turns out great sandwiches for only around four bucks.

We said our goodbyes after lunch, and I went northeast toward Billings while the others headed for Columbus. I checked into a Motel 6 and had dinner alone at a nearby Cracker Barrel where I ate and contemplated the following day and my plans for getting home. I originally thought of stopping at Sturgis to attend the annual bike rally, but since it isn't my type of event and there was nothing there that interested me, I decided to make a wide end-run around it, going as far north as possible without entering Canada.

I left the motel at 5:45 AM, before anything was open for breakfast, and I took Rte 87 directly onto a huge expanse of high plains that continues relatively straight for hundreds of miles. I planned to eventually connect with Rte 2 in Williston, North Dakota. When I spotted a small general store in Roundup with gas pumps out front, I stopped for gas and breakfast – a sausage, egg and cheese sandwich that I found in the cooler and heated in the microwave. I ate at a table with several local old-timers having their morning coffee. We chatted while I ate and soaked up some heat after a cool 60-mile ride before breakfast.

I found Rte 200 just beyond Roundup and followed it for 200 miles – the rest of the way across the Montana grasslands to Williston, North Dakota and Rte 2. I recall following Rte 200 on earlier trips for almost two days across Montana, North Dakota and most of Minnesota. The gap between even the smallest towns in Montana is 75 miles or more, which makes for a long and peaceful ride. The old guys at breakfast warned me to be on the lookout for deer, which they said are plentiful in the direction I was headed, and they are often crossing or standing in the road.

I stopped for lunch in Sidney and got to Williston around three. I learned that there wasn't a vacant room in town, and it wasn't because of the Sturgis rally. It might have had something to do with the Bakken oil shale formation that was getting some activity around that time. The desk clerk where I stopped first said there were definitely no rooms to be had in Williston and the next town of any size with a possible vacancy was Minot, 150 miles east. I got back on the road, and it was 6 o'clock before I finally checked into a Super 8 in Minot after an extremely long day.

Both the day and the ride were far too much for me. I was totally beat after twelve hours and 535 miles. My eyes weren't nearly as bad as they usually get by late afternoon, probably because the sun was behind me during the last 150 miles from Williston.

I called home and said I'd probably be in by the weekend, and I told them I'd try to make it by Saturday night. But after hanging up the phone and checking the maps, I could see that there was no way I would be home by Saturday night, especially if I went south into Iowa, as I thought about doing to give a wide berth to the entire Chicago area, avoiding the morass of interstate highways. I plotted a course toward Iowa using two-lane country roads, and I thought I'd see how the day goes.

It was in the low 50s with huge black clouds around when I started my 24th day, and especially dark in the east. I headed southeast from Minot, keeping an eye on the blackness for the next 2½ hours, without even a sprinkle. I was able to skirt the weather all the way while enjoying a ride through the small North Dakota towns and the vast expanse of farmland.

My gas went on reserve after I hadn't seen a gas station for at least an hour. When I spotted I-94 and there were no gas stations at the intersection, I got on the eastbound ramp to look for gas on the highway. There was none at the first exit or the second, and I was getting concerned about running out when I spotted a small gas-pump icon at the third exit. I got off and saw a similar icon with an arrow pointing south on a narrow, unnumbered secondary road. I followed it, figuring gas couldn't be very far; but after riding about 20 miles across barren farmland, I came to another T-intersection with no follow-up sign for gas, and I thought maybe I missed it.

I was getting really concerned because the final reserve light had been flashing for more than 30 miles. I sat at the intersection figuring how many miles I might have left, and what I should do next, when I saw a mailman stuffing letters into a mailbox. I rode over to ask him if he knew where I could find gas. He pointed to a road less than a quarter-mile away and said I would see a gas station "a little way down on the right." I turned onto the road and rode for 15 miles to yet another T-intersection without seeing any sign of gas. I suspected it was in a side road that I passed, and probably too far in for me to see it.

I was getting even more concerned that there might not be enough gas left to go back for a second look. I was really way out in the country by then! I turned right, but the road petered out to gravel in less than a mile. I stopped again and looked around, feeling somewhat helpless and trying to decide what to do next, when I spotted a farmhouse on one of the larger farms with a boy in his early teens cutting grass.

He had earphones stuck in his ears and he was making circles on the lawn with the ride-on mower, probably in step with the music. I pulled in and waited for him to see me. When he did, he turned the mower off and pulled the earphones out of his ears and sat waiting for me to speak.

I said, "Could you tell me where I might find a gas station?" He looked puzzled and answered that he didn't know but his dad or mom probably would, so I asked if they were home.

"My mom's home," he said.

"Would you mind getting her please?" He got off the mower and disappeared into the house. Moments later an attractive young woman appeared, wearing shorts, a halter-top and sandals and I repeated the question.

She answered smiling, "We have a gas station right here."

"Really? Could I possibly buy some? I'm about to run out."

She said, "Yes, of course. Follow me" and she led me across the farmyard to a pump that was probably used for filling the farm vehicles. I asked if it had a gauge and she said it probably does but the glass is much too cloudy to read. I said I needed around five gallons and I asked if that would be OK.

She handed me the hose and turned on the power for the pump. Gas began to flow into my tank as soon as I squeezed the handle, but seconds later she noticed that the hose was spewing gas at the other end, and she said, "Oh my goodness, we're getting more on the ground than in the tank," and she turned the pump off. I looked into my tank and could see that I had already gotten almost a half-tank.

I said it would probably be enough to get me to a gas station. I reached for my wallet and handed her a $20 bill. She said, "I don't know what to charge. I don't know how much gas is going for nowadays, or how much we pay for it." I answered that if the $20 isn't enough, I'd be happy to pay more. "Oh no," she said, "I meant that I don't know how much change to give you."

"Please don't be concerned about change. I'm very happy to get the gas and I would like for you to accept it." I had no idea how much had spilled on the ground or if she might be in big trouble for using the gas pump with a broken hose and wasting so much.

She took it and offered her hand to shake hands and said, "My name is Ann."

I said, "Hi Ann. My name is Piet. I'm very happy to meet you."

She saw my license plate and asked, "What in the world are you doing in this little farmyard in North Dakota." I told her a little about my trip and we chatted for several minutes. Needless to say, it was another of the nicest encounters I had on the trip. I thought after leaving that maybe I should keep wandering around this beautiful country meeting nice people like that along the way, and the thought crossed my mind – *do I really have to go home?*

Ironically the nice encounter was probably one of the greatest influences in my decision to stay with I-94 and do exactly that – go home! Continuing with the *Then Came Bronson* thing or Charles Kuralt's *On the Road* adventures would take much more time than I was prepared to devote to it; and anything short of that would be anticlimactic to the great time I've had up to this point. But it's exactly the kind of thing I've always loved to do.

I followed her directions on getting back to I-94, and I stayed with it to St. Cloud, Minnesota rather than follow the two-lane country roads into Iowa as I had originally planned where I would be meandering home. It's like when an old plow-horse turns for the barn, it always moves faster than it moved all day. I noticed after reaching the highway that there was a town with plenty of gas just a few miles from where I exited, but I thanked God for my finding gas and for the pleasant encounter.

It was another long day, with 540 miles – even longer than the previous day. I would hold my speed at 80 mph on the interstate for hours at a time. I had to keep a close eye on the gas gauge because the gas mileage drops considerably at those speeds on a lightweight. I checked into a Super 8 in St. Cloud at 4:30.

I located a place to buy a roll of black electrical tape to put on my face shield so I'd be looking through a narrow opening with very little peripheral vision, but it would keep much of the glare of the sun out of my eyes. I was aware of the risks, but the bright early morning sun and the longer days were taking their toll.

The more glare, the less I was able to see by the end of the day – it was a trade-off.

While approaching the Minneapolis / St. Paul Beltway the next morning, the sun was at horizon level and shining directly in my eyes. I couldn't read any of the signs in spite of the tape. I had tried to memorize the highway splits by studying the maps the night before but my memory isn't what it used to be, so I still had to make a few guesses at the last moment. I managed to get onto the beltway safely, and I got around the north side of Minneapolis in pretty good shape, but I made a wrong guess at a highway split north of St. Paul and ended up on I-35E going directly into the heart of the city at the height of morning rush hour.

For my next trick I would have to get into the lane that turns east when the spur I was on crosses I-94. That move didn't happen quite like I had hoped it would, and I got at least two extra-long horn blasts for diving too abruptly for the exit – and probably also cutting someone off. I breathed a sigh of relief moments later when the sun was directly in my eyes again, which told me that I was probably on I-94 heading east.

I got three separate honks for the last few maneuvers, the last of which was extra long – one more reason for disliking the interstates where everyone is in a big hurry to get somewhere. But it's also no place for a half-blind old man on a motorcycle, relying on sixty-something years of experience and 83 years of faith to bring him home safely.

Another reason for disliking it is the bottlenecks, especially at some of the tollhouses. I've been through the Rockford, Illinois toll at least six to eight times in the past 30 years, and I think there was a bottleneck every time. That area has always had the worst congestion in the country. It seems like construction of some kind has been going on continually for years. I remember when the toll was only 15¢. This time it was a dollar, and the traffic was stop-and-go for miles. It cost me at least a half-hour coming into it, and the temperatures were well over 90°.

Other than that bottleneck, I was able to run between 75 and 80 mph most of the day. I got honked at again at a highway split while bypassing Bloomington. I got a motel along I-74, near Champaign, around 4 PM. Truck traffic was horrible all day, but I managed to cover 602 miles, the longest single day of my trip.

I regretted the decision to "slab-it" home several times; especially during the two days I spent on the long self-imposed detour around Chicago where I used I-94, I-39 and I-74 to reach I-70 near Indianapolis. I was making the wide swing around the Chicago nightmare where I always seem to be in the wrong lane. I thought going all the way to I-70 would be safer; but the truck traffic on I-70 was horrendous.

Running between and around trucks on the interstates on a lightweight motorcycle is a challenge, especially with strong side winds when everyone is running close together at high speeds. The gusts ricochet off the trucks from all directions, and you have to be prepared for them. It often makes for a harrowing ride.

Day 26 was more of the same with the trucks, and the traffic was at a standstill between Indianapolis and Columbus for more than 30 minutes in one place. I had planned for it to be a much shorter day with a stop at the AMA headquarters in Ohio, but my visit this time would have to be extra short. I mainly wanted to pick up a few ISDE T-shirts to take home for grandkids and other family members, and to check on my book sales at the museum bookstore.

I did get to chat with a few of the group, but I was unable to get the T-shirts, even after Mark Mederski made a special effort to find the sizes I was looking for. They had no stock on two of the three sizes, so I didn't get any. They were also out-of-stock on at least one of my books, but the girl who is in charge of restocking was on vacation – the visit wasn't as productive as I had hoped.

Knowing about my earlier adventures to remote areas in North America, Grant Parsons suggested that I might enjoy riding to the James Bay area in northern Canada where there are a few Indian villages in an otherwise barren area. He took the time to spread out a huge map across his desk and pointed out several roads and tiny towns way up north. I said that I had thought about going to James Bay several years ago when there were only tire-track roads to get there, and when I would have been the first, or at least one of the first motorcyclists to make the trip; but I suspect that many have been there by now, taking a lot of the exciting adventure out of it.

Another of his suggestions was Prince Edward Island, the only province in Canada that I haven't visited by motorcycle. I've always considered it to be mostly a tourist area with only a few nice "bike roads." He offered several other pointers on places to go and things to see in faraway places, including out of this country. They all sound nice, but I'm convinced that there is still much to see and explore right here in the USA, without making part of the trip by air.

I'd like to spend at least a week on the smaller roads in the Rocky Mountains when the weather is crisp and clear and the Aspen are in brilliant color. I'd also like to spend more time in the small rural areas like Appalachia, meeting and talking with the country folk, which I did once for several days, decades ago, in the coal country of West Virginia – I loved it!

After spending a few hours at the AMA, I headed north on I-71 and stopped along I-76 near Kent, for a room at an old Econolodge. I rode a total of 480 miles that day – my 26th, bringing the distance for my final day down to a relatively easy 450 miles.

After unloading and doing the usual servicing and checking the bike over for the last time on this trip, I looked up and down the road for a place to eat on my last night out. Seeing nothing, I settled for a nearby McDonald's for my dinner meal, which I rarely do.

I turned in early and was sound asleep when a loud, pulsating and piercing sound jolted me from a sound sleep around 2 AM. At first I thought it was the alarm clock, but after pulling the plug on that and the sound didn't stop, I thought maybe the air conditioner was overheating and emitting something that was setting off the smoke alarm. I fumbled around frantically with the cover of the alarm, half-asleep, intending to pull the batteries, but when I got into it I could see it was hard-wired to the house wiring.

I put on some clothes and shoes and figured I'd go to the office and report it. As soon as I got outside, I saw there were many people in the parking lot, and I realized it wasn't only in my room – it was in every room of the motel. I asked the desk clerk what was going on. I had to yell to be heard. She said they didn't know. The fire department was there, along with several police cars.

I stuck around the lobby until one of the firemen finally located the right switch on the panel that stopped the racket, That's when I went back to bed. There was a different desk clerk on in the morning, and I asked her about it. She said they're still not sure what happened but probably someone in one of the rooms set off the smoke alarm.

My last day was uneventful as I traveled a familiar set of interstates to get home. I got in around 2 PM and made several calls to family and friends to let them know the old man was home safely. I had a really great time on the trip with my friends. One of the first things I did when I got home, which I often do even before unpacking, was to get out the maps and look into where I told the guys I'd meet them the next time.

I was totally exhausted and I hurt all over, and that fatigue and pain stayed with me for almost two weeks afterward. My eyesight, which had been in poor shape for years, was never worse than it was on this trip. But I'll say to anyone who might ask, "So why do you do it?" One of the things that comes to mind is Winston Churchill's famous quote during World War II, at the height of the Battle for Britain, soon after a horrendous air raid blitz inflicted heavy damage on the city of London – he said, "Never, Never, Never give in." Herb Gunnison was much more blunt in his book *Seventy Years on a Motorcycle* when he said, "Don't ever let the bastards take it away from you."

I feel much the same about my long distance riding. Giving up something I've loved doing for most of my life is like surrendering to life itself, which I have no intention of doing – if I can help it. Traveling alone on the byways of this beautiful country is what I intend to continue doing for as long as I can get my leg over the machine; and for as long as I can still handle the pain – and for as long as my eyesight holds out enough to find my way out of the driveway.

.

Four

A Fun Ride in The Ozarks

May 11 – May 21, 2009

I left home with the same Suzuki 650 that I had been riding for a year and a half. I was on my way to Joplin, Missouri this time to meet my friends coming in from the west coast for a three-day ride through the Ozarks on a course I had laid out for the occasion. My original plan to get to Joplin was to use several familiar country roads across Pennsylvania, followed by some roads across southern Ohio and Kentucky that I had never ridden. I planned to average 350 miles per day for four days, which was an aggressive plan for me.

When John called to say that they would be arriving at noon rather than late afternoon, the plan became even more aggressive, cutting my time to get there from 4 to 3½ days and raising my average to almost 400 miles of back roads per day, which I thought was probably too much, so I put together an alternate plan using mostly interstate highways, which I planned to use in case the original plan became overwhelming.

After experiencing far too much slow-moving traffic on some of the back roads across eastern Pennsylvania, and pushing myself to hold the schedule, I decided at lunch to switch to the alternate plan. I didn't like the idea of pushing myself that hard for the next three days. It would have been great if I could add an extra day to the schedule, but I had other obligations that prevented it.

It was cool the first day with a few light showers. I used my electric vest and gloves all day and stopped at the same motel in Hagerstown that I've used several times in the past, covering less than 300 miles – most of which was from the original aggressive plan. The sky got dark in the afternoon and a strong storm with lots of thunder and lightening passed through soon after I checked in. I had dinner at Shoney's in the nearby shopping center.

After a quick breakfast I headed into the Cumberland Mountains of western Maryland on I-70. The skies were clear and abundant sunshine was forecast. It was cool though, with fog in the valleys. I exited I-68 for gas in Cumberland and ran into some difficulty finding a gas station. I rode at least two miles up and down hills and taking many turns through the city before finally locating one on the far side of town. After filling up, I got directions from the cashier on how to get back to the highway, which I tried to follow, but I got mixed up and ended up in someone's dooryard. A woman standing outside her garage looked at me sitting there, and said, "Are you lost?"

I said, "I like to think that I'm never lost but at the moment I don't have the slightest idea where I'm at or how I got here." She asked what address I was looking for and I explained how I got off I-68 westbound to look for gas, which I found, but now I'm trying to find my way back to the highway.

She thought for a moment and said "It's a little complicated but I'd be happy to take you there if you'll wait for just a minute." She disappeared into the house and less than a minute later the garage door flew open and she said with a smile, "Follow me," as she got into her car and proceeded to back it out.

I followed her through several left and right turns and up and down hills for what seemed like 2 miles before she slowed at an intersection and pointed left for me to turn up the narrow side street. I gave her a big 'Thank you' wave and a smile, turned onto the street and followed it for less than a quarter-mile to where I saw the sign for the highway and another for the westbound ramp – there are still a lot of good people around.

I traveled I-70, I-68 and I-79 through the Cumberland and Allegheny Mountains, holding a constant 75-mph. The cool temperatures at the higher elevations dropped my gas mileage to the low 40s. It was a scenic ride and different from the norm, making it enjoyable in spite of being on interstate highways – the truck traffic was light, which helped.

I would have liked to reach Lexington before stopping for the day because the weather prediction for the entire next day wasn't the greatest. But I was already tired and I wanted to check in early enough to take my meds. Strong thunderstorms were predicted for later in the day and I hoped to get in before they came through.

I eventually checked into a Super 8 an hour short of Lexington, and a fierce storm with high winds, thunder and lightening passed through a few minutes after I got my gear inside. I covered 410 miles that day.

They served hot biscuits and gravy and a hard-boiled egg for breakfast at the motel in addition to the usual bagel and cream cheese, which saved me stopping for breakfast. It was 55° when I left, and there were lots of dark clouds in the direction I was headed. The sky actually looked ominous in all directions.

I rode through a strong thunderstorm less than an hour later. Not long after coming out of it, I glanced in my rear-view mirror and saw a long black funnel cloud drop out of a flat-bottomed anvil cloud where I had just been. It looked very much like a tornado, and I was glad it was behind me and not in front. I left the motel just in time.

Another strong storm with heavy rain and strong winds came through a short while after I passed Lexington. It was the kind of storm I would normally have looked for shelter from because it was hard to see anything at all. It was especially difficult during the heaviest part of the storm when I couldn't see the road surface. It looked like I was riding on water instead of concrete or blacktop. I couldn't see any of the lines in the road or the edges of the road either – just water – like I was riding on the surface of a pond. Most of the time I was pushing myself to maintain the posted 65 mph speed limit, riding practically blind through the heaviest downpours – it was scary at times.

The rain and wind eased by the time I crossed the Ohio River at Louisville. I had never been through that area before and I thought Louisville looked like a nice town

– whatever I could see of it. The last shower came through as I entered the east side of the city, and it was already beginning to clear by the time I crossed the Ohio River with the city in my rearview mirror.

Soon after entering Indiana I began to look for a place to get gas and a quick lunch. My gas was on reserve when I finally exited for a service center that had a Subway in the same building. I had an Italian half-sub that I ate while chatting with a few people I met. I was exhausted from fighting the weather all morning but I wanted to make it to well beyond the Mississippi River that day if I could, to avoid the morning rush-hour traffic around St. Louis. So after lunch I continued to press on across Indiana and Illinois.

It got very windy in the flat farm country in Illinois, with strong crosswinds out of the southwest. I was already exhausted from fighting the thunderstorms all morning when I began to struggle with the strong crosswinds. I was still wearing a rain jacket over the riding clothes and I wore my extra-tall 17-inch Tingley rain boots rather than the shorter 11" kind because I expected the storms. The temperature was in the mid 80s by then, and I was overheated from far too many clothes. The crops I recognized across Indiana and Illinois were mostly canola with the yellow blossoms.

I crossed the Mississippi on I-255 and used the I-270 beltway around the south side of St. Louis. Not long after exiting from I-270 onto I-44, I spotted a suitable exit to stop for the day near St. Clair, Missouri, and I checked into a Super 8 at 2:15 Central Time after 450 miles in a little less than eight hours. I was satisfied with it under the circumstances because it left me with plenty of time to make the rendezvous at noon. It was certainly a big enough day for me, and I was just about where I wanted to be by the end of my 3rd day – past St. Louis. It was admittedly a tough day because of the bad weather.

I left the motel at 6:20 Central Time after a toasted bagel, cream cheese and coffee at the motel. Another storm passed through during the night, with loud claps of thunder that sounded like a shotgun going off in the hallway. It woke me out of a sound sleep. My first thought was that someone fired a gun, and I woke up wondered what was going on.

From there to Joplin was an easy 235-mile interstate ride. I stopped once for gas and a second breakfast and arrived at the motel at 10:35 Central Time – a few hours early for the planned rendezvous. I learned from the desk clerk that John called earlier to say they were stuck in traffic on the interstate and would probably be a few minutes late. After checking in, I went for a short ride to scout out the back road that I planned to leave town on with the group in the morning.

As I neared the motel on my way back from the ride, I saw the three guys exiting the interstate. I pulled in behind them and followed them into the motel parking lot. After they checked in and got settled, we walked across the street together to McDonald's for lunch, and we sat outside the motel rooms, talking and celebrating the reunion.

John's brother Tom arrived from his home in Weir, Kansas, not far from there, around five. He came to ride with us on our 3-day ride. Someone called a local Papa John's for a couple of large pizzas to be delivered and we ate supper in the parking lot. Before turning in, we agreed to meet for breakfast at seven. Key time for leaving on the ride would be eight o'clock sharp.

I had laid out the 3-day ride from memories of having ridden several of the roads at least a few times in the past. I also used Google to find the "best Arkansas motorcycle roads" and the "best Missouri motorcycle roads." I found several web sites that were helpful in laying it out. I think the Internet would help to plot rides in other states as well.

The roads I chose for the first day were primarily Rte 86 that meanders through the hilly farm country of southern Missouri, and Arkansas Rte 23 that begins near Eureka Springs and heads south with many twists and turns through the heart of the Ozarks. It's a great bike road. Eureka Springs is a tourist town that can often get congested, but we had no problem.

We followed mostly Rtes 86 and 23 for around 85 miles each, with a few interconnecting roads to make an interesting 210-mile first day, and we stopped along Rte 23 at a rustic restaurant near Huntsville for a leisurely lunch. I ordered catfish and fries, and enjoyed it. The restaurant seemed to be a popular eating-place for tourists. It was crowded. The first thing the waitress said as she rushed by our table and dropped off the menus was, "Breakfast is over." I think it was around eleven and almost everyone in the place was still eating breakfast.

We rode a few more tight, twisty sections of Rte 23 after lunch where I stepped up the pace a little to make it more challenging, so no one gets bored. Everyone seemed to enjoy the more spirited ride – especially Jim and John. It's a great area for motorcycling.

I chose the I-40 crossing near Clarksville to look for a motel, figuring they would be plentiful near the interstate with a town nearby. There were several. We chose a Super 8 that looked a lot like a Motel 6 – two floors with parking outside the first-floor rooms – the way the guys like it. There was an exterior walkway in front of the second-floor rooms, also making it look like a Motel 6. I think it was John, Tom and Alan who walked across the street for a bucket of grilled chicken. Everyone thought the grilled variety tasted great – the best new product KFC has come up with in years. It was obvious that everyone liked it.

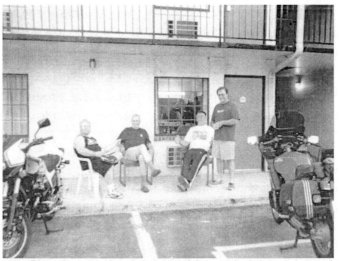

John, Piet, Jim and Alan (left to right) in a typical day-end pose in front of the motel in Clarksville, Arkansas. Tom took the photo.

The weather for our second day wasn't the greatest, with showers in the forecast. It rained on and off much of the day, although not heavily. They served bagel and cream cheese in the lobby for breakfast. We ate at the same time as a group of Harley riders. As we made our way north along Rte 7 later that morning, we pulled in behind the same group. I assumed they planned to ride much of Rte 7, which is one of the best-known scenic roads in the Ozarks. I left it out of our ride because I expected it to be congested.

Traffic was quite heavy and a light drizzle made the roads wet – so the Harley guys were just poking along. When I spotted a gas station, I pulled in for gas rather than blast by the group. Soon after the gas stop we turned northeast on Rte 9, a more rural scenic road with light traffic and only a few houses – a very nice, twisty ride through the hill country of northeast Arkansas.

I stepped up the pace a little more spirited than the day before to make it a fun ride, but whenever I would ease up, John would come alongside and motion for me to slow down. He said later he was concerned that someone might get hurt with so much sand on the pavement from the recent showers – most of which I don't see. I eased up and we still had a great ride.

I planned on stopping for the night at Mammoth Springs, but when we got there and didn't see any motels or even a gas station, we continued across the state line to Thayer, Missouri. It didn't seem to be a suitable overnight stop either, so we eventually rode another 25 miles into West Plains, a much larger town where we found an attractive American-owned motel with reasonable rates. We stopped there and checked in after an enjoyable 285-mile day.

.

Left to right: Alan, Piet, Jim and Tom at our sardine communion in
the motel parking lot in West Plains, Missouri.

Photo by John Dey

During happy hour, Tom took a tin of sardines from
his bag and said it would be an honor for him if I
would share a can of sardines with the group while he
was there, like we had done at Beartooth Pass. Tom
also brought a bottle of blackberry brandy as a gift for
me. We communed in the parking lot and toasted the
occasion with the brandy.

Someone suggested we find a KFC for more of the
same grilled chicken that we had the night before, but
when we found the KFC about a mile away, they
didn't offer the grilled variety. Since we were already
there and they had a buffet, we stayed for dinner.

While John was going over his bike that evening, he
realized the rear tire wasn't safe enough for the type of
riding we were doing, and he felt that it would be

prudent to head back to Joplin and arrange for a new tire before their trip back to California. He had been using an exceptionally soft composition tire that was almost worn out after only a few thousand miles coming across the country and two days of riding in the Ozarks. Alan volunteered to accompany him for the 180 miles back to Joplin in the morning.

The roads I chose for the last day were Missouri Rtes 14 and 76, neither of which I remembered having ridden before. We followed them for 90 miles and 60 miles respectively with a few interconnecting roads to make a total of a little over 200 miles for the day. Missouri Rte 14 was an exceptionally nice two-lane road with sweeping curves and long vistas, while Rte 76 twisted and turned through the hill country not far from the popular music center at Branson.

We were disappointed that John and Alan weren't able to ride with us on our final day. We rode in sunshine and fair temperatures all day and had lunch at a small Italian restaurant off the beaten path, which was apparently a favorite with local people – it was crowded. We got back to the motel soon after John and Tom. Tom left for home a short while later. That night John and Alan rode over to see his place while Jim and I shared happy hour in the parking lot and rode to a nearby KFC for dinner.

I got up at four for my final packing and loading, so that I could get an early start for home. It was only 44 degrees when I stepped outside. I decided to wear the heated gloves and vest when I left, since I'd be riding the interstate for the first hour. While having coffee alone in the lobby at 5:45, I noticed McDonald's across the street was already open. So after finishing most of the coffee I walked over for my usual sausage muffin with egg and orange juice.

When I got back to the motel to see if anyone was out and about, I found Jim there checking over his bike. He got Alan and John up for the goodbyes. They came out in their skivvies for a hug and a handshake just before I fired up and left at first light.

Soon after exiting I-44 in favor of the country roads, I came within inches of hitting a huge coonhound crossing the road. Later, while entering West Plains, all traffic was at a standstill in both directions from a serious accident, and the rescue squad was just leaving the scene. As I inched my way by, I saw one of the vehicles – a car with a badly smashed front-end. I looked around for the other vehicle but I saw only a lot of miscellaneous parts strewn all over the place for a few-hundred-foot radius. Many of the parts looked very much like motorcycle parts. If they were in fact from a bike, I wouldn't have much hope for the rider. It was a somber moment.

I stopped in West Plains for a second breakfast before finding US 160, which I followed to its eastern end just south of Poplar Bluff. I spotted a sign for the Dorena Ferry that I remember taking across the Mississippi in 1988 with Bud Peck on our 15,000-mile back road ride around the US. This time I crossed the river on US 60 into Wickliffe, Kentucky, over the huge confluence of the Mississippi and Ohio Rivers. The highway uses two long, narrow cantilever bridges to get across the two rivers near Cairo, Illinois – first one, then the other.

The Cairo Mississippi River Bridge

It's a sight to behold with all the swirling muddy water where the Ohio River flows into the Mississippi. I was traveling eastbound on Rte 60, which actually runs north-northwest at that point to reach the east side of the Mississippi. It then takes a right turn to the northeast and crosses the second long narrow bridge to get south of the Ohio River into Kentucky. The highway touches three states in an interesting S-shaped pattern while both rivers also make an S-shaped turn there. It's an amazing engineering accomplishment.

After crossing the two bridges, I followed US 51 south to reach Kentucky Rte 80, an old country road that I planned to take most of the way across the state – plus using the parkways to bypass the heavier traffic of the cities. I stopped for the night at a small motel in Mayfield, less than an hour after entering Kentucky, and I checked in at 2:30 after 430 miles of mostly country byways in 8½ hours.

I was up at 4 AM, packed, loaded and out for breakfast by 5:45. It was cool when I left town with the morning sun glistening on the dew-covered alfalfa fields. I love the smells of early mornings in farm country, especially on a nice two-lane bike road with long vistas and sweeping curves. The smell of honeysuckle was in the air, intermingled with the sour smell of fermenting silage and other odors from the barnyards, and from the crops being exposed to the heat of the morning sun. It was one of those mornings when it feels good to be alive – and riding a motorcycle.

The traffic was light and I managed to maintain a fairly good average all day. Besides riding quite a bit of Rte 80, the parkways I rode included sections of the Louie B. Nunn Cumberland Parkway, the Russell Dyche Memorial Parkway, the Daniel Boone Parkway and the Hal Rogers Parkway. They were laid out roughly end-to-end across southern Kentucky, close to the old Rte 80, which had very little traffic.

The parkways reminded me of interstate highways and weren't quite what I had expected, except for the Hal Rogers Parkway that has two lanes with a wide grassy right-of-way that goes into the Appalachians in eastern Kentucky. I was able to maintain a steady 70 for most of its length – as I also did on the last 45 miles of Route 80, which ends at US 460.

I located a Super 8 in Prestonsburg, a few miles after turning north on US 460. I got there at 3:30 EST after 445 miles in 8½ hours. I actually made good time but I lost an hour due to the time change. I got the last room at the Super 8 – a smoking room on the third floor, but I was happy to get it because I was tired and didn't see any other motels around. I sprained my ankle carrying all of my stuff from the bike to the elevator and from there to my room, making three trips out of it. I should have asked for a cart.

After a short rest, I went out for dinner and scouted out Rte 3 that I planned to take east in the morning into West Virginia and deeper into the Appalachians. The road was somewhat obscure, but I found it about five miles north of the motel. I pondered my options for the rest of the trip and eventually decided to abort the plan and follow the superhighways home from there. I was tired and getting anxious to get home.

I was up at four and on the road by 6:30, after much of the heaviest fog had cleared. Even then, I blew through a red light that I didn't see on US 460. I was doing about 70 in the light fog at the time. Fortunately no one saw me, and even more fortunately, no one was crossing at the time. It was 46° when I left the motel and I should have worn my electrics, especially the gloves. It got colder in the fog patches and my hands got so cold the middle finger on my right hand actually went numb. I stopped for gas and a second breakfast at a McDonald's in Weston, West Virginia to warm up. The temperature had risen by then to the upper 50s. I felt better after getting back onto the bike.

I pulled into the Motel 6 in Hagerstown at 2:30 after 430 miles. While I was having a combination lunch and dinner at Shoney's late that afternoon, I decided to ride the interstates home from there, especially since I had nothing to eat in the house and a ton of chores to do after getting home. I got home at 10:45 AM with a trip total of 3,760 miles in 11 days, which is about the same distance and time as my annual trips to Daytona Bike Week. The chain I installed just before leaving still didn't need an initial adjustment and the engine used less than a half-cup of oil on the entire trip.

Five

Las Vegas in December

November 26 to December 13, 2009

I've always enjoyed attending the annual AMA Hall of Fame Induction Ceremony when it was held in Ohio in August. I even helped to sponsor a few of the events, and I would see friends and fellow competitors being inducted. I'd never think of going to the event any other way but riding. When the AMA announced in early 2009 that the event would be moved to the Hard Rock Hotel and Casino in Las Vegas, and that it would be held in December, it raised the bar considerably for riding to the event, but I still wouldn't think of going any other way.

I gave it a lot of thought when it was announced. I wasn't sure that my 84-year-old body was up to the task, especially at that time of year – and that's without considering the interference with Thanksgiving and Christmas, where I'm the senior member of the family and I'm usually home for those holidays. This time my granddaughter and her husband were coming from Alaska to spend Christmas with Grandpa.

If I were to decide to go, I would have to get a better handle on at least a few of my physical issues before I could commit to the tickets or the hotel reservations. Eventually everything fell into place in time, and I was quite sure I could manage it, in spite of concerns about my eyesight and physical issues that had been getting progressively worse recently. The pain in my back would increase after hours of riding, but I felt at the time I could manage it, and I definitely wanted to go.

I began preparations by changing the tires, the chain, the brake pads and the oil and filter on my 650 Suzuki V-Strom. I was still able to do all of it at home without help, although I would get totally exhausted from my congestive heart failure, especially changing the tire, which gets strenuous for someone my age. I'm also bothered by back pain when I'm on my feet too long, or in the mornings after I've spent a lot of time riding the previous day.

I clocked 64,000 miles on the bike in less than the two years that I owned it, but since I never had a problem with it, I wasn't too concerned about it taking me to Las Vegas and back trouble free. My main concern was with the seat and suspension, neither of which were the greatest for long distance riding comfort, and there wasn't much more I could do about that.

It wasn't until a week before I left that I realized my plan called for leaving on Thanksgiving Day, which could affect motel availability. I knew beforehand that I would be sacrificing Thanksgiving with my family but I hadn't thought about motels on that weekend – so I made some calls to try and reserve rooms. After calling a few motels along the route I had planned through West Virginia and Kentucky, and learning that there were no vacancies, I changed the plan in favor of riding interstate highways for the first few days – I was able to make reservations along the interstates.

It was cloudy and 47° when I left home, and the sun began to break through in New Jersey, but not for long. It got foggy again as I descended into the Delaware River Valley, and a heavy cloud cover returned and stayed with me until I reached Virginia several hours later. The temperature was in the low 50s most of the day, which I thought was great.

I began to think about lunch around Harrisburg, and I pulled off the highway several times during the next few hours whenever I would see a sign for any kind of place for food, but nothing was open on Thanksgiving Day, not even a convenience store. Even some of the gas stations were closed. I tried to enter a rest area to get something from a machine, but that too was closed. I thought for a while that I might have to resort to sardines for my Thanksgiving Dinner. I was carrying a few cans, just in case I got snowed in somewhere in the mountains during the trip.

I rode 431 miles the first day to Verona, Virginia and checked in at 2:45. By using the interstate highways I was already ahead of my original schedule. While checking into the Knights Inn that I reserved, the first thing I asked the clerk was about eating-places. I was getting really hungry by then. He said the Chinese place next door might be open, but it wasn't.

I rode around Verona for 10 or 15 minutes looking for a place to eat, or anyone to ask. I spotted a guy stuffing used clothes into a Salvation Army bin, and I asked him. He said he saw a small family place that was serving turkey dinner for $7.99 not far from there. I found it and ordered the dinner, which came with salad, sweet potatoes, stuffing, corn and a big piece of pumpkin pie. They even came around during the meal, offering seconds on the turkey.

When I looked out early the next morning, I noticed that the motel was almost empty, with only one car in the entire parking lot. I asked the desk clerk the night before about breakfast or coffee in the morning. He said a complementary breakfast would be served in the lobby at 6:30. When I got there at 6:45, the office was locked and I had to pound on the door to get in. The breakfast consisted of concentrated orange juice, a small Danish and bland coffee; but at least it lasted until I could find a McDonald's a few hours later for my usual breakfast sandwich.

The temperature was in the low 30s and windy when I left the motel, with lots of fast-moving clouds racing through the sky. Holiday weekend traffic was light along I-81, with very few cars and almost no trucks. The highway patrol was out in force, but they seemed to be allowing plenty of tolerance. Many cars were pulled over, but I kept the needle a little under 80 most of the day and had no problem.

The sky cleared and it got mostly sunny by the time I reached I-40 in Tennessee. Most of the clouds had dissipated and the temperature rose into the high 40s. Traffic got heavier as I got closer to Knoxville. I assumed the traffic was from people returning home from their holiday visits. I used the bypass rather than take I-40 through the city, and I called it a day about 40 miles west of Knoxville.

I learned after checking in that the only restaurant around was once a Huddle House next-door – but the health department had closed it. I checked in, unloaded my bags, lubed the chain and took a brief rest before going back out to find a place to eat. The nearest I could find was a KFC about nine miles and two exits west of there. On my way back, I somehow got onto the wrong entry ramp, probably from being over-tired; and it took me in the wrong direction with the next exit 12 miles farther west. I ended up traveling more than 40 miles for the KFC dinner, which brought that day's total to 410 miles.

I usually stopped for the day around two or two-thirty, so I could take my diuretic and still have at least six hours for it to run its course before I went to bed. I have to take several meds at various times of the day to keep my system functioning reasonably well.

My gas mileage dropped that day from the usual 60 mpg to less than 35 for the first time since I owned the bike, and it concerned me a little. I knew that the speed, the ambient temperature, the headwinds, the weight of the luggage, and even how long since I've changed the plugs could affect it. The plugs had been in for almost 30,000 miles, but I think it's around what the book calls for. It seems that fuel consumption on this bike is far more sensitive than any other I've owned. I was concerned that it could be something more sinister, like a valve tightening up, which could eventually scorch the valve.

Since it continued to run smoothly, both at idle and at speeds, and didn't exhibit other symptoms, I attributed it to a combination of the headwinds, high speeds and the ambient temperature that was mostly around 80; and also to the fact that it's only a 650cc engine and

I've been pushing it like it was a big machine. So I put it out of my mind and pressed on.

I left Kingston, Tennessee with the temperature at 29°. The sky was clear, with practically no wind. Since I had plenty of time to spare, and would gain an hour from a time-zone change, I got off I-40 at the next exit and headed northwest into Kentucky. I had decided to abort the super-slab and ride at least a day without the route sheet or maps, to see where it takes me. I thought at first about taking some back roads to the same motel in Mayfield that I stayed the previous year, but I soon dropped the idea and thought maybe I should see how the ride goes first, before deciding on where to stop. It was a nice day and I had the urge to explore roads I had never ridden before.

After riding northwest for several hours on some nice country roads with and without numbers, I came to US Rte 60 near Paducah, Kentucky; and I followed it west across the same two long cantilever bridges that I used on my trip home the previous year, crossing both the Ohio River and the Mississippi River near Cairo, Illinois. No other vehicles were on either bridge at the time so I rode slowly and enjoyed the panorama and the interesting view of the swirling muddy water where the two big rivers meet.

I stopped for the day around 1:45 at a Motel 6 in Sikeston, Missouri after an interesting and enjoyable 370-mile day. I could have made it to Poplar Bluff or even farther, but I was running a half-day ahead of my original schedule, and I wasn't in a big hurry. It was almost 70° in Sikeston, which felt good.

My gas mileage improved a little with the slower pace on the two-lane roads, and also from the temperature being milder. The bike was back to 40 and 45 mpg, which was still far below what it gets at home, but I figured it was probably normal for the conditions. I also thought it might be from the gasoline recipe, which was probably different.

I had dinner at a Ruby Tuesday and ordered the New Orleans seafood dish with a tall glass of amber ale. It was one of the best meals I had on the road in quite a while. I usually ate my evening meals at places like Shoney's, Denny's or similar family restaurants, and I would try to eat between four and five o'clock, which helps to manage my meds. Eating alone like that where everyone else is in couples or groups often makes me feel out of place, especially at the better restaurants.

I woke up a little after six – an hour later than usual. It was raining, and rain was predicted to continue for most of the day. I dropped the idea of a more scenic route into West Plains followed by a ride on Missouri Rte 14 because of the weather. I originally thought of stopping for the day near Springfield, or maybe Joplin; but with the rain, I eventually chose a more direct route using mostly four-lane highways, and without knowing where I might end up for the day. I was aware that it might put me even farther ahead of my schedule.

It was 8 AM by the time I finally got on the road after eating a handful of raisins and peanuts from my bag and coffee from the office. There was no place around for breakfast. It rained lightly on and off most of the day. I approached Joplin even earlier than I thought I would, so I took Rte 92 along the northern edge of the city toward some unfamiliar back roads in Kansas, rather than stay on the interstate.

I rode around southeast Kansas for a while looking for Rte 166, which I was quite sure would take me into Oklahoma where I thought of hooking up with Historic Rte 66. I planned to follow it for a day or two for the nostalgia. I got totally turned around and eventually dropped the idea and stayed with the unnumbered road I was on. I was curious to see where it would come out and it's always a challenge on unnumbered roads without shadows to go by. I could be heading in any direction. Eventually I came across US 160, which I was familiar with, so I stayed with that for a while.

I stopped in Independence, Kansas at 3 PM, after 420 miles on what turned out to be a very long day that put me farther ahead of my schedule. Besides riding in the light rain, I also rode through a lot of heavy fog around Springfield. The temperature dropped from the 50s in the morning to the mid 40s by the time I checked into the motel. I unloaded the bike, lubed the chain, took a brief rest and realized it was already getting dark; so I rushed out and had one of the only evening meals of the trip at a fast food place so I could get back before total darkness.

It was 28° when I left the motel in the morning and my heated jacket liner and gloves really felt great – it sure beats the old days! I decided to drop the idea of heading southwest into Oklahoma; instead, I stayed on Rte 160 across most of Kansas.

I wasn't thinking about my gas when I went through Medicine Lodge, and I didn't realize until I was eleven miles out of town that I was about to go on reserve. I figured with the poor gas mileage I was getting, I had better not take the chance; so I turned back, rather than try to make it to Coldwater, about 40 miles farther west. The section of Rte 160 west of Medicine Lodge goes across some of the most desolate land east of the Rockies. It's the same general area where I rode through the fierce sand storm a few years back, although that storm was west of Meade. I'd often ride for up to 10 minutes without seeing another vehicle in either direction, or a farmhouse, or even a cow. The relatively deserted two-lane road stretches for 285 miles from Independence to Meade.

I turned southwest on US Rte 54 near Plains, Kansas and decided to pack it in for the day in Liberal where there are lots of motels, and also where I would turn southwest in the morning. I checked into a Super 8 and asked for a room near an exit so I would have a shorter walk with my gear. They had only 10 rooms left, but I was able to get one with a short walk, however it's not possible to see the bike from the room at a Super 8 like it is at a Motel 6. Truck traffic was exceptionally heavy in Liberal. The temperature was 57°, which was the warmest it would be until I got to Las Vegas.

I thought by heading southwest that the weather would get a little milder and the riding would get easier. How wrong I was! I saw some of the coldest weather during those next few days that I had seen so far, which was a harbinger for the rest of the trip.

I left Liberal at barely first light with the temperature in the high 20s – the coldest morning so far. About 5 miles out of town and just before full daylight, I came very close to hitting a coyote. I was traveling a little over 70 mph when I spotted him at the last second on a dead run for the other side of the road. I didn't have time to do anything but yank my foot up to get it out of the way of where it looked like he would hit, and I hung on and braced myself for the collision. Old Wile E. Coyote lived to run another day, as he skidded to a stop just short of my front wheel. Luckily I raised my foot just high enough to clear his head.

The gas stations were scarce between Liberal and I-40, and a few times I came close to running out. Being used to getting better gas mileage, I wasn't watching the gauge often enough. Whenever I would look, I'd realize that I passed a gas station quite a while back and the next one would be fifty or sixty miles ahead. I'd have to sweat it out each time to the next town. I thought maybe the altitude was affecting my brain. The longer distances between gas certainly called for staying alert and planning ahead for the gas stops – but I would forget to look at the gauge.

A snowstorm had hit the area around Tucumcari two days earlier. There was still about 6 inches on the ground when I came through. I noticed after getting onto I-40 that the snow at the edges of the highway kept getting deeper as I traveled farther west and gained altitude. I was totally beat from the combination of the cold and the altitude by the time I got to Albuquerque around two o'clock.

Apparently my congestive heart failure doesn't take kindly to the higher altitudes where my lungs starve for oxygen. There were times when I stopped for food or gas that my hands would be trembling like an old man's hands, and I would have difficulty breathing from the slightest exertion. By the time I checked into the motel in Albuquerque, and I got my tank bag, saddlebags, tank panniers and hippo-hands into the room and lubed the chain, I was totally exhausted. I made a cup of tea for myself and took a half-hour rest before thinking about going back out for dinner. It was a little after four when I walked to a family cafeteria in a nearby shopping center for a pretty nice meatloaf dinner. There was certainly plenty of food to choose from on the line.

The temperature was 15° when I left the motel at barely first light, a few minutes before seven. It was the coldest morning so far. It dropped well into the single digits at the Continental Divide. I exited at Gallup for breakfast after 150 miles in the extreme cold. Even getting off the bike was exhausting at that altitude. I could barely walk into McDonald's for breakfast, and I was breathing heavily all the way. By the time I reached Flagstaff, about 320 miles into the day, I was totally exhausted from a lack of oxygen.

When I crossed the Divide where the temperature was only seven degrees, my knees were cold for the first time on the trip. That's in spite of wearing two pairs of Wickers long johns under high-tech Damart double-force sweat pants and heavy woolen knee warmers. I wore my riding suit bottoms overtop all of the rest. The tank panniers also served as a windbreak for my knees and legs. I was well protected from the weather, short of using heated bottoms, but my knees were still cold, especially with the 70 mph wind chill while traveling.

I had the same problem with my lungs when I stopped for lunch in Flagstaff. The young girl at the counter who filled my lunch order offered to carry the tray to the table for me, so I must have looked pretty bad. I was gasping for breath while I was eating. I stopped for the day at 2 PM in Seligman, not long after a six-mile descent from the high country.

When I got off I-40, I found a nice family-owned motel on the west end of town, along Historic Rte 66. The room next to mine had a small plaque that read, "Will Rogers slept here." I don't know if it was for real, but my room had a similar plaque. I vaguely recognized the name – I think he was an author. I covered 410 miles that day, almost all of which was along I-40. After getting settled, I sat outside my room for a while to rest in the bright sunshine and enjoy the clear air. I felt a lot better than I felt all day. The temperature was only 40°, but it felt comfortable. It was peaceful sitting quietly after a long day in the extreme cold. I suppose the rarified air made it feel warmer than it really was, despite being at a much lower altitude than Flagstaff.

I saw two restaurants within walking distance from where I was sitting. One was next door and the other was across the two-lane historic highway. I walked to the Road Kill Café next door for dinner, and ordered a huge buffalo burger with coleslaw and a glass of ale. The place was decorated for Christmas, with carols playing on a loud sound system.

I walked to the restaurant across the street for breakfast because they had by far the most pickup trucks parked out front. I had a big breakfast that started with biscuits and gravy, and was followed by eggs-over-easy with sausage patties, home fries and coffee. It's rare that I take the time for a full breakfast – and I rarely eat potatoes. There was so much I couldn't finish it, but it was still nowhere near the breakfast I remember having several years ago at a place not too far south of there in Black Canyon City, Arizona where the sausage patties were as big as pancakes.

It was only 10° when I left. I followed Old Rte 66 for 75 miles to Kingman, rather than use I-40. I saw several sets of Burma Shave signs along the almost-deserted Rte 66. In Kingman, I turned onto US Rte 93 for the final 105 miles to Las Vegas. In spite of the

cold, it was an exciting day, especially seeing the huge
new bridge that spans the Colorado River in front of
the Hoover Dam. It had been under construction for
the past five years, and was completed soon after I
went through. Final construction on the new section of
US 93 that would go over the bridge was also nearing
completion.

The Mike O'Callaghan – Pat Tillman Memorial Bridge, under
construction.

The bridge is a truly awesome sight from the top of the
dam. It's much higher and longer than the dam, which
itself is huge. Due to the current terror-threat level, all
traffic approaching the dam was being stopped and
checked, and trucks are not allowed over the dam at
all. Seeing the new bridge was one of the highlights of
my trip. Many people were visiting the area when I
went across the dam, which has always been a popular
tourist attraction, even before the relocation of the road
and the start of bridge construction.

I rode less than 200 miles that day, my eighth and last of the outbound leg, and I reached Las Vegas in late morning on Thursday, December 3rd, which was a day earlier than my reservations at the Hard Rock. The temperature was around 50° in Las Vegas. After an early lunch in town I spotted one of the new Motel 6s a block off the "Strip", and directly behind the huge Tropicana and MGM Grand. I decided to stay there for one night rather than check in a day early at the Hard Rock, especially since the rate at the Motel 6 was less than $30 with my AARP discount, and it was the nicest and most modern Motel 6 I had ever seen.

The TV in the room was a huge new 48" wall unit, and the bathroom and bed were almost as nice as those at the Hard Rock. I saw several motels in Kingman that morning that were advertised as low as $19.95. I paid almost three times that much only 75 miles east, the night before. Most rooms in Las Vegas were priced very reasonable. The nightly rate at the Hard Rock was $99, which I assumed was negotiated by the AMA.

I rode around town during the first afternoon to see the sights, and I rested up from the trip. I checked out of the Motel 6 Friday morning and went directly to the Hard Rock to check in. I parked the bike away from the main entrance while registering, but then I rode it up to the entrance, got off and began to remove my saddlebags, tank panniers, tank bag and other gear. I was putting it all on the sidewalk when a uniformed hotel employee came rushing over with a loud voice saying I can't park there. I answered at least as strongly, maybe even an octave higher, "If you're a bellhop, I'd like for you to get a cart, and put these things on it, and keep them in a safe place for me until my room is assigned. I am a guest here."

His face changed and he answered in a much different tone, "Yes sir." Seconds later he was back with a cart. Unfortunately, it's typical – because of the motorcycle I'm perceived as a second-class citizen.

I asked at the desk about safe parking for the bike and was told where in the garage "bikers usually park." I went there but didn't see a bike anywhere. I chose a spot where the girl mentioned, which was in a dark corner of the garage. I locked it and went to my room where I found my tank bag, panniers and other things sitting inside the room.

During the next few days I walked out into the garage to check on the bike a few times and never saw another motorcycle in the garage. I could hardly believe that we were at a dual motorcycle event – the amateur championship awards and the Hall of Fame induction ceremonies, with thousands of motorcyclists present, and practically no one rode to the event. I almost never saw a bike on the highway between New York and Las Vegas either; nor do I see bikers riding to Bike Week in Daytona in early March nowadays.

The Hard Rock parking garage was almost a quarter-mile from the registration desk. Walking from one area to the other inside the hotel was a bummer – especially for an old guy with congestive heart failure, chronic atrial fib and a bad back.

Most of the slot machines and other games are located in a huge circular pit about three or four steps below the level of the restaurants, coffee shops, conference rooms, hallways and other activities on the main floor. I'd see a person playing a slot machine in the pit, and I'd come by hours later and see the same person at the same slot. I suppose it's an addiction, much like

alcohol, drugs, sex or any other self-destructive
activity. One has to feel sorry for those involved, as
well as for their families, especially if they're addicted.

I hadn't purchased a ticket for Friday night's amateur
championship award presentations, just in case I had
difficulty on the road and couldn't make it in time; so I
asked at the ticket desk if there were tickets available,
and they said there were none.

As soon as the conference center opened, I asked the
girl at the AMA desk to please put my name on the
"standby list". She said she didn't have a standby list
but she started one. She recognized my name and said
she thought she could get me in, but that I would have
to wait. Soon afterward, a gentleman approached me to
say I looked like I needed a ticket. He said his son was
scheduled to get a speedway championship award that
night and the ticket was for his daughter who was
unable to come. I asked if he would consider taking 20
dollars for it and he graciously accepted – so I was in.
It was a very kind and generous gesture, because I
suspect he paid much more through Ticketmaster.

I met many old friends, including Bill Baird, during
happy hour in the outer hallway. I planned to sit with
Bill at the induction ceremonies the following night. I
also met Gloria Struck and her daughter Lori DeSilva.
Gloria is my age and is one of the few who still rides
her motorcycle almost every year from her home in
New Jersey to Daytona Bike Week for something like
the last 60 years. She also rides to Sturgis, South
Dakota and other events. The first thing I said to her
was, "You rode – right?"

She said no – she came by plane, but she said she knew
as soon as she saw me that I had ridden. Lori took our

picture together as she sometimes does at Daytona. Several people approached me, both at happy hour and later, saying they heard I rode the bike from New York. Apparently the word spread quickly.

Earlier in the day I met Gary Homanich, representing the Square Deal Riders from the Binghamton, New York area. We chatted for a while and I learned that he was at the event to accept an award for the most active club. He joined Bill and me that evening for the championship awards dinner. I thought the food that was served buffet-style was very good.

Amateur motocross racer and television broadcaster Laurette Nicoll was Master of Ceremonies for the amateur awards presentation. It started around seven and she kept it going briskly over the next two hours while well over 100 awards were presented. Most of those awards were for young champions, some of whom didn't look much older than seven.

I met Katie Wood, Don Rosene and Tom White in the elevator the next morning and walked to Mr. Lucky's for breakfast with Don and Tom where Craig Vetter joined us. John Penton and his son Jack arrived soon afterward with their families, and they took a table nearby. Jack had recently been appointed as Chairman of the AMHF Board of Directors. John came over to our table to speak with Craig. He seemed to recognize everyone at the table except me, so Craig pointed to me and said, "That's Piet Boonstra there."

John said, "Yeah, I know who he is."

Craig added, "Did you know that he rode in?"

John turned to me and asked, "You did? From New York?"

I said, "Yes. Didn't you ride?" When he didn't answer, I added: "And I think I'm older than you are, John."

He turned and asked, "What year were you born?"

I said, "1925."

He hesitated for a moment and said, "What month?" When I said June, he didn't answer. I think I'm a month older than he is, but I'm not sure. He shook my hand at least twice and talked about spinal problems and the carbon fiber disks in his back, before returning to his table. I didn't mention or compare any of my maladies. It isn't often that anyone ever upstages John Penton, so the brief exchange gave me a little inner satisfaction.

For whoever thinks it's warm in Las Vegas, I have news for them – all three nights I was there the nighttime low dipped below freezing, and one of those nights it was 28°. I had originally thought of taking a ride around the area during the day, but even the days were cool with temperatures in the low to mid 50s, so I rested up instead. The bike never moved from the time I first parked it in the garage until the morning I left.

There wasn't much to do in the daytime unless one wished to try his hand at the slots, and I didn't. There was no other place to sit unless it was at Starbucks, Mr. Lucky's or one of the other restaurants in the complex, so I guess I spent a lot of time in my room, mostly studying the maps and watching the weather.

There was a display of several bikes set up in the hallway outside the conference center, one of which was the Denis Manning built "No.7" streamliner that seven-time AMA Grand National Champion Chris Carr rode when he set the all-time outright world and national land-speed record on September 24, 2009. He had a two-pass average speed of 367.382 mph in the measured mile at Bonneville Salt Flats. The record-breaking machine had much of its cowling removed on one side so that the engine and rider compartment could be seen clearly.

Chris Carr was introduced at the events on both Friday and Saturday nights. The cockpit of the streamliner is barely large enough for his small body. He lies on his back inside, like one might do in a Lazy Boy recliner when the recliner is about halfway down. I would certainly never fit into it, and from the looks of it, getting out would be even tougher.

I had an interesting experience getting into the Hall of Fame Induction Ceremony on Saturday. There were five or six girls checking tickets and assigning seats. I presented my Ticketmaster ticket to one of the girls, and after checking her list she said I could sit at any table that didn't have a number on it. I thought at the time that it meant there was "open seating," but I was confused because Bill mentioned earlier that he was assigned to Table 42. I then thought that maybe it was because he's on the Hall of Fame Board of Directors, as well as being in the Hall of Fame.

But when I looked around, it seemed like the only tables that were without numbers were in the extreme rear of the huge room, and those were all vacant. I sat at one of those vacant tables, but after more than half the crowd entered from Happy Hour and found their assigned tables, the unnumbered tables were still vacant except the one where I was sitting alone – so I thought I'd ask the girl I met the previous night, about the criteria for assigning tables. I felt like I was being relegated to the very bottom of the food chain.

I explained to her that the first girl checked the list and told me to sit at any unnumbered table, and she said, "Oh no, Mr. Boonstra. You can sit at any table in this place. Who would you like to sit with?" I said I had planned on sitting with my friend Bill Baird, but being a member of the board and also of the Hall of Fame, he might be at a specially assigned VIP table.

She looked through her list and said, "You are now at Table 42."

Knowing it was Bill's table. I said, "Are you sure?"

She nodded and answered with a smile, "Yes, I'm sure."

Also seated at Table 42 was long-time board member Andy Goldfine, President and CEO of Aerostich; and Craig Vetter, a member of the AMA Hall of Fame, both of whom I had met previously.

My opinion of the induction ceremony was that it was somewhat of a letdown from the previous night, and the attendance was down sharply, with only about half of the seats filled. The food was good on both nights and I enjoyed the evening chatting with Bill, Andy, Craig and Craig's son. Legendary actor Perry King, also a biker, was the Master of Ceremonies while Rob Dingman, President and CEO of the AMA, handed out the awards. I was exhausted from all the standing and walking when I finally turned in that night.

Rather than call the bell captain in the morning to take my bags from the room to the front curb and load the bike there, I made three trips from my room to the garage instead. I brought the bike close to the rear entrance, inside the garage and not far from the elevator, and I took my time carrying stuff out. I noticed that Andy Goldfine was doing the same from his room to his car. I was happy that he stopped to chat for a minute and wished me well on my ride home.

It was 8 o'clock by the time I got to the highway, after stopping briefly for a sausage muffin with egg during my ride out of town. I entered the Mountain Time Zone less than a hundred miles down the road, losing an hour. The day started with huge dark clouds closing in from the west, with a strong storm predicted to sweep in from the Pacific that seemed to be picking up speed. I was anxious to get on the road as quickly as possible. I chose a more southerly route home to avoid as much of the storm as possible.

About 40 miles short of Wickenburg, Arizona, I was shocked to see that my gas was on reserve and it was too far back to the last town. I had a few close calls with gas on the way out, but this time it looked serious. I spotted a bike and a motor home parked in a rest area, facing like they had come from the other direction, so I stopped to ask if either of them had seen a gas station in that direction, or if they could possibly spare some gas. They couldn't spare the gas, but both thought they had seen a sign for gas about 10 miles back.

I made the 10 miles without running out, and I spotted the sign a few hundred feet off the road in what looked like a squatter's dooryard. I went through an open gate and rode in for about 150 feet, to a beat-up-looking single gas pump where I stopped and looked around. A grungy-looking guy came out of one of the campers and said he had gas, but it cost $10 a gallon, and I can't buy less than two gallons!

I had heard of gas scalpers but this was the first one I ever met. I certainly didn't want to take the chance on trying to make the last 10 to 15 miles into Wickenburg, because I had already been on the final reserve for at least 40 miles, and I never tested it; so I paid the 20 bucks for the two gallons. As soon as he pumped it into a plastic can and poured it into my tank, he grabbed the twenty out of my hand and disappeared.

I located a Motel 6 in Eloy, about 65 miles south of Phoenix, and checked in at 4 PM, after a 370-mile day. The sky behind me was dark all day, which was a constant reminder that the storm was closing in. After unloading and resting for a while, I walked to the restaurant next door where I ordered the dinner special – beef stroganoff. Even that short walk was a strain. I was also constantly aware of the pain in my back and my legs from having been on my feet too long, and also from the ride and from sleeping on so many bad mattresses.

It all seemed to be catching up with me, and carrying the bags out of the Hard Rock through the long hallways didn't help. Even my feet hurt, probably from swelling. I was using more than the maximum recommended dosage of Aleve twice a day – as written on the bottle. My doctor had told me that I shouldn't take any Aleve at all while I'm on the blood-thinning medication because of the condition of my stomach.

I got up early, worrying about the storm closing in, and I loaded the bike as quickly as I could. I raced up the I-10 entry ramp at barely first light like I had stolen the bike, and when I got to the highway I set my speed at a steady 80. The TV weather report said it was already raining in Phoenix and blizzard conditions were predicted for the higher elevations within hours. The sky behind me was getting darker by the minute.

I streaked toward the Continental Divide, holding the steady 80 mph all the way. The only brightness in the sky was a very narrow band of light along the eastern horizon, which I tried for the next two hours to widen, by racing toward it. I stopped for a quick breakfast in Willcox, about 140 miles out, and I thought I might have outrun it. It looked like the sun was about to break through.

It felt colder at the higher elevation, and I stopped at one point to slip on my rain jacket to use as an extra windbreaker. My hands were cold too. I didn't realize until that evening that the heat controller for the gloves and jacket liner had stopped working altogether. I worked on the controller that night but without a meter, I couldn't do much. I decided to bypass the controller and plug the heated gear directly into the battery source, uncontrolled. It worked fine for the liner because I could adjust the amount of heat to my skin, by wearing an extra layer of long johns, but the heat in the gloves was enough to burn my knuckles.

I covered 395 miles in 6½ hours and reached El Paso by early afternoon. The wind was strong all day and I noticed several potential dust storms starting up. The TV weather prediction was for the brunt of the storm to pass just north of El Paso, but the winds were predicted to be strong along I-20, which I had chosen over I-10 after hearing that another storm was coming in from the Gulf of Mexico that would bring heavy rain and winds to Houston. I've been through Houston a few times in heavy rain and wind, and it's no fun, especially if it's during rush hour on the beltway; so I opted for the colder and hopefully drier winds across 1-20, putting me between the storms.

I got very little sleep that night – maybe five hours at most, and I left at 6:45. The strong wind continued and the sun on the horizon was brutal as I rode directly into it, heading southeast toward I-20. It was the first time on the trip that I was bothered by the glare of the sun. I had so much black electrical tape over my face shield that it left very little range of vision.

I was about a hundred miles out when a gust of wind almost tore the handlebars out of my hands. It was around the same time traffic was being directed off the highway into what looked like a weigh station. Everyone was being funneled beneath a huge shelter. There were at least a dozen border-patrol and state police checking vehicles – I suppose for illegal aliens.

I wasn't able to read any of the signs with my face shield taped the way it was, and the wind was blowing me around a lot. My first thought was that I hoped I didn't make a wrong turn somewhere and that now I'm approaching the Mexican border. About that time, one of the border patrol agents asked where I lived and where I was headed. He waved me through, and seconds later, I was back on the highway.

I spotted a McDonald's near Van Horn and stopped for a quick breakfast just before reaching the I-20 cutoff. The temperature dropped about 10° soon after I got onto I-20. I noticed that the roads were wet from a recent shower near Pecos. The wind was exceptionally strong – it was so strong that I was concerned the bike could break traction from it.

Huge tumbleweeds were blowing across the highway. Most of them missed me, but a few hit the side of the bike. They're not heavy but I wondered what might happen if I hit a four or five-foot tumbleweed head-on at 75 mph – would it disintegrate or would it get tangled up in the wheels?

I checked into a Motel 6 in Sweetwater around mid afternoon, after 424 cold, windy miles. It was a rough day. The temperature was in the low 30s and I was totally exhausted from fighting the wind all day with very little sleep the night before. I passed an area coming into Sweetwater where many wind generators were turning. I learned the next morning that there are more than 4,000 in the area, and that most of the power from the generators is going all the way to Florida.

A few minutes after I checked in, I looked out and saw a gust of wind pick the bike up from the side stand and almost blow it completely over. I rushed out and turned it 180 degrees so it wouldn't be lying on its side in the morning. I heard on the news that night that an 89-mph gust was measured in the same area that I came through.

I left Sweetwater in the morning with the temperature at 19° and a wind chill factor that probably brought it down to well below zero. Someone asked me jokingly at breakfast after seeing me ride up on the bike, what the wind chill factor was at 70. I told him I didn't want to know. In spite of my exhaustion and the cold, I rode 430 miles that day from Sweetwater to Shreveport, Louisiana, with the high temperature never getting above the mid 30s. I checked in a little before four.

My old body was beginning to feel the strain. My back pain was getting more severe every day and I was getting weaker every day. At one of the gas stops it took four tries to get my leg over the seat. After checking in and unloading the bike in Shreveport, I spotted a Shoney's that was still serving lunch buffet at 4 PM for four bucks – so that's where I had supper.

I was pretty much of a mess in the morning. My back hurt every morning, but this was my worst morning by far. After I woke up, I couldn't stand up straight from the pain in my back. My lower spine simply wouldn't support the weight of my torso. I managed to get around the room and pack my bags by putting much of my weight on my arms and hands. I'd move around the room like a quadruped, supporting my torso on the furniture, looking like an ape. I packed and got ready with a considerable amount of effort and pain.

I ate a can of sardines from my bag. There was no coffee maker in the room so I made myself a cup of tea that I also used for taking my medication and vitamins. When the pain eased enough and I was finally able to get everything loaded on the bike, I had difficulty getting my leg over it. I made it on the fourth or fifth try. I left at first light and rode three hours before stopping for breakfast. I was afraid that if I stopped, I wouldn't be able to get back on.

The weather cooperated the whole day across Texas, Louisiana, Mississippi and Alabama. Storms raged on both sides of me and in front of me while the darkness seemed to part like the Red Sea before Moses. I rode under mostly sunny skies while the black skies from the two storms kept opening before me. It was cold and windy but I felt that I could handle that part. Even the coldness eased, and it got up to 40° for the first time in almost three days.

I would have liked to stop at the Barber Museum in Birmingham when I passed within less than a mile of the place, but I felt that I probably wouldn't be able to walk around the exhibits with my back the way it was; nor could I walk very far in snowmobile boots with my feet and legs hurting – so I pressed on and stopped for the night in Annison, Alabama, near the Georgia state line. I crossed the Mississippi River at Vicksburg, and I covering a total of 526 miles that day, the longest day of my trip. The traffic wasn't very heavy and the riding was all on I-20, so I was able to maintain highway speeds for most of the eight hours that I rode, giving me an average of more than 65 mph for the day.

The next day I rode 456 miles to Burlington, North Carolina in 7½ hours. The day started with the temperature at 27° and it didn't get out of the 30s all day. I was wiped out by the time I got to the motel. I hadn't taken my diuretic pill the previous afternoon, so I was beginning to build up fluid and getting short of breath. I had gotten in too late the previous afternoon and thought rest was more important than the diuretic.

Since I got into North Carolina early enough, I took a double dose as soon as I got in. I noticed that evening that several of my knuckles had small blisters from the unregulated current in the heated gloves. My gas mileage was worse than any day of the trip, dropping to around 33 mpg. I had problems getting my leg over the bike every time I stopped. I had problems getting off too, without falling over backwards, which I did a few times on the trip.

My most serious problem of the day was when the early-morning sun blinded me so much I couldn't read any of the signs during rush hour traffic coming into Atlanta where I-20 meets the beltway. It was a challenge for my eyesight when all four lanes of traffic were running bumper-to-bumper at a steady 80 mph and I had to switch from I-20 to I-85 without having a clue where the split was, and I was unable to read any of the signs. It actually went well though. I relied on my faith to be in the right lane when the time came to dive out of the 80 mph stream of madness into the relatively sedate cloverleaf at the last split-second.

It's tough when you get old, but even tougher when you can't see! Fortunately, I made some good guesses on which lane to be in and at what split-second to dive for the exit or entry ramps. I learned a week later that well-known Iron Butt competitor Eddie James was killed on the same highway only a few days before I came through. Some of the speeds they were traveling are scary, especially when you realize that many are kids still in high school; and others are older people, bordering on senility – all running bumper-to-bumper, four-abreast at 80 mph with the trucks.

The next day I traveled 176 miles in 3½ hours from Burlington to Prince George, Virginia where I spent a nice afternoon with my daughter and her family. It was 19° when I left Burlington and about 40° when I stopped for a sausage muffin with egg in Petersburg, in the crummiest McDonald's of the trip – the first thing I had to eat all day. I needed the afternoon to rest before my last day, which I knew would be one of the longest, and by far the toughest of my trip. I would finally have to turn directly into the path of the storm that I had been skirting all the way across the country, and it might be considerably colder than it had been so far.

Getting on and off the bike every time I stopped was becoming more of a problem every day because I was getting so much weaker and the pain in my back, legs and feet was getting more severe each day. Donna was getting ready to put the turkey in the oven for our evening meal when I arrived, and we had a nice family dinner together that evening.

It was raining lightly when I looked out at first light. With Donna's help I was able to get the bike loaded and ready to roll by 8 o'clock. Having checked the forecast, I could see it was time to pay my dues. A cold rain was predicted for the entire distance up the east coast, with temperatures in the low 40s most of the way – and then 30s. I could have waited a day for the skies to clear, but I was anxious to get back where I had so much to do to prepare for my granddaughter's arrival from Alaska a week later.

I put on the rain-gear bottoms before leaving Prince George but not the top because of my lack of heat control for the jacket liner. I thought it would get too hot inside both the riding jacket and the rain jacket and I thought getting overheated might sap my strength even more. I was only 20 miles out when it began to rain very hard, and a heavy fog rolled in, dropping visibility to a few hundred feet. I had at least 475 miles to go in this mess, and I was already exhausted. I thought of taking an easier 525-mile end-run using I-81 and I-78 to avoid the I-95 traffic, especially around DC, but with the rain, it would have taken far too long, and I'd either have to leave before first light or ride the last hour in darkness when the roads might be covered with ice in New York.

Even with the more direct route I would have to average 60 mph all day, included stops, in order to get home in the daylight – which meant running 65 and 70 most of the day in the pouring rain and fog without stopping to eat. My best option was I-95, but due to my vision problems, I figured on bypassing the tunnel in Baltimore because my eyes don't adjust fast enough to

the abrupt change from daylight to the dim lighting of
the tunnel, but the detour adds extra miles to the trip.
When I got close, the rain and overcast made it so dark
outside that I figured the difference wouldn't be that
much in the tunnel – so I sailed straight through.

Fortunately it was Sunday and truck traffic was lighter
than usual, but I was hampered by the heavy rain and
poor visibility. I rode without my glasses all day,
relying on the face shield, which also became a mess
after a while. I'd sometimes have to flip it up and take
the brunt of the rain in my bare eyeball (that's singular,
because I see very little with the other eye). A few
times I found myself on the bumpy right or left
shoulder after the lane that I was on ran out. The trick
then would be to get back into an active lane quickly,
but a truck or an aggressive driver would often be in
the lane, neither of whom would give an inch,.

I fought it like that through Washington, Baltimore and
Wilmington and then all the way up the New Jersey
Turnpike. I thought I was home free when I reached
the relatively sedate Palisades Parkway in New York,
but the temperature dropped from the low 40s to the
low 30s, and there was deep snow along both sides of
the road, reminding me that the ground was frozen;
and it was already beginning to get twilight, and I
knew that the road surface would ice up before I could
reach the Bear Mountain Bridge.

As I suspected, I rounded one of the final bends on the
Palisades, less than a mile from the bridge, and there
was a car off the road. It was just beyond twilight. The
EMTs and Rescue Squad were there, and I heard the
flagman yell something about ice and what was I doing
out there. I glided carefully by, trying not to slide out,
and I got through. I knew that I was home free when I

reached the bridge where it was a few degrees warmer and I had only eight miles to go.

I got home at 4:30, just as the last glimmer of daylight faded to black. The trip totaled a little over 6,200 miles. I had an almost empty tank and a very empty stomach when I got in. I stopped twice for gas but didn't stop at all to eat. Fortunately Donna had served me a hearty breakfast before I left Virginia.

It wasn't long after returning from the trip that my stool turned dark. I had started taking iron supplements and thought the darker color might be from the iron, but I was sitting in my living room one evening, feeling very weak and lightheaded, so I took my blood pressure. It was 86/47, which is quite low for anyone, especially me. I reached for the phone and called my doctor. He said to go directly to the emergency room. "Do not ride the motorcycle. Have someone take you – now! I'll meet you there!"

Soon after arriving at the emergency room I learned that the ulcers in my stomach were bleeding badly and I was low on blood. I had taken far too much Aleve on the trip and it burned holes in my stomach, especially since I already had ulcers and I was on blood-thinning medication. I was fortunate that it didn't happen out on the road because I probably would have bled to death before my innate stubbornness would have permitted me to seek help. I was in the hospital for almost a week getting three units of blood while the gastrointestinal specialist worked on stopping the bleeding. I was there for five days before they had enough confidence that the bleeding had stopped – and wouldn't start over again.

Six

Daytona Bike Week

It's the joy of the ride – not just the destination!

It's been estimated that an average of nearly 500,000 people attend Daytona Bike Week annually. Everyone has his or her own reasons for going. After having made the trip regularly for the past 50 years, I derive the greatest pleasure from riding the motorcycle to and from the event. I have a lot of fun after I get there too, mostly visiting with friends and extended family, but the ride has always been Number One.

The photo above was taken on the Blue Ridge Parkway in North Carolina in the early 1990s, when a section of the road was closed for the season. Jake Herzog got his Harley too close to the edge during a blizzard in the mountains, and it slipped off the shoulder. He, Bud Peck and I were able to get it back in a few minutes, and we were on our way again. We came through with great memories, a few laughs and no ill after-effects.

I believe every time the motorcycle is taken out of the garage is an opportunity for adventure, and when it's not, the ride will soon be forgotten. The part of every ride I remember 20 years later is where something exciting happened. Whether it was running out of gas, a breakdown or a minor mishap, it's all part of the adventure of motorcycling. Accept it, make the best of it and keep going! That's what life is all about.

After retiring from active enduro competition in the mid 1980s, I rode Honda Gold Wings for almost a half-million miles, which included four of my eight trips to Alaska, as well as riding two-up with my wife on the back and dual sport riding on dirt and gravel roads with my friends. I retired the last Gold Wing soon after losing my wife to breast cancer in 1999.

At age 76, I bought a new 2001 BMW R1150GS. I was still able to handle the Gold Wing quite well, but my legs were getting weaker and I was concerned about backing it out of the garage safely, and maneuvering it around before getting underway. I've compiled a few highlights of several trips to Daytona Beach since then, and some of the things I did after I got to Daytona.

2001: I've taken shorter and faster trips to Daytona than the 2001 trip, but it was usually when there was a crisis at home for which I needed to get back in a hurry

– like the time in the early 1990s when I arrived at the motel on the beach and called home as soon as I finished unloading my gear. I learned that my mother, who was in her mid 90s, had fallen and suffered a minor stroke. After hanging up the phone, I got a few hours sleep, reloaded the bike in the pre-dawn hours, and left more than an hour before first light. I was in Daytona for part of one night and rode almost 1200 miles in 20 hours to get home the next day – not so much that I was needed, but more to show concern and respect for my mother.

On an earlier trip in the late 80s, I arrived in Daytona and went directly to the camp area where Bill and Millie Baird usually parked their motor home and were having their annual get-together with friends. As I got off the bike, Millie asked, "When did you get here?" – meaning Daytona.

I said, "Just now."

She said, "When do you plan on leaving?"

It was a little after two o'clock when I looked at my watch and said, "In about two hours."

The only thing I stopped in Daytona for that year was to visit with friends for an hour or two and pick up a few T-shirts for my sons. From there, I planned to head across Florida to visit with other friends and extended family. I came mainly for the ride, which took 4½ days of back roads to get there, and the same going home.

I was in Daytona a little longer than that in 2001, but not by much. On Monday and Tuesday of Bike Week, I was still home shoveling snow out of my driveways and off the roofs of my house and garage, trying to stay ahead of the buildup that was predicted, but never materialized. I had a sore back by Monday night. After another six hours of shoveling on Tuesday, I wasn't sure I could even get my leg over the new machine. I actually went out into the cold garage Tuesday night to see if I could get on – and how much pain I would be in when I assumed the riding position. As I winced from the pain, I recalled Bud Peck's words:

He would say, "No problem." Pain was no big deal to Bud. I remember the time when he pulled his little finger back into place after a minor spill on a patch of ice in West Virginia, during one of our earlier trips to Daytona. The finger was bent back so far it pointed at his elbow – totally out of joint. He took hold of it with the other hand and pulled real hard until it popped back into its socket. And then he taped the finger to the next finger with electrical tape and we were on our way. He didn't say another word about it.

The temperature was just below the freezing mark when I suited up and left for Daytona on Wednesday morning. I lost so much time shoveling that I opted for using all interstate highways. By the time I reached the start of the Garden State Parkway I was clear of the hazardous roads, and I had no traffic problems, which enabled me to get into North Carolina before stopping for the night – about halfway – 565 miles.

There was thick frost on the seat in the morning with the temperature in the mid-20s. I saw no other bikes on the road until I got well into Georgia, and even then I saw less than a half-dozen before the Florida state line. When the temperature rose to 70° around Jacksonville, I took off my snowmobile suit, but I still wore the long johns all the way into Daytona.

Being a Thursday, I went straight to the Alligator Enduro start-finish area to visit with friends and pick up a few alligator T-shirts as gifts. Riding around the parking area and looking for friends gets more difficult every year because I'm no longer able to recognize faces farther than about 15 or 20 feet.

When I heard a familiar voice call my name, I stopped for a brief visit with Pat Moroney, who had just finished the enduro. He said there wasn't a bit of mud in the entire run, and he said that the whoop-dee-doos were fierce. He spent most of the day diving in and out of huge dips that were too wide to just hit the high spots, and after a while the ground got chewed up and the holes got deeper from everyone landing in the low spots and blasting the throttle.

I traveled to Daytona alone in recent years and stayed with my nephew, Bob Conklin and his wife Renee, about 30 miles north of Daytona in Bunnell. That year I arranged to use a small camper parked in their back yard. Luckily I got there just before dark because they live on a road with soft sand, and I don't see the ruts very well at night.

Bob was in training that year for a long-distance trucking outfit, and he wouldn't be home for several days. Renee and a friend, Lorrie, were there. Lorrie had been living temporarily in the camper, but she gave it up for the two nights I was there. That night the temperature dropped to 29° and I didn't think of asking how to start the heater. I found some light blankets, but I woke up around 1 AM thinking I was in my tent at the Arctic Circle. It was only 40° inside the motor home. I put on my hi-tech long-john bottoms and three layers of long-john tops and crawled back into bed. I was comfortable then, but I woke up around four to use the camper's bathroom, and I could see my breath.

After enjoying a day with friends and riding around, I spent a second night in the camper that was much more comfortable. I got up, packed, said my good-byes over coffee and headed for the AMA museum fund-raising breakfast in Deland. Bill Baird was recovering from a recent stroke, but Bill and Millie managed to make it, and they saved a seat for me at their table.

Joe Leonard was featured. He certainly changed a lot since I saw him last as an intimidating charger on the racetracks of the 1950s when he earned a spot in the AMA Hall of Fame. He was overweight, gray, and walked with a cane; and he could hear very few of the interviewers questions due to a hearing impairment – and he wasn't wearing his hearing aid. Some of the stories he told were amusing. He also described the disastrous career-ending crash that occurred in March 1974 when he hit the wall during a race at Ontario, California while doing around 180 mph in an Indy car.

Our club's contribution to the AMA Hall-of-Fame Museum was shown as an associate sponsorship of the breakfast. It appeared in the program as, "In Memory of Ed "Mac" McIntyre, from RAMS Motorcycle Club." I left for home right after the breakfast. It was still chilly enough at 10:30 to wear hi-tech underwear and the snowmobile suit. I didn't see a single bike on the entire return trip, except in trailers and pickups. I saw guys loading their bikes on pickups alongside the road north of Jacksonville, and a few others got as far as the Georgia Welcome Center before quitting. I'm sure that some would ride out of Daytona for the image, and then load the bike on the trailer when they weren't having fun anymore.

There was frost on the seat in the morning in Florence, South Carolina. I stopped later at my daughter's in Virginia and spent the rest of the day and night with her and the children. I left Monday morning in full winter dress, stopping for a brief visit in Alexandria with one of my stepbrothers. I was home by mid-afternoon Monday. The trip took less than six days – two days down, two days there, and two days back.

The BMW was a constant source of amazement to me. It would whisper along at 80 without the slightest hint of vibration or sound. The aftermarket Aeroflow fairing did an excellent job of keeping the wind off my head and shoulders. The only buffeting I got was while riding behind the huge semis traveling at 70 mph. It was then I realized the bike was lighter than the Gold Wing. It would get thrown around more in the wind, and the tank bag would rock from side-to-side. Strong crosswinds blew the bag clear off the tank. I felt the stiffness of the stock seat after the first 2,000 miles.

I wasn't sure at the time which bike I'd take to Alaska for my grandson's high school graduation later that spring, since I still had the Gold Wing. If I were ten years younger, I would choose the BMW in a heartbeat, but I would be 76 in June, and my old body wasn't what it used to be, preferring the comfort of the heavier machine, especially with the arthritis and stenosis in my lower back. When the time came for the Alaska trip, I chose the BMW, and it was a superb ride. The Gold Wing gathered dust until I sold it.

2003: I left for Daytona a few days earlier than usual – Saturday rather than Monday, due to the weather. A mixture of rain and snow was predicted for Sunday and Monday. I quickly rearranged my itinerary and route sheets to reflect the extra time before leaving. I rode 475 miles directly to my daughter's home in Virginia and spent the afternoon, evening and morning with her and the kids. One of the boys still had a stomach virus that ran through the family during the previous two weeks, which I was a little concerned about catching. We went with the other four children to brunch at a nearby country buffet on Sunday morning.

In the afternoon, I rode 70 miles east to Portsmouth, for a brief visit with another stepbrother and his wife. She made a delicious pot roast for dinner, and I stayed overnight. Their condo is on the banks of the Elizabeth River where huge aircraft carriers often pass very close to their picture window in the narrow waterway. From their 3rd floor balcony, it's possible to have a normal conversation with sailors on the flight deck as the ship eases by.

I left after breakfast on Monday and thought about riding the remaining 720 miles to Daytona, but when I got as far as Georgia, it looked too much like rain, and I didn't want to descend dripping wet on Bob and Renee just before bedtime, especially considering they get up early for work. I rode the final 200 miles on Tuesday in steady rain – heavy at times. It was foggy too, and visibility was poor, especially where the truck traffic was heavy and throwing up a huge spray.

I stayed with Bob and Renee on Tuesday, Wednesday and Friday nights. Friday evening we went together with Bob's oldest son and his girlfriend to the Outback in Palm Coast. During the time they worked, I visited with friends in the area. One of the days, I went with two couples to an interesting waterside restaurant in Daytona called *The Boondocks*.

On Thursday morning, I practically buried the BMW in mud between tech inspection and the sign-up tent at the enduro start. The pit area was a sea of mud. I talked with several friends, including a Canadian rider who I competed with in the 1960s. After watching the start of the enduro, I rode 110 miles south to Barefoot Bay for dinner and overnight with friends from New York at their vacation home. It was warm, and I got sunburned riding with only a T-shirt. I left their place around nine on Friday morning and headed back to Daytona to pick up a few T-shirts as gifts. It was pouring at the track, so I ducked under a display tent and hung around until the rain let up before heading for Bunnell.

For many years, I rode to Daytona and back on almost all back roads – sometimes as far west as Kentucky. It struck me recently, during the last few years that I had been riding the interstates, how few people ride to and from Daytona for Bike Week any more. Twenty years ago I would see at least a hundred bikes on the way down and the same on the way back. In 2003 I saw none on the highway north of Georgia, either on the trip down or the trip home. I saw only one Harley in southern Georgia on Tuesday, riding in the rain, and three Gold Wings in central Georgia – and that was it. I didn't see any bikes on the ground in the rest areas either, or at the motels where I stayed.

2006: I was 80. I had been put on morphine in August of the previous year when the Lyme disease got into my central nervous system and the pain level went through the roof. A month before Bike Week I almost gave up hope of making the trip because of the risk of traveling under the influence of the painkiller. As the date got closer, I went practically cold turkey off the morphine. The withdrawal was fierce, but the pain was tolerable – so I packed my bags and got ready to leave.

The temperature was 20° when I left. I was still weak from the six-month bout with the two diseases when I almost spun out in heavy rush-hour traffic 10 miles from home. I was following a car and didn't see a ridge of snow between the tire tracks. When I hit it, the back end swung sideways and I almost lost it. Luckily, my reflexes cut in quickly enough to save it, but it certainly woke me up. A few miles later, my gas went on reserve with the odometer showing only 20 miles since the last fill-up. That's what I get for leaving the key in the bike! Someone apparently siphoned the tank almost dry while I was laid up.

Crosswinds were strong on the Tappan Zee Bridge. I bypassed most of the New Jersey Turnpike because bikes were banned due to the wind. I stopped for lunch a few miles short of the Delaware Memorial Bridge where the wind was very strong; and it was even stronger crossing the Susquehanna River in Maryland where it threw me around a lot. I reserved a room in Ashland, Virginia after my daughter called to say she had three down with the flu, and she advised me against stopping. I rode only 370 miles and checked in early. I had dinner at the same Ponderosa where the infamous DC sniper shot a guy in the parking lot.

The temperature was in the low 30s when I left, but it was comfortable without the balaclava, scarf or electric vest. It eventually got up into the mid 60s. I noticed that my gas went on reserve far too soon, and I figured there might be a problem. When I stopped for gas, I the engine was running a little rough, so I decided to make a quick check of the valves, just to make sure. It was a year and a half after taking the bike to Alaska, and the total miles were beginning to mount up.

I went across the street from the gas station and pulled into a Shoney's parking lot to work on it. Two of the Allen screws holding the left skid guard were frozen.

Consequently, I snapped one of them off getting to the valves. The valve adjustment on the left was okay, so I quickly put the cover back on, and tried the right side. The intake valve there had no clearance at all. I readjusted it by feel and was happy that I found it in time before any damage was done to the valve.

It was less than a 30-minute pit stop. The engine ran well after I started it, so I quickly buttoned it up and headed for the highway entrance ramp, glancing down to check for oil leaks as I rode. Whoops! I noticed oil had already covered my left boot. I pulled over onto the grass and found that one of the seals hadn't seated properly. The oil was down a little from the leak, but I refilled it that evening at the motel in Florence.

I left Florence at 8 AM in light rain. As I pulled out, I noticed that the clutch lever was engaging at the very end of the swing. I hoped it would get me home later that week. I rode in steady rain for about an hour and a half and chose to bypass Jacksonville because I thought I might miss a turn in the city due to my poor eyesight. Ironically, only 20 miles later I found myself on a strange boulevard, heading north. I turned east, thinking it would take me to I-95, but when I realized I was in Jacksonville Beach, I was able to reorient myself and get back on course.

I pulled into Bob and Renee's in Bunnell around three. They had both finished work for the day, and we had dinner after a few beers. Bob made an excellent antipasto salad. He said he emptied the refrigerator in it – lettuce, tomatoes, olives, cold cuts, cheese, etc. We turned in early, as they had to get up at four. I took a long back-road ride on Tuesday before heading back to Bunnell for dinner that evening, when Bob steamed several pounds of fresh giant shrimp.

Wednesday morning I went into Daytona to meet
Jessica Prokup for breakfast. She was the managing
editor at RoadBike Magazine at the time. She arrived
on a Honda that her magazine was testing. She is an
amazing young woman who I have a great deal of
admiration and respect for, and I've always felt proud
to be her friend. Our breakfast together, which I looked
forward to every year, flew by much too quickly.

Jessica described our unusual friendship best when she wrote in
one of her editorials, "What can I say – we get along."

Jessica said she'd try to get to the museum's fund-
raising breakfast on Friday if she could possibly break
away from her work. I promised to get her in without a
reservation if she showed up. We had our photo taken
together just before we split.

I also made arrangements to have lunch with Renee
that day while she was at work in Denny's. It was a

light lunch, after which I headed for Gustafsson Plastics in St. Augustine to have another windshield made for the small BMW F650, to replace the one that got smashed when I hit the sheep. Leif made the new windshield in a half hour while I waited.

Thursday morning, I went directly to the Alligator Enduro where I met several friends, including Jim Bellach, who had come all the way from California. After seeing most of the start, Jim and I joined several of his friends at a pit stop along the enduro course. They're a friendly bunch – generous with their beer. I had to leave at three, following my liquid lunch to get back to Bunnell in time to meet Bob and Renee for dinner at the Outback.

I attended the fund-raising breakfast in Deland on Friday where Mark Brelsford was the featured guest, and Dave Despain interviewed him. It was a great show! I met many old friends and cleared the way with the powers-to-be for Jessica to join us, but unfortunately she couldn't make it. I joined Bill and Millie at their table – front row center.

I ran into Gordon Razee at the breakfast, and he made a call to his BMW shop in Rhode Island to ask about my clutch, but his mechanic was out. I decided to go into Daytona to talk with the BMW service people there. I learned after finding the place, that Lee Florin, a friend and fellow club member from the Crotona Motorcycle Club, was the service manager. He took the bike in immediately. Meanwhile I walked around the vendor area on Beach St and had lunch. When I got back, the verdict was that the rear engine seal was leaking on the relatively new clutch, causing it to wear prematurely. The mechanic said it would probably get me home, but not much farther.

I decided to abort my plan for visiting the gulf coast, to avoid putting too many extra miles on the clutch, especially in stop-and-go traffic. I left on Saturday morning for home. The most notable event during my return trip was when a Lexus SUV in North Carolina changed lanes to pass a car while I was halfway by. I had to swerve onto the rough, sandy shoulder at 75 mph to avoid a bad scene. The woman simply didn't see me. I'm getting too old for that kind of thing!

2007: The temperature was around 25 degrees when I left home at first light, riding the BMW 650 Dakar for the first time on the Daytona trip. I had meanwhile determined that the R1150GS was already getting a little too heavy for my legs that were being affected more and more by my spinal stenosis. The 1150 also had 105,000 miles on it, and it had already cost me a bundle for repairs. The prediction was for cloudy skies on the trip down. I took the highways directly to my daughter's, making the 475 miles in 8 hours. I left there at 8 AM for a visit in Portsmouth, and left Portsmouth around noon, getting to Florence by 5:30. The Motel 6 that I used so often was getting pretty-well rundown. The entry door was still open a quarter-inch when it was closed and locked, and the phone didn't work. I got another phone from the desk that wasn't much better. I never carried a cell phone.

I left at first light and ran out of gas on the highway about five miles from Santee. I've rarely run out in more than a million miles of riding, but it happened on the interstate with heavy traffic running at about 80 mph. They would be past me and long gone before they could ever think of stopping. Several brake lights went on, but with other cars and trucks bearing down on them, they couldn't possibly stop.

I stood for almost a half-hour, hoping that a police car might come by. I locked the bike and started to walk the three miles back to where I saw an exit. As soon as I could, I switched to the other side by running across the active lanes when there was a break. Luckily the center divider was dry. Much of it in both Carolinas is often waist-deep with water. I wondered what the Lord had in store for me that day, realizing that God is always in total control – not only for my running out of gas, but also for how the adventure plays out.

After walking at least a mile, I noticed that a car had stopped about 500 feet ahead of me, which is how far it took for him to stop safely. My ankles were about to give out and my back and legs hurt. I had begun to wonder how far I could walk in the heavy riding clothes, carrying the helmet. I tried to walk faster and even tried to run, but I couldn't. I finally got to the car and got in with great effort and pain. It was a luxury Infinity, and the guy driving was in his late 30s, wearing shorts and sport clothes.

After locating a convenience store with gas pumps, I borrowed a can from the attendant, filled it, and we headed back to where the bike was parked. On the way back, I said, "I hope the Lord rewards you well for this good deed."

He said, "Let me tell you something – the Lord has already been exceptionally good to me, and I figured this was an opportunity to give some back. I consider it payback-time." His answer surprised me. It was certainly worth the hour-or-so delay and the painful walk to hear his testimony. It reaffirmed for me that it's the ride, and not the destination. The exits were far enough apart to have taken this guy at least 30 miles out of his way, after also returning the can – all to do a favor for a stranger.

2008 – The ride to Daytona seemed to get longer every year, and it's not without problems. My first problem of this trip happened on the first day while I was suiting up after a quick lunch. I took my glasses off to put my helmet on, setting the glasses on top of one of the saddlebags. I forgot to put them on before leaving, and I realized a few miles down the road that I wasn't able to read the signs, and that I had lost the glasses. I went back in search of them, but no luck. I'm almost blind in one eye and don't see well out of the other, and I was starting a 12-day, 4,000-mile trip without glasses. At least the spare pair of reading glasses I carry in my bags would be enough to read menus. I kept going for the next 11½ days without glasses.

It was the first time I rode the Suzuki 650 V-Strom on any kind of trip. In spite of being the most reliable of all the motorcycles I have ever owned, it was very uncomfortable; and this trip would tell what I would need to do to fix that. I described the problems and what I did about them in Chapter 3.

I spoke briefly in Florida with an enduro friend of the 1960s about his five-day ride from western New York. He takes the same time to get down as I used to take. I decided never to ride the interstate highways to Daytona again – if I could help it. It had become the main downside of my Daytona trips in recent years. I had gotten into the habit of heading straight down after my bout with Lyme disease, and I've always been a proponent of the ride being of foremost importance; and I wasn't getting much enjoyment from the ride any more, especially on the latest bike that was getting thrown around in the wind more than any other. It was also the least comfortable of any. In any case, I vowed to try to go back to using the back roads both ways.

I took 200-mile day trips on each of the three days I spent on the east coast of Florida, exploring many lightly traveled roads. I'd take a different loop each day, getting as far west as Ocala one day. I also visited with friends on each of the days, but I spent most of my time riding around and enjoying the 70-plus degree temperatures – a break from the winters in New York.

On Saturday morning I left Bunnell for my niece Susan's home in Gulfport over an impromptu 200-mile back road ride that I made up as I went along. Wind gusts were so strong on the ride across the six-mile causeway between Tampa and St. Petersburg that it picked up water from the bay and blew it across the highway. It was a challenge to keep the little Suzuki in a straight line and clear of the cars.

Susan cooked on Saturday night, and we had a late breakfast at a nice little place on Boca Ciega Bay in the morning, and later we went out for an early dinner at Sculley's on the boardwalk at Madeira Beach, which overlooks a busy inlet that's used regularly by gambling boats and fishing trawlers. The food and ambiance are great. We chose inside seating this time because it was quite windy on the balcony.

2009: The weather forecast was not good for several days before I left, with predictions of a storm, probably with snow, sweeping across the south during at least two of the five days I would be on the road riding down. Had it been twenty years ago, I'd have no problem with it, but my legs weren't nearly as useful as they used to be for sliding around on ice-covered roads and bridges, and the Suzuki isn't designed for it.

I planned the trip through farm country, including the many horse and turkey farms of western Virginia that I remembered so well from the old days. Some of the ride was on back roads in the Blue Ridge Mountains of Virginia and North Carolina. When I left, I hoped to be able to follow my route sheet for at least the first day, and maybe the last one or two days of the trip down, in spite of the storm tha was predicted. The greatest uncertainty was in Virginia and North Carolina.

The first day was partly cloudy with a high in the mid-30s. It was 28° when I left at 7:45 AM on Saturday. I hadn't used the back-road route that I chose across northern New Jersey in several years, and I missed a turn halfway across the state, due mainly to my inability to read the road signs. I was able to reconnect a few miles later but I missed another turn on a remote farm road in Pennsylvania – luckily, the sun was out, which helped me to reconnect, and I got to my lunch stop in Pine Grove in good time.

The strongest objection to my taking this particular trip came from my eye doctor, who insisted that my eyesight was not good enough for riding to Daytona Beach. I told her that not going to Daytona was simply not an option, and that I'm not about to give it up yet. She made last minute arrangements for me to see a specialist that I hadn't seen in seven years.

After hours of retesting I met with him in his office and he recommended that I get an up-to-date MRI of the optic nerves behind my good eye, because the MRI technology had improved a great deal since my last one, and it should show much greater detail. I agreed to have it done, and he said that he would set it up and call me. I said, "Okay, but I thought she sent me here because there might be something you could do before I leave for Daytona Beach next week."

He said, after a brief pause, "That's not why she sent you here."

I said, "Yes it was. That's what she told me."

"That's not what she told me," he answered.

"What did she tell you?"

After another pause, he said, "She wanted me to talk you out of riding the motorcycle to Daytona Beach." I looked down at the floor and shook my head. He continued, "My father rode a motorcycle practically all of his life – up until he was 84 years old – your age – and he could no longer get his leg over the bike. It broke his heart. If somehow I could get him back onto that motorcycle, I would do it." He smiled, and said, "There's no way I would ever tell you not to ride to Daytona Beach. Have a good time, and stay safe."

I learned later that she also called at least one of my other doctors. I suspect they told her that any attempt to talk that stubborn old goat out of not riding anywhere would be an exercise in futility. They're both in favor of my continuing to ride. When I got to Daytona, I sent my eye doctor a postcard with a picture of the beach, and I wrote on the card, "Having a wonderful time, wish you were here." She's actually an excellent doctor and a very nice person, and I know that she was mainly concerned about my safety.

I was totally exhausted when I stopped for lunch on the first day. Rather than push myself, I rode the interstate for the rest of the way into Hagerstown, bypassing about a third of the scenic route I planned for the day. The back roads were familiar to me and I was already very tired. When I got to the motel, the sky was dark and the temperature was in the low 30s.

It was snowing when I got up in the morning, and an inch of snow already covered the bike and the ground. I waited for a few cars to make tracks in the parking area before riding to breakfast. I was on the road by 7:45, but I almost dumped it on an interstate highway overpass about a quarter mile from the motel.

It was the deciding factor for my aborting the back road route for at least part of the day in favor of I-81. The TV reported that many activities were cancelled and places were closed, and that most of the back roads were treacherous. Snow mixed with rain was falling when I left. I soon learned that the interstate was also slick in spots, and the trucks threw up a heavy spray, mixed with oil and road grime, that coated my face shield and obscured my already poor vision. I stopped often to clean the shield during several showers – the heavier the shower, the more trouble I had with the face shield. A blanket of snow covered the surrounding countryside, making it look like a winter wonderland.

The sky darkened around Roanoke and it got even darker near the intersection of I-77. I had to decide whether to take I-77 and go over Fancy Gap into North Carolina or stay with I-81 and reconnect with my back road route. A heavy snow shower helped me to decide when huge flakes covered my face shield faster than I could wipe them off. I was near the Whytheville exit at the time, so I took it and went directly to a motel that I used before. I barely made it up the steep driveway as the snow began to stick to the road surface.

I had three options at that point: first, to reconnect in the morning with my original route; second, to take I-

77 over Fancy Gap toward Charlotte and reconnect with my original route farther south; or third, to stay in Whytheville for an extra day if it got really bad, in which case I'd forget about the original route sheet and use the interstates for the rest of the trip. The peak of the storm came through that night. TV reports in the morning said roads around Charlotte were a mess, with trucks and cars in ditches all over the place, and traffic at a standstill. I was glad I didn't attempt going over Fancy Gap on I-77, which was still slick.

There was an inch and a half of snow on the bike in the morning and the motel driveway was a mess. It was cold and windy all day, with lingering snow showers and a high of 20°. The motel had no plans to plow or salt the steep driveway or parking areas. Needless to say, I opted for the alternative of staying put for a day. There was a Bob Evans Restaurant within walking distance where I could get breakfast, lunch and dinner, although even the walking was treacherous.

After waiting for several cars to make it up and down the driveway safely, I walked to breakfast around 9:30. With snow on the driveway it was even treacherous walking. It wasn't thawing very fast, but it was windy, and the ground wasn't frozen, so the snow disappeared quickly. I managed to get out for a short ride in the afternoon to check out the highway. I intended to fill the gas tank while I was out.

The bike was hard starting with the temperature around 14°, and the front brake calipers were frozen, causing the brakes to drag. The interstate didn't seem that bad, but when I got to the gas station, I couldn't turn the ignition switch off because the lock was frozen in the 'on' position and the key was frozen in the lock. My spare key was at the motel, making it impossible to gas up. So I went back to my room and thawed the lock with a hot wet towel and got the key out, and I decided to deal with the problem in the morning.

The temperature Tuesday morning was 3°, with a wind chill of minus 12. After walking to breakfast, I loaded the bike and got totally suited up before trying to start it. I used a hot wet towel to thaw the lock enough to get the key in and turn it. The starter barely turned over, and I was concerned it would run the battery down before it started. For at least a full minute, it just popped once and failed to catch. It took eight or ten tries before it finally started. When it did, I left the motel wearing just about everything I had with me. Thank goodness for the electric vest and gloves. I wore my heavy woolen knee warmers under the riding suit. They're badly moth-eaten, but they still do the job. My mother knitted them as a Christmas gift 30 years ago.

The road was clear and dry, but it was close to zero when I turned onto I-77 and started over Fancy Gap. When I got near the Blue Ridge Parkway crossing, I saw a shiny thin film on the road that looked like black ice. It glistened in the morning sun, and it was far too cold to be water. The trucks were running 70 mph, and the road was straight, so I held my breath and stayed with the trucks for the next nine miles. I breathed a lot easier and the circulation returned to my knuckles when I began to descend into North Carolina.

The gas was getting very low in the tank, but I nursed it as far as I could, hoping the temperature would raise enough to thaw the ignition lock. When it didn't, I pulled in for gas anyway and left the motor running while I filled the tank using the spare key that I dug out of my bag the night before to unlock the tank cap. Luckily the tank lock wasn't frozen.

I continued on I-77 to where it ends at I-26, southeast of Columbia, South Carolina, and I stopped for the day in Orangeburg – about halfway to Daytona Beach from where I started the day. I delayed lunch and pulled into the motel at 1:30. It was a short but stressful 5½-hour day. The temperature had risen into the 50s by the time I checked in, after 350 miles.

It was 27° when I walked to the lobby in the morning for a light continental breakfast. I stopped for a second breakfast after reaching I-95, near the Georgia state line. After finding a seat at McDonald's, the people next to me remarked on "all the motorcycles heading south" – almost all of them were on trailers. One of the guys said I reminded him of "the guy in the movie about the fastest Indian." He was surprised to learn that Burt Munro was a real-life character, and that *"The World's Fastest Indian"* is a true story.

When I reached Bunnell around two o'clock, Bob was working and Renee carried most of my bags into the house. I must have looked like I was about to collapse. The truth of the matter is that I was in bad shape, with a great deal of pain in my lower back and I could barely stand, let alone walk and carry the bags.

I did my usual visiting for a few days, and Friday morning I headed out early for the Hilton on the beach where the museum's fund-raising breakfast was being held. Parking is at a premium anywhere near the beach, and bike security is always a problem. I parked in a 3-story municipal parking garage a quarter-mile walk from where the breakfast was being held. I wasn't even sure I could walk that far. There's no safe place on the bike to leave my outer clothes so I carried the helmet, gloves and heavy riding jacket, and I wore the heavy riding pants over my street clothes.

At least 200 people were seated when I picked up my nametag – late as usual. Millie had saved a place at their table – a great spot for the show, which was a dual interview with Jay Springsteen and Scott Parker, dirt track aces from different timeframes. I thought it was the best show since Jim Pomeroy in 2002.

After visiting with several friends at the breakfast, I headed out for a ride through the state park and picked up a few items, including a card for my eye doctor. I also stopped for a quick lunch before heading back to Bunnell. We chatted until it was time to head for the Outback, where I really enjoyed the rack of lamb with sweet potatoes, fresh green beans and Australian wine.

Saturday morning I packed and loaded for the ride across Florida to Susan's in Gulfport. I went northwest first to pick up a pint of fresh orange blossom honey at a roadside stand in San Mateo. The prices are marked and there's a locked box with a slot that says, "Pay here" – the honor system. I stopped for a quick lunch in Ocala and got to Susan's around 1:30. She was still at work but she told me where to find the house key. I serviced the chain before unpacking and changing into more comfortable clothes. Susan was able to leave work early, and she arrived at four. Meanwhile I took the opportunity to soak up some sun in the back yard as the temperature rose into the mid 80s – what a difference from Whytheville! After freshening up, we had an early dinner at Scully's in Madeira Beach.

The next morning, we went to a Greek restaurant in Gulfport for breakfast. I packed around eleven for the 50-mile ride to cousin Bev's home in Hudson, arriving before noon. I suggested we go for chicken wings, so after unloading, we went with her car to Hooters in Port Richey, and we spent the next few hours relaxing, chatting and eating hot chicken wings and curly fries. It seemed like only a few hours later we were at Red Lobster, enjoying lobster tails.

I was up at five for an early start for home. Leaving before first light was a challenge. It wasn't long before I took a wrong turn in the Spring Hill suburbs, but using the brightness of the sky in the east, I was able to find my way to US 41. Later, riding east along Rte 50, it was the blinding glare of the sun as it broke over the horizon. I finally reached I-75 and followed it to beyond Ocala where I exited in favor of the old Rte 301. I followed it the rest of the day into Statesboro, Georgia. After checking into a motel at 2 PM, I went to a nearby Captain D for a fish dinner.

I woke up at 3 AM and couldn't get back to sleep thinking about a chain problem that had been getting worse every day. I should have changed it before I left on the trip. I was carriing a used chain, and I picked up a chain tool at J&P Cycles in Daytona, knowing that the change was inevitable. I was just waiting for the right opportunity to make the switch. I got up at five and was the first customer at Shoney's for breakfast buffet, which put me on the road by first light.

I continued on US 301 to US 321 in South Carolina, and then into North Carolina where I spotted Rte 18 in Lenoir. I remembered it as a great bike road, so I aborted my planned route and took Rte 18 into Sparta. A short time later, the chain began to sound really bad, so I nursed it into Galax, Virginia for a 425-mile day, and after finding a motel, I decided it was time to make the switch with the chains. I had put it off long enough.

It didn't take long to see that the problem could have been prevented if only I had taken the time and effort to inspect the chain closely before leaving on the trip, when it first started to show signs of stretching. The master link had simply run out of grease and wore an oblong hole in the link next to it. It was a small miracle that the chain didn't come apart while I was out on the road – blessed again! After removing it, I got the spare chain from my bag, but noticed that the master link that I brought was the rivet-type, and I didn't have the riveting tool with me.

I had recently signed up for the new AMA Roadside Assistance program, so I called the number on the card, but they needed a member number. The AMA had told me to use my AMA member number, but the tow company said they had no record of that number. I then called the AMA, who gave me another number to try, which was also rejected. While talking on the phone with the tow company and getting nowhere, I was going through my bags with my free hand, and I came up with the right master link. Old enduro riders always carry extra master links. I simply hung up the phone and went out to finish the job. When I got home a few days later, my new roadside assistance card was in the mail, and I realized the number the tow company was looking for had an "A" suffix, which was added to my number when I became an "expert enduro rider" in the early 1960s.

The next morning I could barely get around from the pain in my back and both legs. I had a sausage and egg sandwich at a fast food place called *Aunt Bea's* before getting underway. I took US 221 from Galax to Roanoke, which was a nice ride, and I used the Blue Ridge Parkway to bypass the morning traffic in Roanoke. I followed US 460 east from there most of the way to my daughter's home in Prince George.

I learned that night that my stepbrother in Portsmouth, who was in his 90s, had just been put on hospice. I waited until morning to call, and I asked if he was up to a brief visit. I left for Portsmouth around 9:15. He was doing well and we had a good visit. I was back at my daughter's by 2:30. The next day, Friday the 13th, I decided to scrub my 2-day back-road route home that I had taken many times in the past, and I left at first light – snow was predicted for the first 200 miles along I-95.

It was snowing when I left, and by the time I got to Fredericksburg it was coming down quite heavily. The roads were getting slick, and the visibility was poor. I decided to get off I-95 and head northwest on US 17. The forecast west of there was much better. Luckily, I ran out of it about 30 miles west of Fredericksburg, and I enjoyed a good ride the rest of the way home. It's about 75 miles longer that way, but I still made the 565 miles in nine hours – my longest single day of the trip that totaled 4,175 miles in 14 days.

2010: This was my first trip after the Las Vegas trip when I had so much trouble with pain, and I needed blood transfusions soon after the trip ended. The roads were a total mess. It snowed all week and was still snowing on Saturday. Places near my home got as much as 30 inches in five days. I probably could have gotten out Saturday, snow showers and all, but I wanted to spare the chain and engine cases from the salt brine – so I delayed it a day and left on Sunday. My sons did a great job of shoveling and sanding the driveway to give me a safe exit to the street.

I made a last minute decision to replace the rear tire with a used one that I found in the garage that had a few thousand more miles left on it than the one on the bike. It might have gone the distance, but it would have restricted me from taking side trips. The tire I found looked to have at least 6,000 miles left on it, so I took a few hours of effort to change the tire.

I left a little before 8 AM during a snow shower, with the temperature at 30°. I rode interstates for 518 miles to an Econolodge along I-81 in Salem, Virginia, getting in around 4:20 – too late for my diuretic. It was windy all day and the temperature was still in the low 30s when I got in. I rode mostly 70 to 75 mph, but later in the day I rode with the traffic at an indicated 80.

The only stop I made was north of Harrisburg where I stopped in the middle of a rain shower for lunch at the same McDonald's I once swore I'd never use again because of an intestinal bug I got from a double cheeseburger there a few years earlier – but I had an empty tank, an empty stomach and a full bladder, and it was raining. I ordered their McChicken and a salad.

I was tempted to go all the way to Bunnell the next day, which would get me there a full day early, but I'd have to skip the diuretic again. I decided instead to kill time by turning onto US 301 in Orangeburg, South Carolina and use the back roads, with an overnight stop in Jesup, Georgia. When I got about a half-hour from Jesup, I took the diuretic, even though I had been depriving myself of fluids all day, but I figured I'd be in the motel with plenty of time to get fluids.

Unfortunately, when I got to Jesup, I didn't recognize the town, and I got onto US 84 heading west, which wouldn't have been a problem, except for having taken the diuretic and my bladder was already filling. I spotted US 341, which crosses I-95 in Brunswick; so I headed for the highway to find a motel as quickly as possible. I was already dehydrating big-time and it would be almost an hour before I could check in.

When I finally got to the motel, I went directly for the sink and turned on the water, and I started to take the thin plastic covering off the drinking glass as quickly as I could. Before I could get the water, my legs buckled and I went all the way to the floor – out like a light! I didn't know where I was when I came to; but I saw the glass halfway across the room and crawled over to it – and then to the sink to drink three glasses in quick succession. I crawled to a chair and sat quietly for at least a half hour before attempting to unload the bike. My legs were like jelly and I could barely stand. I made a cup of tea and rested before unloading the bike. I walked next door to a KFC for barbecue chicken and carried it to the room – after 560 miles in 9½ hours.

It was pouring when I woke up. I checked the TV for weather and it said the rain would taper off by ten – so I took the extra time to rest up and have a few cups of tea. I ate tropical trail mix and smoked salmon from my bag, along with a small donut and coffee from the lobby. I loaded the bike just before ten. The rain had stopped by the time I got on the highway.

After getting up to 80 mph with the traffic, I realized I was still a little light-headed, so I stopped for a more substantial breakfast. The rest of the way into Florida I stayed in the right-hand lane, so if I began to feel another bad spell coming on, I could pull over and stop quickly enough. I got to Bunnell shortly after lunch.

My gracious hosts went to work the next day and I left soon afterward for a ride in the country and attended to a few chores. I stopped for a visit at the RV Park near the Destination Daytona complex where some of the

RAMS stay in the wintertime, arriving just in time to go for coffee in Ormond Beach with a group of four.

On Friday, I walked into the fund-raising breakfast 20 minutes late, looking like a tired old cowpuncher coming in off a cattle drive, wearing my tattered riding clothes and carrying the helmet. The program had already begun, in which AMA Chairman of the Board Stan Simpson was interviewing random attendees with a roving microphone. He spotted my helmet soon after I sat down – or maybe he saw me walk in. He came over with the microphone and asked several questions, starting with how many miles have I ridden in my lifetime, to which I answered, "About 1¼ million." There were rounds of applause after each answer.

When the interview was over, Tom White, the MC on the stage, added that I recently rode across the country and back for the Las Vegas event, which brought more applause. Later, Rob Dingman, President and CEO of the AMA, came by my table to shake hands and say a few words, as did Chairman of the AMHF Jack Penton and a few others. I was asked to stay for autographs with the Hall of Fame people but I declined because I had a lunch date with five Dutch girls at my cousin Margo's condo in New Smyrna Beach. I ate quickly and left so I wouldn't be late for lunch. It took almost a half-hour to break away because I kept running into friends and well-wishers on my way out, getting me to Margo's a few minutes late.

I had no problem finding the address because she and one of her daughters were waiting outside for me on a park bench. Another daughter arrived with her fiancé, soon afterward, riding two big Harleys. Ten people were invited, but two were stuck in traffic coming across Florida. They arrived as I was leaving for dinner at the Outback. I had a fabulous time at lunch, eating and telling stories, but it was tough to break away because I was leaving while the others were arriving.

With five of my Dutch cousins in New Smyrna Beach

From the time I got up on Friday morning until I got to bed that night, the day was one of the greatest I've spent in years. How would I know the following day would be a disaster? I left Bunnell at 8:30 AM for an easy 3½-hour ride to Sarasota to visit with Susan, who had recently moved from Gulfport. I had her new address on a piece of paper, but an hour after leaving, when I stopped for a second breakfast, I looked for the paper and couldn't find it. I figured – no problem – I remember the name of the road she lives on and the general vicinity from having looked it up on the Internet at home. If I had trouble finding it, I'd simply call her mother for the address.

I got to Sarasota around the time I promised, but the gated-community's gate was locked. A few people came in and out, operating the gate with a portable device like a garage door opener, but I didn't want to "sneak in" if I could help it – no telling who might be watching and what they might do – not to exclude a possible call to the police, Not having the exact address, I would have to look for her car.

I found a small directory box near the gate and looked for her name, but it was a faded LED that I couldn't read. I stopped a car going in and asked the guy to read it for me, but her name wasn't listed. After waiting around for 10 or 15 minutes, hoping she would come out to look for me, I went to the nearby shopping center to find a pay phone, only to learn that pay phones no longer exist, or at least I couldn't find one.

I went back and tailgated a car through the gate and looked around for her car but couldn't find it. I rode around for a while hoping she would see me. After at least three complete circuits and asking about an office in the community and finding that it was closed on Saturday, I went outside to wait, hoping she would come out to look for me. I waited for almost two hours, but finally gave up and headed for home. I had a date with Bev in Hudson on Sunday, but when I saw her the previous day and she wasn't sure she'd be back in time, I skipped that too, and I was out of there.

I called home from a motel about 175 miles up the road and learned that everyone was in a panic because I failed to show at Susan's, and they had no way of contacting me. The highway patrol had an APB out, and they were checking every county between Bunnell and Sarasota for accident reports, hospital entries, etc. I was also on what they call a Senior Alert, which is something like an Amber Alert, but used in Florida when an elderly person is missing. A highway patrol detective was questioning Bob in Bunnell at 8:30 PM when a message came over the police radio that I had been located at a motel in McIntosh, Florida.

There was also an alert sent out on three different motorcycle forums on the Internet that many of my friends monitor. I couldn't believe how many people had gotten involved and how many cared, which humbled and embarrassed me. I had never owned a cell phone, but seeing how much it means to my friends and family, I bought one – I haven't used it yet.

2011 - The aging process began to accelerate and the geriatric issues increased during the winter. In an effort to ease the damaging effect the small Suzuki was having on my pelvic area, I ordered and received a new custom seat during the winter, but it was two inches higher than the touring seat I had been using for three years, and it wasn't comfortable that way. I didn't have enough time before Daytona to return it for an adjustment, so I tried using it on the trip.

The first problem I had was an inability to see the gas gauge or the odometer for almost the entire day, and I ran out of gas long before I expected. Since I couldn't read the gauge, I planned on stopping for my first fill-up at the same place I've stopped several times in the past. I was two miles short of the exit when it ran out, which stranded me in farm country, and I had to walk about a quarter-mile uphill across rough fields to find a way to get the gas. The walk was far too much for my heart condition, and it put me in rough shape. If I didn't have good arteries and a strong heart muscle, I probably wouldn't be here! People at the place where I stopped offered to call 911 because of my labored breathing, but I declined. I was able to get a few gallons and a ride back to the bike on a big quad.

I continued my journey from there, but getting on and off the new seat became more difficult as I grew more tired. I had to struggle at every stop. I could barely get my leg over it after a while, and I knew when I got very tired, I wouldn't be able to get on the bike at all. There were times that I would try four and five times just to get my foot onto the seat, and then I'd have to try to work it over to the other side from there. Once, I even climbed onto the gas-pump island to get on, which gave me about an eight-inch advantage for throwing my leg up.

Pain also became a problem. I got injections in both sacroiliac joints three days before I left, but after the first day, the pain was greater than it was before I got the shots. I can usually handle pain, so the pain alone wasn't the problem. The problem was that the more pain I got in my lower back, the more difficult it became to get my leg high enough to get it over the seat. I figured by the time I got to Florida – if I got that far – I wouldn't be able to get on the bike at all, or maybe I would become stranded somewhere.

I decided at the motel on the first night that rather than get stranded along the road or have to abort later, I would bite the bullet and abort the trip there. I thought I was probably an accident waiting to happen anyway. There were several other geriatric issues that I didn't list here because they're more than the reader needs to know, but suffice it to say that it was one of the most difficult decisions I've ever had to make. I knew that it could possibly spell the end of my long distance riding. I rode the 285 miles home in the morning with a list of things on my mind that needed to be done before trying it again.

Epilog: I sent the seat back to California as soon as I got home from the attempt to ride to Daytona, and I asked to have it lowered two inches. I got it back two weeks later and figured I'd see how the summer goes. My doctors have encouraged me to keep riding, and they've adjusted my meds accordingly. My eye doctor hasn't mentioned it lately, but I think she's now in favor of my riding. I've had four operations in the past four years and as many as ten epidural and steroid injections, which no longer work. I had two titanium rods put between the vertebrae in my lower back, which didn't work either. I've started physical therapy to improve my ability to get my leg over the seat and lessen the pain. I stopped taking pain meds because my system can only tolerate the narcotic type, and I'd rather bear the pain than be numbed out.

In June 2011, about 10 days after a hernia operation, one of my sons needed parts for his KTM, and I offered to pick them up for him in Newburgh. I hadn't ridden since I aborted the Daytona trip. My surgeon told me that I should stay off the bike for at least two weeks, but I thought it would be cool to take a ride to celebrate my 86th birthday. I wasn't even sure I could get my leg over it, or back the machine out of the garage when I reached for my helmet. I threw my leg up to get on and the other leg buckled. I almost ended up in a heap on the garage floor – but I got on, and I got the bike started. I shook the leg that buckled and backed it out of the garage; hoping the leg wouldn't give out again while I was turning it around.

After getting it in position, I carefully eased it into gear and recited the Lord's Prayer as I rode carefully down the driveway. I took a deep breath and started up the street. I had been feeling weak since the operation, and

I met with the surgeon the previous day. He said to walk more, and get more exercise. I told him I don't have much desire to walk or exercise, and I asked if he meant that I should push myself. He said, "Yes. Push yourself." So after taking a deep breath, I said aloud, "Push yourself," and I headed for Newburgh.

I felt a little out of it as I passed a school bus and a string of cars going up Storm King Mountain above West Point, and I wasn't sure that I should be pushing quite so hard. After picking up the parts and chatting with friends at Moroney's, I felt a little more normal. When I got back out to the bike and was able to get my leg over it without incident, I felt confident enough to take a longer way home. I had traveled only 25 miles so far – so I headed west instead of south.

By the time I got past Stewart International Airport, I had already decided to turn north and go at least as far as Modena on the back roads. That started a series of similar incidents where I'd think of the same two words – push yourself, and I kept going north, beyond Kingston where I was already 60 miles from home and didn't have a destination in mind yet.

I came to a roadblock where six state troopers were inspecting vehicles, I pulled in and turned off the engine – I wasn't wearing my hearing aid and wanted to hear what was being said. One big guy said, "Don't turn it off," as he walked around to the right side of the bike, while several others stood in a line on my left side. I said as the big guy walked around the bike, "It's over on this side, at the top of the fork leg."

He said, "I already saw it. Do you have a motorcycle license?" I laughed and said, I sure do. I've had one since they "grand-fathered" me in more than 50 years ago, and I reached for my wallet. He said, "I don't have to see it."

I said, "I'm out taking a ride to celebrate my 86th birthday" – which got a few smiles and at least one "Happy Birthday" as I restarted the bike and said, "Have a nice day," and I left.

I stopped for gas north of Kingston and went across the river into Dutchess County, wondering which roads I'd like to ride on my birthday; and I thought of the doctor's words again. I knew he meant to walk more; but riding isn't nearly as strenuous as walking. By the time I got to the east side of the Hudson, I had already decided to head north into Columbia County and stop for lunch at the Farmer's Wife, a country deli where I've eaten several times before.

I had a lightheaded episode and wondered if it could be from low blood pressure that I've had since coming out of the anesthesia – or it could be dehydration – but I had coffee when I stopped for gas – or it could be weakness from having skipped breakfast. Stopping for lunch should tell the story. I got there at noon and the place was empty. I put my order in for a Rueben with an orange juice, and I ate outside on the porch. By the time I got back to the bike, I felt better.

It was 80° and sunny, so I decided to make a full day of it. I took some back roads northeast to Sharon, Connecticut, and then several of my favorite country roads near the state line along the Mizzentop ridge towards home. I got to where Birch Hill Rd descends from the ridge and found it to be blocked with cones. A storm the night before was apparently quite strong in that area, and many trees were down – not to mention branches. I went around the cones and started down the mountain where I passed at least six trucks and more than a dozen guys clearing debris. No one objected as I carefully picked my way through it all.

I turned west on Rte 164 toward Luddingtonville and home, clocking a total of 210 miles in a little over six hours on what turned out to be a really nice 86th birthday ride. I still had barely enough energy to attend a joint birthday party for my grandson and me, with pizza and ice cream. We share the same birthday, 74 years apart. I had no negative aftereffects from the ride and I felt that I was back in the game.

A few months later, I went out for my usual daily ride and after getting started I came up with the idea of maybe visiting five states that day, and also test my ability to still ride at least eight hours in a day. I didn't have the ride planned, so I would figure the route as I went along. I headed toward the northern tip of New Jersey where I considered stopping for a quick second breakfast before the long day, but instead, I headed across the state line into Matamoras, Pennsylvania and then back across the river into New York using the old Rte 209 bridge into Port Jervis – three states so far, and it's still early, so I headed northeast.

Ellenville was the next possibility to get something to eat, but it was already be too late for breakfast when I got there, so I thought I'd stop in Red Hook for gas and lunch. But after crossing the Hudson, I went right through Red Hook and took Rte 199 to the Taconic Parkway and headed north towards Massachusetts, stopping for gas at one of the parkway exits. The only thing I could find at the gas station to eat was a small cheese Danish. I didn't want to take the time for a sit-down meal at the diner next door, so I ate the small Danish standing, and I got back on the Taconic for another few miles to Rte 23, which I took into Great Barrington, Massachusetts for state number four.

Since it was early enough when I got there, I got the idea to head north for Bennington, Vermont instead of south for Connecticut, which would add another 125 miles and make a total of six states rather than five. So I went back to Rte 22 and headed north. The road was rough for about 30 miles through Rensselaer County, and I was almost sorry I included Vermont because it was wreaking havoc with my arthritic back. But by that time it was too late to turn back; and I pressed on and made a U-turn on Vermont Rte 9, coming back over that same rough section.

On my way back, I used County Road 62 and US 44 to get into Connecticut, making it state number six. I took another U-turn at the outskirts of Canaan and rode US 44 west to the Taconic Parkway and then NY 301 and US 9 to get home by 4:45. I had only the small Danish to eat all day, and I didn't drink anything. I carry water only for emergencies, and I didn't need it because the temperature only got into the low 80s. I rode 387 miles in 8 hours. Considering my 86 years, and very little riding in the previous six-month period, I thought it was a pretty good day.

I was able to continue riding in 2011, and I managed to eke out another 16,000 miles, most of which was after the 86th birthday ride in June. But it was not without a lot of pain, and not without heart-wrenching tradeoffs between my passion to continue and what my body has been telling me for years that it's capable of doing.

CPSIA information can be obtained at www.ICGtesting.com
Printed in the USA
LVOW071843070113

314711LV00032B/2060/P